MIDNIGHT IN MOSCOW

Rebecca Buckley

R. J. Buckley Publishing
San Tan Valley, AZ

www.rjbuckleypublishing.com

R. J. Buckley Publishing
1451 E. Poncho Lane
San Tan Valley, AZ 85143

© 2010 by Rebecca Buckley

First Printing May 2011

For information about special discounts for bulk purchases, please contact the publisher at: rjbuckleypublish@aol.com.

ISBN:978-0-9819654-8-2
Library of Congress Control Number: 2011906493

Works by Rebecca Buckley

NOVELS - "New Year's Eve" Series
Midnight at Trafalgar Square (2005)
Midnight at the Eiffel (2007)
Midnight in Brussels (2009)
Midnight at Trafalgar (revision - 2010)
Midnight in Moscow (2011)

COLLECTIONS of SHORT STORIES
Love Has a Price Tag (2006)
Bits & Pieces of Me (2008)

ANTHOLOGIES
The World outside the Window
2008 WOW Anthology
2009 WOW Anthology

STAGEPLAYS
Little Katie McMullen
Opposite Ends of the Rainbow
Café Dustyefsky

SCREENPLAYS
Peace in the Valley
Where Do We Go From Here

ACKNOWLEDGEMENTS

Kudos to the magnificent Metropole Hotels, which are my favorite. But then I love old world surroundings, opulence, and feeling that I am transported back to an elegant bygone era. I would rather spend the money for the ambiance and comfort of a Metropole than on anything else. It is well-worth the expense.

In the writing of this novel, I returned once again to a Metropole: last time it was in Brussels, this time the sublime Moscow landmark with its luxurious environment near Red Square and the Kremlin.

One of the novels in my *New Year's Eve* series will be set in Monte Carlo, and of course it goes without saying that I will be staying at the Monte Carlo Metropole. Can't wait! (*Malibu is next, but no Metropole in Malibu.*)

DEDICATION

To the memory of those who have passed, and to those who have been left behind.

"Those around you may be full of ideas about how you're supposed to grieve, and how not. You may be told that grief comes in clear-cut stages and you may even be given a name for the stage you're supposedly going through. You may hear advice like "Be strong!" or "Cheer up!" or "Get on with your life!" rather than be encouraged to allow your grief to run its natural course. It's important for you to be clear that this is your grief, not theirs. You'll grieve in no one's way but your own."

James E. Miller

"And after the grief, whatever the loss, in our own good time we will find there is still an abundant and wonderful life ahead of us. This the universe promises. We're made to love, not wither."

Rebecca Buckley

FOR

Trish Alden, Linda Hainline, Marianne Lindstrom, and Barbara McKee . . . my best buddies.

We can do it, girls, we can do it! It's our turn!

MIDNIGHT
IN
MOSCOW

PART ONE
Rachel O'Neill

Chapter 1

Even with her eyes closed Rachel could see all four of them plain as day, just as they were when they were alive. Her Irish father Neal - tall, lean, and freckled, with a grin revealing his dry sense of humor. Her spiritual Blackfoot Indian mother Lily - tall as Neal, with a long braid hanging down her back, teaching children on the reservation in Montana. Her dear friend Ethan in all his British rotund joviality and clumsiness, always in a rush. Her fiancé Pete - tall sexy Pete, her Liverpudlian lover with his forearm tattoos and dangling cigarette. All four of them she had loved, but now they were dead and gone.

She was still in the last stages of grief over Pete, the last stage of acceptance. But as always, when she thought of one, the memories of all four would resurface, dredging up the grieving processes all over again.

A sick feeling and heavy cramping was growing in her belly as she thought of them. It was making her want to double over. Stress affected her that way. She breathed deeply but could feel the emotions moving up into her stomach combining heartbreak with heartburn. There was a moment she felt as if it would explode through her chest. Her throat closed down on it, trying to suppress it, but she knew she had to let it go.

In her imagination she saw them in a pile of dead bodies.

1

In her dreams she would tug and pull at the bodies, trying to separate them one from the other.

In her conscious mind they were bundled together, one memory sparked the memory of the other and the other and the other - all four of them, dead in a heap.

The dreaded nightmares began right after her fiancé Pete Bell was shot and killed in Brazil. He was in South America on assignment to collect plant life in the jungles for the Eden Project in Cornwall; his lifelong dream was to be of service to the world, to aid in preserving plant life for future generations. Pete and Rachel were to be married that Christmas in Paris. Rachel had always dreamed of being married on Christmas Day, same as her mother and father . . . but just a few weeks before the wedding was to take place, Pete was killed.

Now it had been almost a year since his murder. She kept telling herself that she should be able to deal with it by now. But not only was she not dealing with his death, she still felt bereavement for the loss of the ones who had died before. Pete's death seemed to bring it all back to her. So now her bereavement was four-fold.

Rachel shook her head at the ridiculousness of the continual mourning and swiped her eyes in protest, blinking back the next wave of sorrow that threatened to follow the previous one.

She pushed her thick auburn hair behind her ears away from her face.

She didn't know why the crying jags kept coming. It wasn't as if she was the type to weep, whimper, and wallow in misery and depression. She was like her father in that respect, able to mask her feelings, to get on with life. Sure she succumbed to the grief the night Pete died, to the extreme. She'd taken an overdose, but that was a fluke, she would never do that again no matter what. It was just that it was one more tragedy piled up on the others, too many too soon. That's what it was.

But these recent emotional outbursts had to stop. She was an upbeat person, had always looked on the bright side of things. Everybody said that about her . . . *'Nothing can hold Rachel O'Neill down for long.' 'Rachel is a survivor.'*

"This is ludicrous!" She grabbed a wad of paper towel that lay on the table and used it to wipe her eyes and blow her nose. Nonsense! She had to get control. It was time to move on.

Rachel stood up from the lawn chair, gave one last nose blow then scrunched up the towel again, throwing it at the table in a brusque, deliberate motion.

The wad bounced and landed in the grass. She stared at it for a moment as it lay in its spiked, green nest like a misshapen egg. A sigh of resignation escaped her lips and she scooped up the towel and plopped it back on the table as if she were punctuating the end of a sentence in one of her manuscripts.

Her cell phone rang. She stared at the phone for a few seconds before picking it up.

Finally, "Hello?"

"Rachel, it's me, Maxim."

"Oh my goodness, how are you, Maxim?" She closed her eyes and changed phone hands. "What are you doing?"

"I'm calling you, of course."

Rachel took a deep breath and held it. "So, are you in Brussels or Moscow?"

"Neither. I'm in London on business and I thought I might come down to see you afterwards, if you don't mind? Do you?"

"When?" She frowned and began to pace while nervously running her free hand through her hair.

"I can be there tomorrow, if that is all right with you."

"Tomorrow? Uh, okay. Sure. That'll be all right."

"Good! Then I will call you early morning to let you know when I arrive. I will fly to Newquay and take a train to Penzance. I am told that is the best way."

3

"Yes, it is." This was catching her off guard; the last person she wanted to see was Maxim Ballenchine. She didn't need any interruptions in her life at the moment and she wasn't fit for company.

"I'll call you in the morning then. Bye," he said, and then he was gone.

Stunned, Rachel listened to the dial tone. She couldn't believe that Maxim was actually coming to Cornwall to see her.

They'd met the previous New Year's Eve in Brussels; Maxim a widower, Rachel in the throes of her own grief over the death of Pete. Her friends Mandy and Richard had convinced her to come to Brussels for their wedding on Christmas Eve and she ended up staying with them till the week after New Year's. So she had become acquainted with Maxim during that week. And now, he was coming to Cornwall.

God, I need to make a list! She grabbed her pen and notebook and quickly jotted down what to get at the market and what she needed to do in preparation for his arrival. As soon as the grocery opened in another hour, she'd go. But for now, she decided she wasn't going to let anything or anybody interrupt her daily morning routine. Not even a rich, handsome Russian like Maxim Ballenchine. Her mornings were her time for reflection and meditation.

Taking a deep breath, she stood up again and inhaled the cool, crisp June morning air that smelled of sea and flora. She lifted her pointed, straight nose towards the sky and closed her eyes. Regardless of where she went in the world, this was her favorite place to be, at her Heart's Ease Cottage. No matter how distraught she would become, this was where she found solace and peace. This was where she came to soak up the environment and be inspired, to heal and gain strength. This was her haven.

She leaned forward against one of the four garden chairs surrounding the glass covered wrought iron table. With her hands atop the curvature of the chair's iron back, she gazed out across Mount's Bay towards Saint Michael's Mount. She never grew tired of the view of the Mount.

There it was . . . Saint Michael's . . . standing majestically on a rocky mound off the coast of Marazion across Mount's Bay. It once had been a Benedictine monastery granted to the famous Mont St. Michel of France across the English Channel. In addition to Saint Michael's earlier glorious life, since the seventeenth century the medieval castle belonged to the St. Aubyn family of Cornwall. Rachel had fortuitously met a member of the family when she came to Cornwall - Margaret Trimble, a second cousin to John St. Aubyn.

She made a mental note to give Margaret a call and tell her Maxim was coming for she knew all about the story of the meeting in Brussels. Rachel sighed as her thoughts shifted to her dear friend Margaret who had just recently married a present-day Spanish nobleman. *There's a fairytale for the older set*, she thought to herself, amused. Rachel loved fairytales, collected books of them - Grimes, Andersen, Perrault, and others. She even owned a book of Russian Fairy Tales that she'd purchased the last time she was in St. Petersburg.

Even after Margaret Trimble married the Count, Margaret continued to manage the Godolphin Arms in Marazion. In fact, the newlyweds lived at the Godolphin, although they were permitted to use a sectioned-off portion of the castle along with the rest of the family, away from the tourists.

Margaret's husband, Felipe, was hardly ever around. Rachel could count on one hand the times she'd seen him. But when he was there, it was always fun to kibitz with him. He had such a great sense of humor, reminded Rachel of her father Neal. Margaret and Felipe made a splendid couple.

Rachel's hands shielded the sun from her eyes as she focused, trying to see the tiny Marazion village past Penzance on the far shore of the bay. She could barely make out the Godolphin where the view of Saint Michael's was a clear shot across the man-made granite walkway. At high-tide the causeway was hidden beneath the water. So crossing the bay to the sea-bound castle could be an adventure in itself. At mid or low tide one could walk in the footsteps of those who had crossed the causeway throughout the ages, but when the tide flooded over the historic footway, row and motor boats ferried tourists to where trading ships once anchored at the medieval village at the base of the Mount.

Since that first memorable visit to Marazion, Rachel lunched at the Godolphin quite regularly for more reasons than one: she loved the history, she loved talking to Margaret, she loved the food, she loved the view of the Mount, and she loved nosing around the quaint bayside town, had made friends with many of the local merchants.

As it turned out, Margaret and Rachel shared a belief in reincarnation; they both felt strongly that they were connected in past lives. The familiarity between them was much too strong for that not to be true. They both believed in the premise that they were part of a group traveling together from one lifetime to another, her beloved Pete Bell included. Like Rachel and Margaret, Pete had been a believer and, in fact, had introduced the two women to each other, knowing they had something in common.

Since Rachel first moved to Cornwall, she had spent many hours visiting the towns and villages in the south of England, even traveled from the west to the east coast meeting people with whom she instantly felt a previous connection. She was convinced more than ever she had lived in Cornwall in the seventeenth century. Even her dreams hinted at it. Investigations suggested it. It felt like she belonged there for more reasons than one. Open mindedness and eagerness to accept was the key to the belief she adopted long ago when her mother first introduced her to the theory.

Sounds of a car horn in the distance broke into Rachel's thoughts, bringing her back to the present. Sounds were magnified and echoed loudly in the Newlyn bay area.

She stepped to a nearby stone wall in her garden on which sat some of her favorite potted plants. She lifted a small pot of hyacinths to her nose, a hand-painted decorative pot she'd found in an art shop in St. Ives. She had intended to place it on the white filigree table that morning before she had her morning coffee and slices of toast, but she had forgotten.

Rachel was all about setting the table as beautifully as possible, whether she was alone or with guests. She used porcelain china and crystal, tea cups instead of pottery mugs, silver instead of stainless . . . even outdoors. Plastic was not an option. She used cloth napkins instead of paper. The paper towel she'd used earlier was there because she kept a roll of it nearby for spills on the glass-top table. But she loved pretty things and surrounded herself with them, they made her feel good.

The sweet smell of the hyacinths soothed her as she breathed in the aroma. The perfume of all flowers soothed her soul and lifted her spirits, whether from a bottle or from the actual bloom.

It had been years since Rachel first set foot on the British Isle and had immediately fallen in love with the English gardens wherever she went. So when she moved into her cottage in Newlyn, she worked diligently to create her own blossom-filled space in her own little corner of the island.

Her garden was picturesque with the emerald grass and multi-colored flower beds stretching to the magnificent magnolia tree perched near the edge of the bluff. Surrounded by the climbing vines and roses, the sounds of the seagulls and fishing boats bobbing in Newlyn Harbor below, and the varying shades of blues in the sky and sea beyond ... it all came together to create a picture-perfect world. Rachel's picture-perfect world.

Yes, Rachel loved Newlyn - her charming town in her own boot of Cornwall - that part of England reminded her of the shape of Italy . . . although a bit different, more like a backwards boot. Still, with an imagination one might visualize a boot.

Newlyn laid claim to having the largest fishing port in present-day England. W*here winters are wild and raging, summers are mildly engaging.* Rachel had written the rhyming description of Cornwall in one of her feeble attempts at writing poetry. It seemed her creativity ran rampant in England, but rather than her paltry poetry, she wrote romantic novels and screenplays. At times she even dabbled in oil and acrylic painting as well.

Rachel had first made the trip to Cornwall's seacoast with her dear friend Ethan Philips, during the Christmas holidays. She had come from the States for an extended stay, just after her father died.

She frowned. *Too many dead.* She attempted to drown out the emerging death thoughts by singing dramatically at the top of her lungs . . .

"Oh what a beautiful morning . . . oh what a beautiful day . . . I've got a beautiful feeling . . . everything's going my way."

It worked.

Usually did.

But she hoped no one had heard her melodious outburst. That would be embarrassing. Of course if she didn't see anybody watching her, then it wouldn't matter. She wouldn't know who they were, would she? She usually sang to herself as she walked to the villages of Newlyn and Penzance from her cottage, but she sang quietly, not belting out as she just did. She figured someone had definitely heard her, though, because there is always someone watching and listening, no matter what.

Sighing heavily, she poured another cup of coffee from the glass cafetiere that sat on the table, hoping the coffee would still be warm. She moved to the lounge chair, sat, and leaned back, allowing only pleasant memories of her first trip to Cornwall with Ethan slip back into her thoughts. *Only the good thoughts, please.*

She remembered how she and Ethan had arrived during a wicked storm, one of the most violent storms that had hit the region in years. It pounded the coastline of Mounts Bay the entire week before Christmas and continued on through New Year's Day.

Of course Rachel had always loved the romance and drama of stormy weather - the high seas, the waves crashing over the granite boulders and pebble-strewn beach and up over the coastal road. It reminded her of Daphne du Maurier's Cornwall, her dramatic, romantic novels set in the region. Daphne, too, had lived and written in Cornwall. Rachel felt a connection to her.

But her friend Ethan hated storms. He wanted to go back to London and spend the Christmas holidays with his sister and mother, and insisted they do that.

Needless to say, Rachel couldn't pull herself away from the Cornwall coast, she was fixated. So she remained at the Queen Hotel in Penzance and Ethan returned to London to be with his family.

It turned out to be the best Christmas week and New Year's Eve Rachel had spent in years. Growing up with an alcoholic father, who spent nights and holidays tending his pub, left Christmas something to be desired, never to be experienced. Her young adult Christmases were just as vacant, although she did try to make them as nice as she could for her son over the years.

But for her, personally, those first holiday nights with the locals at the Ship Inn in the tiny fishing village of Mousehole were exciting. While meandering through shops and pub-crawling the few days before Christmas after Ethan left, she had learned from the shop and pub people that Mousehole was the place to be on both holiday eves. Not being a religious sort, Rachel's mode of celebrating the holidays fit right in with the Mousehole celebrants.

Now she was living just a mile from Mousehole and a mile from Penzance—in between the two towns—in Newlyn. Her dreams had come true, literally come true. Yes, she was exactly where she wanted to be, she was where she belonged. She knew it the moment she arrived that day in Cornwall with Ethan, but it took her three more years to finally make it her home. She'd lived in Cornwall four years now.

Again her reverie was interrupted, this time by sounds of lines beating and clanking against the boat masts below in Newlyn Harbor. The winds were picking up. Sounds of squawking seagulls as they pillaged for food filled the atmosphere too, mingling with the memories of that first visit and of Ethan.

All of a sudden a vision popped into her head - Ethan lying dead in the hospital morgue. She shook her head and stood up.

Ethan had died in a car crash just after Rachel moved into her cottage, was on his way to visit her. She remembered it as if was yesterday. They hadn't seen each other in quite some time, not since she and Pete had committed to each other. And Ethan was at last coming to see her and she was glad, she still cared for him. But in his haste, the unexpected happened, a heart-breaking tragedy. He'd had an aneurism while driving and rolled his car just a few miles east of Penzance, pronounced dead on arrival.

She squeezed her eyes shut and rubbed her temples before lifting the bottom edge of her chambray shirt to wipe emerging tears from her already sore, reddened eyes. A deep, dull ache was again growing deep in her abdomen. She bent over, arms clenched across her belly.

Loud voices and laughter wafted up the steep bluff from the harbor below, instantly distracting Rachel's increasing stress. She walked to the edge of the cliff.

She heard the cheerful voices, gladly letting them steer her imagination to visions of the *Mayflower* pulling into the harbor for fresh water as it had in 1620.

This was how her mind worked … jumping from one subject to another, from one imagination to another, from one feeling to another. It wore her out at times. But she'd given up trying to tame her fleeting thoughts and feelings; it wasn't conceivable nor plausible. Even as a little girl, her father had given up trying to quell her hyperactive actions and thoughts, he'd push her off onto the housekeeper to get her out of his way, to silence her. In those days he was a serious drinker at the pub he owned, as well as at home, so he didn't have the patience or time for an inquisitive little girl who seemed to have an interest in everything. Not until his later years when he sobered did they become loving friends, father and daughter.

Why she was thinking of the *Mayflower* right at that moment, she had no clue. But it came at a most opportune time, eradicating the death images of Ethan, which would inevitably bring on the death images of her father, mother, and Pete . . . all in a pile of dead bodies.

She sat on a nearby boulder.

The *Mayflower*. She'd been reading about the history of Newlyn Bay, maybe that was why the thoughts of the *Mayflower* came to mind. She allowed her historical thoughts to wander.

The *Mayflower* had anchored in Newlyn to take on water because the supply in Plymouth was contaminated. Rachel loved history and she'd read that the journey from Plymouth, England to Plymouth in Cape Cod Bay on the eastern coast of North America took two months when they finally were able to make the trip after several attempts. They actually first sailed from Holland on a different ship, the *Speedwell* (a contradiction), then transferred to the *Mayflower* in Plymouth because the *Speedwell* was leaking between the planks.

The pilgrims were separatists, branching off from the Church of England. They had fled to Holland to worship as they wished, but wanted to go to America for complete religious freedom, which was their ultimate goal.

She visualized Captain John Smith and John Alden—of the Priscilla Mullins and Miles Standish love triangle. Alden had been a member of the crew on the Mayflower, a barrel-maker. Priscilla was seventeen years old when she boarded the ship. Being the military advisor of the new colony in Plymouth, it was said that Miles Standish's unrequited love for Priscilla never came to fruition. According to Longfellow's famous poem, whether it was true or not, it was Standish who convinced Alden to propose to Priscilla for him, only to have Priscilla tell Alden to speak up for himself. As it turned out, John and Priscilla were the third couple to be married in Plymouth and they had ten children.

In Rachel's imagination she saw the story and history unfold that had begun right there in the bay below where she lived. She could see the men, women, and children on the ship. She saw John Alden and all the eager, hopeful faces staring up at the hills and cliffs of the bay around them, not realizing the dangers ahead on the long and grueling journey they were about to take. They lost two lives at sea and more than half of the remaining settlers that first year while anchored in Cape Cod.

Sighing heavily, Rachel returned to the table and poured herself another cup of coffee. She sat for a few minutes, sipping the contents from her favorite teacup. She lifted the saucer and closely perused the tiny pink roses in the yellow and blue flowered pattern - the gold scrolling and solid pink background around the edges. *Lady Carlisle* was stamped on the back of the saucer - Royal Albert Bone China. She had seen the same china used in quite a few British movies and was thrilled to have the set. She took the last sip of coffee and set the cup and saucer on the table.

Standing up, stretching her arms, and reaching for the sky, she breathed deeply. Then she bent over and easily touched her toes. She placed her hands on her hips and turned from side to side to the count of twenty.

One of the most difficult things was to take time away from writing to do physical exercises. It took effort to maintain her ideal 5-foot 4-inch, 120-pound body. She loved gardening and walking, but she didn't feel that was enough to keep her in shape after spending such long hours, thinking and writing. Her thought processes were as much a part of her writing as the actual physical act of putting pen to paper, or fingers to keyboard, whichever the case might be, depending on where she was writing. Her imaginings and dreaming played bit parts in the concepts that unfolded in her stories.

Again at the cliff's edge she did more stretching and bending, thinking she should be jogging which would never happen in a million years of course. She'd leave that to the Stephen Kings of the world, who jogged every day for miles before sitting down to write. Not her. Besides she believed that jogging bruised the insides, jostled it all around, not to mention broke down the feet and knees. Plus . . . she was sure jogging would bruise her soul. No thank you.

She dropped to the grass and lay flat on her back, arms outstretched. Silent film star Gloria Swanson said the only exercise she did to maintain her slim, svelte body was to stretch like a cat before she got out of bed every morning. That was the extent of her daily exercise.

As Rachel lay splayed on the lawn, she closed her eyes, trying to calm and relax her mind and body. Visualizing a color with her eyes shut was a good trick. She'd think of a color until all she saw behind her eyelids was that color, bright and sparkly. She could even change the hues with her thoughts, and the concentration would eliminate all other thoughts. Sometimes it worked, sometimes it didn't.

It wasn't working.

Again she stood up, this time turning and heading towards her cottage. She stopped and pinched off a few stalks of tiny, pink rose buds from a climbing vine, inhaling the handful of fragrance as she passed through the open French doors that led into the master bedroom of her small, cozy house.

It had been four years since her fiancé Pete Bell had emailed her about the availability of her Heart's Ease Cottage while she was in Montana.

Four years.

She plopped down onto her pink satin duvet cover, lying face down, crossways on the bed, her nose buried in the bunch of roses still clutched in her hand.

She rolled over and stared at her bedroom walls covered with wallpaper of pink and pale yellow rosebuds, chintz draperies to match, lacy curtains covering the diamond-shaped panes in the windows between the panels. Pete had called it her cotton candy world.

Yes, just four years since she bought the cottage after her dear mother died. Four years since Rachel had gone to the Blackfoot Indian reservation in Montana for the service honoring her mother and the contributions she'd made to her native Indian nation. Rachel was half Blackfoot and half Irish, her father being the O'Neill side of the family which explained her rust-colored hair, her olive brown skin—easily mistaken for a deep tan—coming from her mother's side.

Both dead. Too many deaths.

Tears filled her eyes again as she remembered her dear parents, and how she missed them more than ever. She squeezed her head with both hands, trying to rid herself of the visuals and the emotion.

"That's it!" she said aloud as she jumped up and hurried into the dressing room to splash cold water on her face. She stared into the mirror. Who was this haggard, red-eyed, red-nosed, sad-looking creature standing before her? Whatever happened to the happy-go-lucky Rachel, the one who could suppress her feelings, always show a bright smile and a happy face, no matter what? That had always been her claim to fame. Where was that person? This one was looking old and haggard.

She would be forty-nine in September. Maybe her problem was the proverbial change of life, the chemical changes that were going on inside her body, screwing up her emotions and her good looks.

"Get over it, will you?" She yelled at herself in the mirror and wiped her eyes and nose again with her shirt tail.

She grabbed the bunch of roses from the bed, and went into the kitchen to get a vase.

The kitchen wall phone rang.

"Hello?"

"Hi. What are you doing?" Belinda Newland asked across the wires, sitting Indian style on a settee in her shop.

"Taking a break from writing, putting some roses in a vase. How about you?" Rachel sniffed and blotted her nose on her sleeve.

"Are you crying, Rachel?"

"No, I just had a sneeze attack."

"Well, I was thinking maybe you'd like to go to an early lunch with us in Penzance? Mama's visiting, she's at home with the boys, so we thought we'd take advantage and go into town for some R & R. What do you think?" Belinda grinned at her husband, Paul, who was standing on the bottom stair of their workshop galleries in Mousehole - his painting gallery upstairs, her sculpting studio on the ground floor.

Cradling the phone against her shoulder, Rachel ran water into the vase. "Sure. Sounds good to me. When are you going?"

"We'll pick you up at half past eleven."

"Okay, works for me." Rachel looked at the clock on the wall. "I'll be ready."

"See you then," Belinda said and hung up.

Rachel put the roses in the vase and set them on the kitchen table. Resting her hands on the back of a chair, she remembered when she and Pete had found the white-washed table at an antique shop in St. Ives, along with a wall mirror with the same fanciful carvings. Pete had hung it on the wall next to one of the heavy pine ceiling-to-floor bookcases that he had built for her.

Exhaling, Rachel turned and headed for her bedroom. No time to dawdle.

She quickly changed into a clean pair of faded blue jeans, black sandals and a black scoop-neck T-shirt. Decided that the chambray shirt she had been wearing and had used as a handkerchief all morning just wouldn't do. She tossed it into the wicker hamper.

After splashing more cool water on her face, she brushed her reddish-brown hair straight back from her face.

I can't believe Maxim is coming here. I just cannot believe it!

She searched through her drawer of scrunchies, grabbed a black and blue plaid one and fastened a pony tail to the nape of her neck.

Tomorrow, for God's sakes!

She added a touch of pink lipstick. It never took her long to get dressed and put on her minimalist makeup.

She went back out to the garden, cleared the table, and grabbed the shopping list she'd made. After plopping the cafetiere and the dishes into the sink to soak, she headed for her car in the small detached garage near the lane that ran in front of her house.

Then after driving the walkable distance to the Newlyn co-op market, stocking up on the provisions she figured she'd need for the weekend, she returned to the cottage—total trip thirty minutes.

While waiting for her closest friends—Belinda and Paul—she straightened the living room, returned books to bookshelves, restacked magazines, and fluffed the pillow cushions on the overstuffed chairs and sofas.

She just finished vacuuming the living room and giving the pastel Persian carpets in the bedrooms a once-over when she heard a car coming up the lane, so she grabbed her bag and out the door she flew.

She was exhausted. It had been an emotional roller-coaster morning.

Chapter 2

Lunch at the Admiral Benbow Pub on famous Chapel Street in Penzance was always entertaining and festive, whether it was because of the ambiance, the patrons, or the wait staff. One felt as if he had entered the hull of an old wooden sailing ship, the comfy captain's quarters of course. Wining and dining in the dimly lit alcoves amongst nautical memorabilia collected from shipwrecks going back 400 years was the pub's primary allure. However, the huge selection of brew was an attraction unto itself.

Rachel and the Newlands frequented the place as often as they could. It was their favorite haunt in Penzance. A great way to waste away an afternoon and they'd done it a time or two.

Penzance was situated on the shore of Mount's Bay flanked by Newlyn and Mousehole harbors to the southwest and Marazion to the southeast - Penzance in the middle.

In Rachel's research she'd learned that Marazion and Mousehole had once been more important than Penzance as ports, but in the eighteenth century the tin trade increased the preference of Penzance harbor to the others. She also learned that it was Sir Humphrey Davy, born and bred in Penzance, who was the inventor of the miners' safety lamp in 1815. Not only known for its tin mining industry, Penzance was known for its shipbuilding till the nineteenth century.

"So, what do you think Penzance's main industry is now, since tin and ship building has disappeared?" Rachel asked Paul as she gazed at the interior of the ship-like pub.

"Pasties," he said with a chuckle, his blue eyes gleaming.

"Oh Paul, be serious," Belinda smiled, her big green eyes sparkling up at Paul.

"So which is it? Past-ies or Paste-ies. I've heard it pronounced both ways? Rachel asked

"Past-ies," Paul said. "And people do come to Cornwall for a meal of pasties, Belinda. That's a fact."

Belinda laughed. "Well, I think the draw is mainly tourism now, Rachel. Used to be fishing, but that's gone by the wayside."

"But Newlyn and Mousehole are still fishing," Rachel said as she noticed that Belinda had lost more weight.

"Except for the closing of the pilchard factory. That was big at one time. Over all, I think fishing is in a decline," Paul added.

"You're probably right. When I first came here, the pilchard loads were still coming in. I really do miss going down to the wharf and talking to the packers and fishermen." Rachel picked up her menu and glanced at its offering.

She didn't want to think of pilchard fishing, it reminded her of Pete. She'd first met him near the wharf standing in front of The Swordfish Pub. Her heart had skipped a beat when she first saw him - his rugged looks, tattoos on his arms, and a cigarette dangling from his mouth. There was just something about him that was sexy as all get out. That first sight of him she'd never forget. He had explained to her that pilchards were the Brit term for young sardines. So talking about the pilchard factory only reminded her of Pete and that was totally off limits.

"So what should we order?" Rachel asked as she changed the subject.

An entree of wild boar and a vegetable plate, along with a starter of hot, smoked mackerel were the meal choices they decided to share. Paul ordered beer, the girls ordered wine.

"So, Rachel, what do you hear from Maxim?" Paul asked as he sipped his beer, waiting for the starter.

Rachel hesitated. "You aren't going to believe this. He called this morning, he's coming tomorrow. I'm shocked. I didn't think he'd ever come to this part of the world, such a departure from Brussels and Moscow. I really am shocked!" She lifted her glass of wine and took a gulp. "And I'm a bit uneasy about the visit."

"Why?" Paul reached up and brushed back his lengthy blonde hair that had fallen over half of his face.

"Well, it was fun meeting him in Brussels at New Year's, sort of filled a void, you know. And it was nice seeing him again in the spring when I was there visiting Mandy and Richard. But now that I've had a chance to think about it … well, I—I really don't know much about him other than the fact that his wife died ten years ago and he deals in diamonds. That's it, that's all I know, basically. Plus he's handsome as all get out." She grinned widely.

Belinda raised her eyebrows. "And he is extremely rich." She grinned at Rachel.

"Well … yep. He is that." Rachel blushed. "But that doesn't matter to me, and I'm not ready for another relationship; it's too soon. So what's the point of it all? It's making me nervous, that's all."

Belinda reached across and squeezed her best friend's wrist. "Well, you don't have to do anything but be a host, just stay in the moment. You like to entertain, and it'll be good for you to have company . . . especially the handsome, rich, virile widower that he is." She giggled.

"Belinda!" Rachel blushed again.

"Well, just remember, we're right here if you need us. Nothing wrong with being friends with him, is there?" Belinda winked at Paul.

Rachel took another hasty gulp of wine. "I know. I just need to relax and see what happens. Right!"

"I wonder what he'll think of our little paradise," Belinda said and then set her glass on the table.

"It's certainly a far-cry from what he's accustomed to, that's for sure," Paul said. "When are you going to Moscow, Rachel? You are still going?"

"Yep. I'm working on the Russian novel now, so I need to go pretty soon. I was hoping to be there already, but I had to make that unexpected trip to Los Angeles last week, had to postpone my plans for Moscow."

"So what does your agent say about the movie deal?" Belinda asked.

"She says it's a go, they're definitely going to make a movie of my second novel and possibly the third one. I can't believe it. It's a dream come true."

Paul lifted his glass towards the girls and said, "Let's toast our resident movie writer, shall we?"

"Oh no, I'm not going to write the screenplay, someone else is doing that. It's just based on my book. And that's okay with me. I don't want to go to Hollywood, don't want to get into that scene, I'm staying right here," Rachel said with determination. "They can do whatever they want with it, as long as I get the credit for the book, and I get the money."

"How does that work?" Belinda asked.

"I'm not sure, but my agent is an expert in all that. She said I'll get money up front and a percentage of box office, as well as a piece of the film and the DVD sales. So looks like she's got me covered. My attorney in L.A. is looking over the deal right now. The best part of it all is that now all my novels could be picked up and made into movies. My foot is in the door. Thank God!"

Paul reached across the table and gripped Rachel's hand. "That's incredible!"

"We're so proud of you, Rachel," Belinda added.

The young waiter brought the food while silence prevailed as he set it before them, then they began eating.

Rachel couldn't help beaming at her two dearest friends in the entire world - Belinda and Paul. Both had been there through her personal tragedies in the past few years. In fact the two of them had had more than their share of sorrow, too.

She first met Paul in London on another New Year's Eve at Trafalgar Square. It seemed as if her New Year's Eves, one after the other, were monumental occasions. That particular one was life-changing when at the stroke of midnight Paul turned and faced her in the crowd that had been shoving her forward, right into his backside. He looked down at her and commenced to give her a celebratory kiss that would have knocked her socks off if she had been wearing any. Then the throng pushed them apart while he motioned for her to follow, to no avail. Rachel happened to be with Ethan that New Year's Eve. He had been stuck a few rows back with a couple of willing ladies and of course didn't witness the passionate kiss between Rachel and Paul.

Then it was a couple months later that Rachel inadvertently ran into Paul on the seafront walk between Newlyn and Penzance, he was with Belinda. Paul remembered Rachel from New Year's Eve, and of course Rachel remembered the explosive kiss, but even without the kiss Paul was memorable— a blue-eyed, tall, tan hunk of a man with blond shoulder length hair. He could have been a model for the book cover of a period romance novel.

That day on the boardwalk, they had stopped and chatted—Paul, Belinda, and Rachel. It was the beginning of a strong, loving, friendship between the three of them. It was as if they had known each other forever. They had talked about it and all three believed they had known each other in past lives. They were believers, too, same as Rachel. To Rachel it was one more convincing incident supporting the past life theory and the fact she belonged in Cornwall.

It was interesting how Rachel's mother Lily was a firm believer and on the other hand her dear step-mother Lee wasn't. Rachel had explained it to Lee many times, but Lee being raised as an Arkansas Methodist, staked her beliefs on how she interpreted the Bible. As all hard-core protestants she believed when you died you went to heaven or hell, literally, and that was that. That was the end of it. Rachel loved Lee, and she would never argue with her. Besides the two beliefs weren't that far apart anyway. Both were spiritual, both believed in the after-life, they only differed on the reincarnation part of it. And what did it matter, anyway? Neither belief hurt anybody. Whatever felt right to Lee and felt right to Rachel was all good. Neither was a bad way to go.

"Try a bite of this boar, Rachel," Paul offered.

"Just a little piece . . . no, no. Less than that." The smell of the Bordeaux wine sauce that soaked the meat was making her mouth water.

"How about you, Belinda?" Paul asked.

"Sure, same size as the piece you gave Rachel. Yes, that's fine."

"Oh, my gosh! This is so good, isn't it?" Rachel closed her eyes as she relished the morsel melting in her mouth. She sipped her wine and sat back to relax and savor the meat and the moment. "You haven't told me what the doctor said yesterday, Belinda." Rachel was concerned about her weight loss.

Paul reached for Belinda's fragile hand that was resting in her lap.

Belinda darted a glance at Paul and then said to Rachel, "Well, I have to go back in for some tests next week. Something is going on, so they want to take a better look. Blood tests, you know. Same old stuff." She looked again at Paul. "But I'm not worried. Lymphoma is a slow one; it can come and go forever. So whatever the verdict is, I can deal with it. Nothing to worry about." She reached over and patted Rachel's hand, "Now don't you start worrying. We're not." She began eating again.

Rachel looked at Paul, watching his reaction to what Belinda had just said. He was looking down at his plate, not moving, not eating. That told her more than she wanted to know.

Belinda grasped Rachel's arm and said, "Now, Rachel. I mean it. I'm going to be okay. If I have to have more treatments, then so be it. I can do it. I made it through the last bout, I can do it again."

Rachel wondered about that. Belinda still hadn't fully recovered from the last round of chemo the year before. She was too pale and too thin, still wasn't as energetic as she was before, it was way too early for more treatments. How could her body take it? The remission was supposed to last at least five years. It had only been a year.

"I won't worry," Rachel said as she patted Belinda's hand. "You're going to get through this. I know you are."

Paul's glance was teary and fearful as his eyes met Rachel's.

"Hey, enough of this grim stuff!" Belinda interrupted. "You haven't told Rachel our good news, Paul. That's the reason we're here having lunch, remember?"

"You're right," he said. He shook himself loose from his sad thoughts.

Rachel's raised eyebrows and widened eyes revealed her eagerness to hear what he had to say. "What is it?"

"Well . . . we've been contracted by one of the most prestigious art distributors in the world, little Miss Rachel

24

O'Neill. What do you think about them apples?" he said, sounding more American than ever. He laughed and hugged his British wife to him. "Both of us. My paintings and Belinda's sculptures. We'll be in the wholesale catalogs they send to all the galleries."

"You're kidding me! So what does that mean?"

"It means they'll do the promoting, marketing, duplicating and selling for us, all we have to do is paint and sculpt and appear at the major shows."

Paul reached across the table and touched Rachel's hand. "So, we've got a huge favor to ask of you."

"Shoot! I'm up for whatever it is," Rachel said as she placed her other hand over Paul's.

"We need to meet with the distributor in London next week, and we'll have to be there a few days. We were wondering if you could watch the boys?"

Belinda chimed in. "My mother has to be in Hastings all week, so she won't be able to babysit for us, or we'd take the boys with us and leave them with her in London."

"That isn't a problem. I'd love to have them. You know that. No problem at all."

"But do you know how long Maxim will be staying?" Paul asked.

"It doesn't matter; I'll take the kids whether he's here or not. Don't you worry about it. You were here first, and they're my godchildren."

"Good, then that's that. I'm happy." Belinda grinned up at Paul and leaned her head on his shoulder.

Rachel reached for her glass, "This is terrific news! Shall we make another toast? My god, all three of us have something to celebrate today. What are the odds, huh? All our dreams coming true?"

Chapter 3

For at least the fifteenth time Rachel looked at the clock in the station and saw that it was five minutes till Maxim's train arrival. It was the same the last time she looked.

Maxim Ballenchine was arriving from London in five minutes. It was true, he was coming. He telephoned her earlier that morning to let her know the schedule.

She hadn't seen him since she'd gone back to Brussels in the spring to check on her investment in *Mandy Malone Designs* and visit her dear friends Mandy and Richard Miller. Maxim had joined them for dinner one evening while she was there and had taken her to lunch twice.

During that week, Rachel and Mandy discussed plans for opening two more *Mandy Malone Designs*, another one in Brussels and one in Bruges where it had all begun . . . where Mandy as a tourist learned how to make lace at the Kantcentrum, and where she and Rachel had first met.

Mandy was also considering opening a shop in Paris after the Belgium shops were making a profit. The first Brussels store was remarkably successful and Mandy had paid Rachel's loan back in full. Richard had wanted to pay the debt for Mandy earlier, but Mandy was insistent that she do it herself, she didn't want to use her husband's fortune in her business. She wanted to keep her independence. It had been long in coming and not without a price.

Rachel was fascinated with Mandy's ability to have come from such humble beginnings in Arkansas all the way to Belgium to make lace and design clothing. What were the odds of that happening? Very, very slim. Mandy's mother had been a seamstress in Arkansas up until her death when Mandy was a young girl. She had taught Mandy as a girl how to sew and embroider fabric, but Mandy learned the rest on her own.

And now the girl actually lived in a castle, a wedding gift from her wealthy American husband Richard. It was incredible where she was now and where she was headed. Mandy was one determined young woman. Rachel admired her for doing what she loved most in the world, and for finding the love of her life during the process. Mandy had found purpose and passion at such a young age; Rachel wondered if she knew how lucky she was.

In many respects Rachel envied Mandy because she seemed to have the perfect life and knew exactly what she wanted, but mostly she was proud of her and had taken her under her wing. It was like having the daughter she never had.

Thinking of Mandy made Rachel think of her son. She hadn't talked to Devin since she'd returned from the States the week before, but she'd meant to call him. Devin had met her in Brentwood at her father's estate while she was there. Her son Devin and his wife used the house quite often when they flew into L.A. from Denver. In fact they were spending the next two weeks there.

She hurried to the rest room at the train station one last time, didn't want to have to go to the loo right away when they returned to her cottage.

Nothing worse than your guest hearing your toilet habits.

That was one thing she wanted to fix in her house. If someone was in the living room, they could hear what was going on in the bathrooms and every other room in the house. It had to be the doors, because the walls were eighteen inches thick. Had to be the doors with the big gaps underneath. She needed new doors.

When she returned to the platform from the ladies room, it was noon straight up. She could see the train coming 'round the bend towards the Penzance station. Her heart quickened. She breathed deeply. Johnny Cash singing *I hear the train a comin'* came to mind. She laughed.

God! I hope he likes the guest room. It's small-time compared to what he's used to.

Her mind was racing over the plans she'd made for the weekend and going over the special provisions she'd made in her home for Maxim. She didn't have many guests, so she hoped she hadn't forgotten anything.

Oh dear, there he is!

Rachel waved at the elegant silver-haired gentleman that stepped from the train carrying a valise - an old fashioned, but new, camel-colored leather valise, not a suitcase, not one of the standard black four-wheelers. A weekender, a valise, with straps and buckles. *Classy.*

He was wearing a short leather jacket to match, tan shirt open at the collar, light brown slacks and brown Italian leather shoes.

Wow! He is something, isn't he? Wow! Margaret's Spanish nobleman came to mind. He dressed the same way - the elegant style of rich European men.

Rachel questioned her own choice of blue jeans and black top, maybe a bit too pedestrian compared to Maxim's attire.

"Maxim!" She hurried towards him, waving, catching his attention through the approaching passengers.

His stride picked up speed when he saw her and he flashed a wide grin showing his sparkling perfect teeth as he raised his hand in the air.

"Rachel! Here!"

Chapter 4

The Ship Inn in Mousehole was quiet that afternoon as Rachel and Maxim sat at a corner table in the pub waiting for Belinda and Paul to join them. Rachel had decided to drive to Mousehole before going home, to meet up with the Newlands and introduce Maxim. Of course she was stalling, and she felt she desperately needed fortification before taking him to her cottage where they would be alone.

So, first she killed time by showing Maxim the little seaport village of Mousehole, going through the tourist shops. They stood at the sea wall near the Ship Inn, gazing out at the boats attached to strong ropes strung in the tiny harbor, giant ropes as thick as a fist connected to the rock and mortar sea wall fronting the village. However, there wasn't any sea water lapping up on the narrow beach below the rock wall in the semi-walled harbor because it was low tide, and most of the boats were sitting askew at the end of their ropes on the sandy bottom with exposed hulls. But nearer to the narrow harbor entrance, other boats were afloat in water tethered by ropes stretching out to them. It was a sight that captivated Rachel every time she went to Mousehole. Truly an artist's paradise. She had spent many hours viewing the boats in the harbor and wandering the little village.

Mousehole, one of the most picturesque harbors in England, was a couple miles west of Penzance around Mount's bay, just past Newlyn where Rachel lived. Mousehole was known for its Christmas illuminations when the boats were decked out in holiday lights and décor and paraded around the harbor.

But now she and Maxim were enjoying the dark rustic interior of the Ship Inn, one of her favorite pubs. She felt safe. She loved dark pubs. They calmed her, and there was something to be said about the coziness and romantic shadowed corners. It gelled well with champagne and candles and someone of the opposite sex.

Maxim was holding Rachel's hand across the table as he talked about his trip from London to Cornwall earlier in the day. There'd been a delay with the scheduled flight to Newquay, he said, and so he missed the first train from Newquay to Penzance, and had to wait for the next one. He wasn't complaining, he was just making small talk. He always gave the impression of being a happy, positive man regardless of the circumstances.

Rachel liked that about him. She had already noticed he was able to take pretty much everything in stride. Nothing seemed to rattle him. He was the same every time she was with him—pleasant and charming—almost too good to be true. But then she was the same way, whether she felt it or not, putting on a happy face when inside she was withering.

So she wondered if there was a horrible dark side to Maxim, a violent temper lurking somewhere behind his façade. Her father had once told her to be cautious of a man who seemed too good to be true.

"Did you know that 'The Little Country', by Charles de Lint was set in the village of Mousehole?" she said, searching for things to say 'till the Newlands arrived.

"I'm not familiar with Mr. Lint. Is he a popular writer?" Maxim asked.

"Well, actually, I'm not all that familiar with him either." She laughed. "He writes fantasy and horror. Not my preference. But I did read the novel when I found out it was set in Mousehole. It's about a female musician, Janey Little, who discovers a hidden book in her grandfather's Cornwall home. A magical book. From the pages leap a chain of events that takes her across the sea to America and to Madrid. A fantasy, actually. An urban fairy tale, if you will, but sinister. But enough about that.

"I just want to say that it's so nice of you to come to Cornwall, Maxim. I know you're a busy man, and I want you to know how much I appreciate it. I love showing off my home and my friends."

"It is my pleasure, believe me." Maxim squeezed her hand before letting go to reach for his glass of Scotch. "And this is probably one of the best Glenmorangie on the market - Highland Park Scotch whisky. I am surprised we found a bottle in this far corner of the world. Would you like a sip?"

"No, thank you. I'm not a whisky person. Can't stand the smell of it, actually."

He set the glass on the table. "I'm sorry; maybe I should have had a glass of champagne with you. I wouldn't want to offend your sense of smell."

"No, no, no. I didn't mean it that way." She touched his arm. "I can't smell it on you. What I meant was, I can't get past the smell to drink it myself. No problem. Really. I'm glad they had it here for you. Cheers!" She lifted her glass to meet his.

"This just happens to be the best Scotch in the world. From Scotland of course."

"No kidding? And it's here in Mousehole? See, I told you, you would like this place." She was beginning to feel the effect of the champagne. "You know, on second thought, I'm

32

thinking maybe I should have a cup of coffee now, too much champagne, I'm feeling a bit woosey. Do you mind?"

"Not at all." He stood up to go to the bar and at the same time Belinda and Paul came through the doorway.

"Oh, they're here!" Rachel stood, reached for Maxim's hand and moved toward her friends with Maxim in tow.

After an early evening meal of fish & chips at the Ship Inn, the two couples drove in separate cars the mile and a half to Rachel's cottage for dessert.

"You baked this yourself?" Maxim asked while devouring a slice of lemon cake with lemon butter-crème frosting and topped with candied cherries and a mint leaf as garnish.

"I promise you, I did. Baked it last night. Lemon is my favorite and I'm glad you like it too. There's more if you want another piece. Plenty of it."

"I believe I will take you up on that, thank you." Maxim gobbled the final bite, and took a sip of coffee while handing his plate to Rachel.

Paul added, "Me too, Rachel," he said as he lifted his plate.

"How about you, Belinda? Seconds?" Rachel hesitated in front of Belinda before heading for the kitchen.

"I'm okay. But it is delicious. The best, yet."

"You can take some home with you, then. If it stays here I'll eat it all. You know how I am with lemony desserts. Just can't resist them. Anyone want more Champagne?"

The three yes's were in unison.

"Paul, will you do the honors? There's another bottle in the bar fridge, the ice bucket's on the bar. And I'll bring more coffee too." She left the room.

"Rachel said you were in London on business?" Belinda said to Maxim as she took in his tan and gorgeous gray-blue eyes. They were more silver than Paul's - whose eyes were nearer an aqua shade. Her green eyes, the guys' blue, and Rachel's hazel were quite an assortment under one roof, she was thinking. Of course her interest in eye color carried right over into her sculpting, creating subjects of metal with eyes of multicolored chunks of Canadian Ammolite. Her rainbow rocks she called them.

"Yes, I was in London for several days meeting with diamond merchants," he replied.

Paul took the bottle of Champagne from the small refrigerator. "So, tell us more about the Russian diamond industry, Maxim. I didn't realize diamonds were such a Russian commodity."

"Oh yes! Both diamonds and amber."

Paul popped the cork and took the ice bucket to the cocktail table.

Maxim continued: "The diamond mines are mostly in the Sakha Republic – a section in the northeastern corner of Russia. Are you familiar with Sakha?"

"No, I'm not. Don't know much about Russia at all," Paul said as he poured a glass for Belinda.

Maxim motioned towards his own glass. "I'll have some, too, thank you. Sakha has its own president and is the largest subnational governing body by area in the world at over a million square miles, yet it has only a population of 950,000. Its capital is Yakutsk and it's under the jurisdiction of the Russian Federation."

"I didn't realize Russia was so huge, and you're talking about only a section up in the northeastern corner?" Belinda asked.

"Oh yes, Russia is the world's largest country, comprises one-eighth of its inhabited land, and shares boundaries with fourteen countries." He took a sip of champagne. "And Sakha is over-flowing with raw materials, so it is very important to

Russia. The soil contains large reserves of oil, gas, coal, diamonds, gold, silver, tin, tungsten and much, much more. Nearly all Russian diamonds are mined in Sakha, accounting for over one quarter of the world's diamond production."

Rachel entered with the cake and served the men. "Sounds like we should all go to Russia and invest in mining. Who would have known so many minerals were in such a remote part of the world?"

Maxim took a bite of the cake. "Problem is, although it's easy to fly in to Sakha's International airport, it's difficult to travel around the region because of the constant permafrost. Blacktop roads are non-existent. The roads are dirt and therefore, mud. But the waterways are a well-used mode of transportation, many rivers. Over forty percent of the republic is above the Arctic Circle."

"So then, all the diamond mines are in the Sakha Republic?' Paul's interest was obvious.

"Yes, that is true."

"And you personally deal directly with the mines in the region? I mean, you go there?" Paul asked.

"Yes, my company, Ballenchine Brothers, is partnered with Alrosa which is a major Russian mining company. We deal with the selling of rough diamonds to Antwerp, London and New York City. Alrosa owns all the Russian mines and a few in Angola and Namibia. Our biggest competitor is DeBeers, you've heard of DeBeers, who owns over twenty diamond mines in Africa and many others around the world, Canada, especially." Maxim took another sip of Champagne.

Belinda lifted her glass and said, "Diamond mining in Canada?"

"Yes, Canada. But most of the world's diamonds are from Australia." Maxim eyes lit up as he talked about his favorite subject.

"Australia? That's a surprise," Belinda looked at Rachel with widened eyes. "Did you know that, Rachel?"

"No, I didn't."

"The Argyle diamond mine in Kimberly, Australia, is the world's largest producer. It also produces 90 to 95 percent of the world's pink diamonds," Maxim said.

Paul was intrigued. "Amazing. Australia. I figured its only products were beef, wool, didgeridoo, and kangaroo."

They all laughed.

"So what about blood diamonds, Maxim? I've been doing some research on that. Is Alrosa involved in them since it owns a mine in Africa?"

"Well, my dear, we aren't interested in mining diamonds to fund conflicts and wars. We have very little to do with what is going on in Africa. Even though we have small interests in mines there, there is nothing of any great magnitude. So I will say, no, we are not involved in the blood diamond trade."

"Good. I'm glad to hear that. In my new novel I'm touching on blood diamonds in the story. But I really need to see a diamond mine, Maxim. Is that possible? In Sakha?"

"I shall arrange it when you come to Moscow. But I must warn you, the mines are above the Arctic Circle, it is cold, isolated, and not very pleasant."

"I can handle it." The thought excited Rachel.

"I have meant to ask you about the diamond pendant you wear." He reached to look at it more closely. "This is a beautiful stone. Do you know the history of it?"

Rachel took a deep breath, "Yep, it was given to me by my fiancé Pete Bell. It was in my engagement ring. I had it made into a pendant." Tears clouded her eyes. *No, no, please don't cry. Not now.*

"It was made from a raw diamond mined in Brazil," Paul added, seeing the direction Rachel was going emotionally he stepped in. "Pete was there on assignment and bought it from one of the mining companies. He took it to a jeweler in Belem and had it cut and polished and made into a ring. So she's the first to wear it. A beauty, isn't it?"

"Yes, it is." Maxim had pulled a loupe from his pocket and was inspecting the stone resting in his fingers.

Rachel regained her composure. "I always wear it now; a jeweler in Penzance designed the pendant setting a few months ago."

"Brazil has had its share of illegal prospectors and killings, even up to last year," Maxim said as he turned the pendant and viewed the back of the stone through his magnifier. "It could be dangerous to be caught in the crossfire of the illegals and the Cinta Larga Indian reservation where mining is ongoing. Under normal circumstances, only the Indians are allowed to mine the diamonds. So, the government stepped in after forty illegals had been killed, and the hostility lessened somewhat. But smugglers abound in Brazil. The diamonds are actually making it to Belgium illegally." He sat back and put the loupe in his pocket. "Yours is a lovely one. The cutting is superb. Are you aware it is called a Cushion Cut?"

"No, Pete never said what it was. And I just dropped it off at the jeweler, told him the setting I wanted. I don't even know how many carats it is."

"First, the Cushion Cut is an antique cut that resembles the Old Mine Cut, deep with large facets - common in the late nineteenth and the early twentieth centuries - and a modern Oval Cut. It is sometimes referred to as the candlelight diamond, designed for sparkling in candlelight before electricity came into being. It is not as fiery or brilliant as newer cuts, but it has a marvelously romantic and classic look and definitely stands out from the crowd of round brilliants. And I would say it is at least five carats. A magnificent stone."

"Thank you, Maxim." She reached up and held the diamond pendant, rubbing her thumb across its surface. "And I thank Pete for extending his stay in Brazil so he could bring it to me in Paris on New Year's Eve to propose to me. But now I'm wondering if it was the poachers or the Cinta Larga who killed him. He was near the reservation; he'd emailed me about it." She hesitated for a moment. "I will tell you this; Brazil is definitely not on my list of countries to visit. Ever."

Maxim placed his hand on hers and with abundant empathy exuding from his kind blue eyes, he said, "I'm so sorry you lost him, my dear."

Chapter 5

When Maxim came out of the guest room the next morning, breakfast was ready. Rachel had heard him in the shower and had timed the food just right. But she was surprised to see him in jeans and polo shirt, since he usually dressed in slacks and expensive silk shirts.

"We're having breakfast outside under the magnolia tree. I hope you don't mind. It's a beautiful view and a beautiful day," she said as she picked up a tray of food.

"Please, let me," Maxim said as he took the silver tray from her.

"All right then. Through the French doors and onward!" She dramatically motioned to the open doorway off the dining room.

There were two sets of French doors, one set leading from Rachel's bedroom to the garden, the other from the dining room. The day was already warm; in fact, it was being reported as a heat wave, so both sets of doors were wide open letting in whatever breeze came their way. Usually being that close to the sea was a godsend, because no matter how hot it got, there were still cool breezes off the ocean to be had.

39

Not to mention that Rachel loved airing out the house in the mornings, even during the cooler months. The first thing she would do when she got out of bed was put on the coffee and open up the house—she opened draperies and blinds, and flung open the doors and windows.

The garden table was already set with placemats, china, and silverware, so Maxim put the tray in the empty space on the glass tabletop.

"Sit where you want," Rachel said as she came up from behind him with another silver tray holding a plate of American biscuits and butter, honey, jam and jelly. "I'll go back and get the coffee. Be right back."

Maxim watched her scurry back to the cottage, impressed at her energy and her lovely backside. She was wearing black leggings and a blue chambray shirt hanging open and loose to mid-thigh, a black tank top underneath. Her shiny, auburn hair was thick and wavy and fell casually just above her shoulders. He was also impressed at the beauty of the table setting, the well-tended garden full of blossoms, the unbelievable view of the sea. It didn't look real. None of it looked real, including Rachel, not to mention the table of delectable food spread before him with an artistic flair.

He couldn't remember when he felt as good as he did right at that moment. Rachel was a wonderful hostess, that couldn't be denied. She was smart, clever, artistic, pretty . . . all the rare qualities rolled into one, hard to find in one package. At least that had been his experience.

Of course his wife had been a kind woman when she was young, and was a beauty at one time, she had talents, but she had always been more of a house frau than a career-minded, multi-faceted female like Rachel. Katarina had been content to live in their country home outside of Brussels with her menagerie of animals and birds, and she didn't care to travel or entertain. She had finally become a total recluse, had gained weight, hardly moved from room to room, wouldn't walk although there was nothing wrong with her legs. She went from bed to wheelchair to chair or sofa. Alcoholism played a major part in her condition and isolation; Maxim had dealt with her problem for over twenty years.

Katarina and Maxim didn't have children, due to a serious infection she had during her twenties. The two pregnancies she had didn't last past three months. Surgery became necessary, removing her reproductive organs. Maxim had always wanted a son to carry on the business like he had for his father. Katarina was from a large family and became dangerously depressed over not being able to bear children. So she withdrew from Maxim's sexual advances, alcoholism and more depression followed.

At first Maxim felt guilty about his dalliances. Their lives were separate in every sense of the word and had been for many years. He told the women he met that he was a widower, just as he told Rachel.

But Maxim provided for Katarina's well being, made sure she had what she needed to make her comfortable in her habitation, she had the best care, the best doctors, the best therapists money could buy, but that was the extent of it from him. Most of the time he lived his life as if she didn't exist, as he was doing in Cornwall at that exact moment.

Rachel and Katarina are as different as salt and pepper, Maxim pondered as he picked up the linen napkin and placed it on his lap, feeling a pang of guilt.

"Here I am!" Rachel said brightly. "Oh, go ahead and help yourself, you shouldn't have waited for me. There's sausage and bacon in that covered dish, scrambled eggs and sliced tomatoes in that one, fried sweet potato over there, and toast and scones in that one, and you must try my biscuits. Have you had American biscuits? With gravy?" She began pouring the coffee.

41

"No, I have not."

"Well, you have to try them, at least have one. Here I'll fix it on a separate plate for you. The biscuits are my dear stepmother's recipe. When I first came here the British thought I meant a cookie when I said biscuit. They call their cookies, biscuits." She laughed. "I guess an American biscuit could be described as a type of scone without sugar, at least that's all I could think of to describe it. Here you go. Biscuit and gravy. Homemade, not out of a can or box."

"I shall not be able to get up from the table if I eat all this," he laughed.

"Oh, I forgot the orange juice. Go ahead, I'll be right back."

After they'd eaten and the plates and tureens had been cleared away, they sat back, basking in the morning sun, sipping coffee.

"So, you'll be traveling to St. Petersburg, and then to Moscow?" Maxim asked.

"Yep, there's still a bit of research I need to do in St. Pete, for a week most likely. Then I'll be coming to Moscow."

"You will let me know in advance when you are to arrive?"

"Of course I will. I'll know as soon as I get to St. Pete and organize my schedule. But I'll be communicating with you before that, so you'll know where I am, if that's all right with you," she said in-between sips.

"I am not looking forward to leaving on Tuesday," Maxim said softly.

Rachel replied, "Then by all means, stay longer." She was beginning to like his company; he was easy to be with. It felt natural and familiar.

"I wish I cold stay longer. But I must be in Brussels for a meeting with DeBeers, and there is still much preparation to do for the meeting. I was hoping to stay at least a day or two longer, but the phone call came this morning saying the meeting is to take place as planned and how important it is that I be there in advance. Alrosa is trying to increase the percentage of Russian diamonds we're allowed to place in the Antwerp market. DeBeers is always holding us at a ridiculous minimum, while it controls sales in all markets around the world. We're in direct competition with them. It's an ongoing dilemma and an important meeting. But I do not want to bore you with talk about business." He leaned back and sighed heavily. "Believe me when I say I would love to be here with you for at least a week, my dear, if not more." He reached for her hand.

"I would like that, too." She felt she meant it, but was feeling a little awkward holding his hand. It wasn't that his touch didn't feel good to her, because it did. And although she had been able to resist his charm and the sexual attraction, her resistance was growing less by the moment. It was inevitable that they would make love, but she didn't want that yet, it was too soon. And then again, Maxim hadn't initiated it. So there was a chance he wasn't even interested, but she doubted that. All the signs were there. But it didn't matter, she wasn't interested.

"Remember, we're meeting Belinda and Paul for a late lunch at the Godolphin in Marazion," she said as she stood up. "So if we're going to check out Penzance and Marazion before that, and I definitely want you to see Mount Saint Michaels and meet Margaret, we'd better get going. What time do you have?" She didn't wear watches.

Maxim looked at his Patek Philippe watch. "Half past nine."

"Okay, I'll clear off the rest and let the dishes soak. Oh, would you like more coffee while I'm straightening up?"

"Yes, that would be perfect. I'll enjoy this wonderful weather and gaze at the boats, unless you need help?"

"No, you stay here and relax; I'll be back in a minute. Here you go." She poured the coffee and headed for the cottage, glad to get away to catch her breath.

It felt strange having a man sleeping in her house again, not to mention sitting on one of the heart-filigreed garden chairs her lover Pete had given her.

She was confused about her feelings for Maxim, and was feeling guilty.

Chapter 6

On the drive to Marazion, Rachel detoured through Penzance rather than skirting the town on the coastal road. She wanted to show Maxim a few historical landmarks and a close-up view of the harbor.

She was feeling relaxed and felt more in control of the emotions and fears that had plagued her the day before, the fear of being alone with Maxim. Maybe she felt okay about it now because they were out in the public away from the cottage of memories and the close proximity, although they were pretty close in the car. But that was different somehow; she didn't feel as vulnerable in the car for some reason.

"I love this lane," she said as she drove up Chapel Street towards the main part of Penzance. "That's St. Mary's Church sitting there in all her glory, the same as in the seventeenth century, and that small chapel at the end was built in the thirteenth century. Some of the oldest buildings are on this street. I walk this way to downtown Penzance at least once a week. I just love it."

Maxim was spellbound by Rachel's enthusiasm. "It would be pleasant to stroll along the sea and on your Chapel Street. Maybe we can do that one morning while I'm here."

"Sure. Tomorrow, if you like. We'll come to my favorite café for breakfast tomorrow. A traditional English breakfast - eggs, sausage, bacon, black pudding and mushrooms, baked beans, hash browns … I mean it is tons of food, all on one plate." She laughed.

"Can we order a la carte?" he smiled.

"We can order whatever we want. I never eat all that stuff, and especially not the black pudding. There's something about congealed blood that just doesn't appeal to me. So I usually have toast and bacon or just a scone and coffee. Oh, that's the Egyptian House built in 1836. Amazing isn't it? Did you know that the mother of the Bronte sisters lived on Chapel Street? 37 Chapel Street . . . it's right up here. You know who the Brontes were, don't you?"

"Yes, that I do know - Jane Eyre, Wuthering Heights - very talented family of writers. You seem to be very fond of England and its history." Maxim rested his hand on Rachel's shoulder, his twinkling eyes perusing her countenance from his perspective in the passenger seat. "You make it come alive when you speak about it."

"Yep, I do love England, and I love Cornwall. I really do. Can't imagine living anywhere else in the world. So we'll drive down Main Street and then out by the harbor and on to Marazion. Penzance isn't a very large town, the population is around 22,000. So it doesn't take long to drive through it. We still have time to cruise around Marazion a bit before we meet up with Paul and Belinda. We can do that on foot, though, Marazion is a tiny burg, only about fifteen hundred people. But it's Britain's oldest, did you know that?"

"No, this Britain is all very new to me, and I know nothing of Cornwall. This is my first experience outside of London." Maxim chuckled at Rachel's child-like exuberance. It had been years since he had seen such a spark of raw spirit in a woman.

Rachel glanced at him with a broad grin. "I lived here in a past life, you know. Or didn't I tell you?"

Maxim laughed, "No, you didn't tell me. But you must."

So she told him of her dreams of Newlyn and Marazion, Mount St Michaels and Charlestown. How the dreams had started when she lived in California. How she was drawn to Cornwall while living and working north of London with Ethan Philips. How she came to Cornwall and was convinced that was where she belonged. How she and Pete had gone to the manor in Charlestown at Margaret's suggestion and found out that she had possibly been married into the founding Rashleigh family in the eighteenth century. She told him about meeting a Rashleigh descendant, the elderly Lord Evans, at the manor. She told Maxim of the giant painting still hanging in the great estate house. How it was an uncanny likeness of her, in a gown with exactly the same jewelry that she'd seen in her dreams. She said she was convinced more than ever why she felt so at home in Cornwall. She believed she had truly lived there in a past life.

After they spent a half hour driving around Penzance, they drove on to Marazion. She parked the car and they walked through the little village on Mount's Bay where they had an early beer at a pub tucked up the lane in the east part of town. Then they found the spot where Rachel believed her prized Lamorna Birch watercolor of the Mount was painted. She told Maxim she'd show it to him when they returned to the cottage.

Then they went to the Godolphin to meet up with their friends for a late lunch.

Margaret of the St Aubyns was already sitting with Paul and Belinda when they arrived and was privy to the story of who Maxim was and how Rachel had met him in Brussels. Margaret stood and greeted the couple as they entered the Seaview Room and signaled to the waitress to bring champagne on the house, knowing how Rachel loved her champagne.

Drinks were sipped happily with the delectable tapas Margaret had prepared for them. Conversation ran the gamut from the art world of Paul and Belinda to Maxim's diamonds in Russia and Belgium. Margaret told Maxim about St. Aubyn history and the background of her Spanish husband who was at the moment in Spain tending to royal business.

Margaret suddenly glanced towards the entrance and immediately stood, her face brightening even more than it already was. "My God, it's Lord Evans!"

Coming through the doors was the man himself in all his grandeur. His mail coach style cravat of dark blue silk positioned gracefully around his neck, looped, and stuffed down into the front of his light blue shirt; yellow sweater vest, grey slacks and navy blue sport coat with a coat of arms embroidered on the breast pocket topping off the look of affluence he so graciously represented. His silver hair and grey eyes matched his attire.

"Over here, George. Look who is here." Margaret called out to him.

The Lord George Evans dismissed his driver and joined the group with all eyes upon him.

Hugs, greetings and introductions were made as they settled into a superb luncheon, a meal that was fit for a King . . . or a Lord, as it was.

Questions were asked of Rachel about her writing, about the plot of the latest novel, and the film that was in production.

Lord Evans brought them up to date on what was happening politically in the region. He also spoke of Rachel's connection to his family.

Maxim answered questions of Russia.

Paul and Belinda answered questions about the art distributor in London. Maxim and Lord Evans both expressed their desire to purchase some of their work.

All in all it was a catching up and getting acquainted session. A pleasant time that ended too soon, but Rachel still wanted to take Maxim across to the Mount.

So they all said their goodbyes and off they went, back to their normal routines, except for Rachel and Maxim who headed out across the causeway towards the castle atop St Michael's Mount.

As they walked along the rocky pathway, Rachel told Maxim about the movie she'd seen with Jean Simmons and Josh Ackland - *Daisies in December* - that was set in the region and one scene was shot on the Mount. Told him what an impression it had made on her and had only fueled her feelings that Cornwall had once been her home in a past life.

As they traipsed through the site of the original harbor at the foot of the mount that had once serviced the castle, Rachel pointed out the buildings that had been converted to cater to the thousands of tourists and visitors each year. She guided Maxim into one of the shops and he bought a small bottle of wine to have when they reached the top of the island. They found a couple of tourist mugs they liked, a bottle opener, and off they went, bag in hand.

It was a beautiful, cloudless day. The sun was shining, their tummies were full, and their spirits were high. After touring the castle, they perched on a stone picnic table in a grassy area and sipped wine together while viewing the ocean stretching out to sea and across the bay to Penzance, Newlyn, and Mousehole beyond.

Rachel felt as the Jean Simmons character felt in the movie, sitting at the same table. There was no confusion, no doubt, she was elated. How could anyone have negative thoughts in that environment?

"It doesn't get any better than this," Maxim said.

Chapter 7

They returned to Rachel's Heart's Ease cottage after spending the afternoon in Marazion and were standing near the bluff watching the sun disappear into the sea.

The scant clouds that were forming low on the horizon enhanced one of the most beautiful sunsets Maxim had ever seen. Hues of red, orange, pink, and yellow appeared to have been brushed by an artist across the sky, the rich colors reflecting in the water.

"Never have I seen such a magnificent sunset! Now I understand your feelings for this Cornwall of yours."

With Maxim's arms holding her close, they stood side by side beneath the magnolia tree, marveling at the majestic seascape stretched out before them.

"It's just as beautiful during the summer storms. Sometimes I'll sit by my windows for hours watching the wind and rain pelt the shoreline. I get such energy and restoration from them." At that very moment she could feel the synergy from the earth's elements and from Maxim. It made her body buzz with excitement.

Maxim stepped back and held her at arms length, facing him. He looked long and hard into Rachel's eyes.

"That phone call a few minutes ago was to tell me that everything has been moved up a day. I'm afraid I must leave tomorrow morning instead of Tuesday."

The truth of the matter, the call was from his wife's doctor, saying that she had been critically injured, had fallen down a flight of stairs and was in the hospital.

Maxim spoke in a whisper as he moved closer to Rachel, still looking into her eyes, "I will miss you very much."

"I— I will miss you, too." She was transfixed by his tone and gorgeous lips as he spoke.

It felt natural to come together in an embrace, as natural and exciting as one could feel while the zings and thrills of touch coursed their bodies. Maxim tilted Rachel's face up to his, and they were still gazing into each other's eyes when their lips met. At first the kisses were soft and tender, and then escalated to hard and eager. Their lips and tongues stirred up long overdue passion within each other. Their bodies seem to morph with each breath and heartbeat.

Rachel was the first to pull away. Her rampant thoughts and imagery had them already naked in the bed and she panicked. She couldn't bring herself to desecrate the memory of making love with Pete in her cottage. She just couldn't. It didn't seem right.

"Maxim, I— I can't. I just can't. I'm sorry."

He reached for her hands and held them to his lips, gently. "You needn't, my dear. Please look at me. I will not impose myself upon you. I do not want to spoil our friendship. Trust me, yes? For I only want what you want. Do you understand?"

Rachel nodded, teary-eyed as she turned away. He placed his arm across her back and shoulders and they walked together toward the cottage.

Before they entered the French doors, Maxim took her hands again. "Now let us have champagne from one of the special bottles I brought for us, and then we will go to the Ship Inn in Mousehole for a light supper. Yes?"

"Yep, that sounds good." Rachel entered the house, Maxim following.

For a moment she stopped and stared at the painting of Saint Michael's Mount hanging next to the mirror in the dining room. "This is the Birch painting I told you about in Marazion."

"It depicts the Mount perfectly."

She told him how it had been a priceless find as she had rummaged through a quasi antique shop mostly filled with cast-offs nobody wanted. It was one of those *one person's trash to another person's treasure* sort of shops. The painting was a view of the Mount from a hill in Marazion. His usage of muted shades of golds, browns, blues, and greens captivated her and she told Maxim she often thought if she became a serious painter she would capture all of Cornwall's glory on canvas just as Birch had done, using those muted colors.

She had wondered if Birch had ever painted Newlyn Harbor. She knew he had been in Newlyn early on in his career when it was known as an artist colony. Samuel John Lamorna Birch was his full name. He'd taken the name of Lamorna from the village where he lived when he returned to Cornwall after a year of study in Paris.

"I find it amusing that his assumed name was to set himself apart from another painter called Birch," she said.

She wasn't surprised and could fully understand why he would return to Cornwall to live out his life. She, too, found that it exuded a peacefulness and inspiration hard to find anywhere else in the world.

She continued, "He must have painted the harbor in at least one of his thousands of pictures, but I haven't found one yet."

They walked towards the bar. Maxim reached for the champagne resting in an iced bucket.

"I'll call Paul and Belinda while you're doing that, they want us to come over for dessert later. Is that all right with you? I'd love for you to see their house."

"Yes, of course," Maxim said as he poured their drinks. "And then we'll come back here and enjoy a nightcap and conversation before we retire into our . . . separate bedrooms."

Rachel stopped and turned; her sparkling eyes looking into Maxim's.

He was puzzled at the sudden stare and moved towards her.

"Why are you so perfect?" she finally said, grinning from ear to ear.

"Why are you so enjoyable?" he said with champagne bottle in hand, and he kissed the tip of her nose.

Chapter 8

It was a gorgeous morning as Rachel drove Maxim to the airport in Newquay. The sun was bright, the air was cool, not a cloud in the sky. He had decided to fly directly to Brussels rather than do the train to London and then fly.

They were on the road very early, which would get her back in plenty of time to pick up the boys so Paul and Belinda could be on their way to London for the week.

As she drove, Rachel was sorting in her mind the activities she was planning for the boys. She was going to take them to Marazion for lunch one day, take them to the castle, maybe to the Eden Project - although she wasn't sure of Eden, it might be too much for toddlers, might be too much of a reminder for her, still.

"You are in deep thought," Maxim said as he reached across the top of the seats and touched her shoulder.

"Oh, I'm sorry. I was thinking about my week ahead with the boys. I'm a bit excited about it. Sorry." She looked over at him before turning onto the airport property. "I hope you've genuinely enjoyed your stay in Cornwall."

"Yes, I most certainly have, and I look forward to coming again, if you will have me," he clutched her shoulder and leaned to kiss her on the cheek. "I will miss you."

Rachel pulled to a stop at the curb in front of the airline terminal. She touched Maxim's face, "I'll miss you, too." She leaned and softly kissed his lips. "But we'll see each other soon in Moscow."

"Not soon enough, my dear." He hugged her, kissed her forehead and then opened the passenger door. "I will get my bag, you stay in the car." He hesitated and then leaned back in to kiss her again, this time on the lips. *"Horoshij poka, moya l'ubov',"* he whispered and then quickly exited as if he was afraid to linger one more moment, afraid he might not leave at all.

She threw him a kiss when he looked back at her and waved, and then she watched him go through the terminal doors and disappear out of sight. *Good bye, my love,* she thought in English what he had said in Russian. *Horoshij poka.*

"Okay, that's enough," she said aloud after he was out of sight. She pulled away from the terminal and headed back to Newlyn.

Her mind shifted to Baby Jake, although he wasn't a baby anymore, and to Paulie - Paul Junior. Her heart felt full as she remembered she was the god-mother to the five- and three-year old boys.

It took less time than she figured to get to the Newland's three-story house on the hill. The castle on the hill, Rachel called it. Paul had been lucky to literally steal the house from a friend whose mother had passed and left it to her son along with several other properties. His friend wasn't crazy about Cornwall so he sold it to Paul at a low, ridiculous price, not needing the money, but wanting to be rid of the house. It had an unobstructed view of the bay, of Penzance and Marazion, Mount St. Michaels's, Newlyn and the forever openness of the sea and sky.

She pulled to a stop at the entrance and hurried towards the front door. Paul opened it before she was able to ring the doorbell.

"Here she is," he called out and he hugged her.

Belinda appeared, holding Baby Jake's hand and carrying Paulie. "And here they are," she added with a giggle. "Yours for a week. I hope they're not too much for you to handle."

"I'll get their bags," Paul said as he went back into the house.

"They won't be too much for me, not at all. I'm looking forward to it. Okay, let's load up, boys." Rachel took Jake's hand and led the way to the car.

Paul hurried past her, carrying bags and a car seat. He adjusted the car seat in the back and placed the bags on the floor.

Belinda smothered Paulie's face with kisses before she fastened him into the car seat.

His big blue eyes were twinkling as he said, "Bye-bye, Mommy, bye-bye." He giggled and waved.

"He loves to ride in a car," Belinda told Rachel.

"Great, we'll be doing a bit of that. I've got a busy week planned for them. It'll be fun."

"Hug daddy good bye, Jake," Paul said as he lifted Jake into his arms. "You help Auntie Rachel take care of Paulie, okay?'

"I will. I'll be the daddy," he said seriously, as he put his arms around Paul's neck and gave a tight squeeze. "Don't you worry. We'll take care of Paulie."

Belinda's eyes began to tear up. "I'm going to miss my babies," she said as she took Jake from Paul's arms and gave him another big hug.

"Oh, you'll be back before you know it," Baby Jake said.

They all widened their eyes and laughed at another of the boy's adult comments that usually astounded them.

"Yep, they'll be back before they know it. I agree." Rachel winked at Paul and Belinda. "He's growing up so fast, isn't he?" She took him from Belinda's arms and lifted him into the front seat onto one of the suitcases Paul had set there. She fastened the seatbelt.

Paul put his arm around Belinda and said, "They're growing up too fast."

"Okay, we're off." Rachel got into the car and they all waved as she drove down the hill to the street leading back to her precious cottage on the bluff.

Chapter 9

The week was passing fast for Rachel and her godsons. Today they were going to have a picnic on the grass next to the lawn bowlers near the Penzance public pool on the beach.

Dudley was meeting them, bringing the food. He had insisted on providing the picnic lunch. Rachel adored Dudley; he owned the rock shop next door to the Newland's Studio in Mousehole and was the boys' godfather.

Ever since Baby Jake was born Dudley had been Johnny on the spot for Belinda and Paul. He took the baby off their hands every time they needed a break, or if they had to run errands and what not. Dudley would take the boys to the park or to the beach in the afternoons to give their mom time to concentrate on her work, he'd take them for a ride in his car since they loved riding, he'd take them to the Mousehole harbor and tell them Mousehole stories - bought them *The Mousehole Cat Story* book telling them the story over and over and entertaining them with the pictures.

Based on an old Cornish legend, *The Mousehole Cat Story* is told through the eyes of the cat, Mowzer. One winter, the Great Storm-Cat comes snarling and leaping at the harbor walls so that no boat can go out to fish. When all the food in the village is gone, the cat's master Tom Bawcock decides he must brave the terrible weather. As they sail into the mountainous seas, Mowzer sings a lullaby to calm the Great Storm-Cat of the sea. Tom catches enough fish to feed the entire village. And to this day the people of Mousehole hold a procession and feast every Christmas in memory of brave Tom Bawcock. The boys loved the story and listened to it over and over. Especially with Dudley's antics and voices he'd use in the telling of it.

Dudley would even take them into his own lapidary shop next door to their parents' art workshop and tell them stories of the different rocks and where they came from.

He was a godsend to Belinda and Paul when Rachel wasn't available or Belinda's mother wasn't visiting, but when grandma came from London, the boys stayed up at the house with her.

And Dudley had been Pete Bell's best friend. So that drew Rachel to him all the more. She'd known Dudley since the day after she met Pete.

"Over here, Rachel!" Dudley called out to her when she and the boys arrived and were getting out of the car. "Do you need any help unloading?"

"No, I've got it!" She lifted the boys from the car and off they ran to Uncle Dudley, leaping into his arms and almost knocking him over. Dudley was a bit on the frail side, due to his years of alcoholism, had a ruddy complexion and a heart of gold.

He had lived in Mousehole for ten years, had tired of the traveling rock shows and fairs, and had chosen Mousehole in which to open a shop since it was a tourist village. He'd married early on in life but never had children, divorced in his late twenties, and had been single ever since.

When Pete was alive and ran the pub where Rachel originally had met them both, Dudley spent more time at the pub than he did in his shop, about which Pete continually teased him. They were close buddies, talked about everything and anything.

So when Pete died it was a tragic blow to Dudley too. If it hadn't been for Belinda, Paul, and the boys, he would've fallen off the wagon and once again immersed himself in spirits and sorrow. Being chosen as Baby Jake's godfather was what had inspired him to quit drinking in the first place, and he learned how glorious life could be outside the bottle. He was grateful to Paul and Belinda for giving that freedom to him.

"Do you want a biscuit, Jake? How about you Paulie, want one?" he asked as he pulled the box of cookies from the bag.

"Dudley, no cookies before lunch. You are so bad." Rachel laughed and hugged him. "Let's eat, shall we? I'm famished. Did you bring anything besides cookies?" She grinned widely.

"Fish and chips, luv." He reached into the basket and pulled out newspaper wrapped fish and chips. He spread them on the table and then grabbed containers of juice and water for the boys and cola for himself and Rachel. "There we go. And we have biscuits and cake for dessert. I brought some fruit and cheese, too, whatever you want, we've got it."

"You do know how to do lunch at the beach, my friend. Where did you get the fish and chips?"

"At the Ship Inn, of course."

Rachel sat the boys on the blanket she had spread on the grass, and prepared their food before them. "Okay, my little ones, you can gobble it all up. Gobble gobble gobble."

The boys giggled at her gestures when she said gobble gobble gobble, and began to cheerfully mimic her and eat their chips."

"Eat the fish, too, for Uncle Dudley. I brought it especially for you, you know," Dudley said as he moved to the blanket beside them. "Do you need a fork or can you eat it like I do, with your hands?" He showed them how he did it.

They giggled and followed suit. They loved their uncle Dudley and would do almost anything he told them.

"That's it, don't worry about the mess, aunt Rachel can clean it up." He chuckled.

Rachel gave them all a teasing look of disapproval. "Uncle Dudley can clean it up, that's what he can do. I eat with a fork like humans are supposed to do. He's teaching you bad habits."

Dudley dramatically licked his fingers and the boys did the same, giggling all the while.

"Oh no! I can't stand that," Rachel said. "Use your napkins."

Dudley and the boys broke out in hearty laughter.

PART TWO

Della Doheny

Chapter 10

Della Doheny watched the villages shoot by in a blur. Here she was, on the train from St. Petersburg to Moscow, fantasizing about hopping off anywhere along the line to live with the Russians. She was dreaming of dropping out of her life. She was thinking she could learn their language and could be perfectly happy living as a poor peasant in the Russian countryside.

This wasn't the first time she felt that way. She had fallen in love with Russia three trips back, wanted to drop-out even then. Anyplace was better than New York City, she told herself every time. Everybody at the office teased her about her *grass is greener* tendencies.

But even more this time, she was tired of the complicated, rat-race life she had created for herself in Manhattan and wanted to escape it, at least for a while. She felt she desperately needed a break, more than just a few weeks' holiday, possibly a permanent break.

As usual she had managed to overload herself with commitments and deadlines in her publishing world. Her mind, body and soul ached under the weight of it all. It wasn't easy being an independent publisher in the midst of the majors in New York City.

Miley Daugherty, her senior editor had insisted she take a vacation when one morning Della lost it in a department heads' meeting and was on the verge of fatigue collapse. Knowing how much Della loved Russia, Miley suggested she go there for some serious R & R.

It didn't take much insistence because as a matter of fact since Della was already obsessed and passionate about Russian culture and romantic history, she jumped at the chance. In fact her Manhattan condo was already filled with Russian art and artifacts. She even collected novels and all sorts of books on and by Russians.

So here she was, back in Russia again. She was in heaven. She was in a happy place.

It had taken a few months to make the arrangements through the appropriate consulates and to obtain letters from the hotels that she'd booked in St. Petersburg and Moscow. It never was as easy to go to Russia as it was for foreigners to visit the United States. She wondered about that.

And now after spending an ecstatic three weeks in St. Petersburg she was on her way to Moscow. At first she was thinking of taking one of the cruises to Moscow traveling the Volga River, Russia's most famous waterway, which also utilized a number of lakes and canals to link both of Russia's capitals. But she opted on the quicker trip by train, and she was so glad she did. It only reminded her of how she had felt in the Russian countryside when she'd been there before. She'd forgotten. Besides, she'd done the river cruise as a teenager on her first trip with her mother.

Della leaned back and closed her eyes, remembering what a disastrous holiday that had been. Her mother had been one of the unhappiest people she'd ever known. Early on she was happy, when Della was a young girl, before she became a teenager. But then the day came when she stopped smiling, stopped laughing, stopped being the vibrant person that she had always been. Instead she became depressed and angry.

Della's father had arranged that first European holiday including a tour of Russia and China with her mother, and Della had always wondered if it was to get rid of both of them for three months. On looking back, she felt her father must have had someone else, another woman in his life, maybe that was what changed her mother. But Della never found out the truth.

Now here she was in Russia again, several trips and many years later. And since leaving the U.S. this time, she hadn't thought about book deals and deadlines, timelines, marketing strategies, royalties, advertising or hectic schedules. It had been easy to switch off that part of her brain. Maybe too easy, she was thinking. Maybe she'd like to switch it off completely.

In the past couple of years her interest in her work had waned. The business didn't have the kick it had in the beginning. The passion was gone. It was more of a drudgery than anything else. In fact the thought had crossed her mind several times in the past two years to faze out of publishing. She wasn't sure what she'd do instead, but she really didn't have to worry about money. Her folks had left her quite well off.

She didn't worry about Kaman either. *The jerkoholic can go to hell for all I care.*

She turned and looked out of the window. *Being in Russia, what more could I want? I love it!*

Her attention was drawn to a woman in a red and white polka-dotted dress sitting in front of her. The woman stopped the waiter, speaking English with a Russian accent.

"I would like glass of champagne, please." She was obviously practicing her English, since the train staff was Russian.

"I am sorry, madam, champagne is by the bottle, not by the glass."

The woman looked disappointed. "A cup of coffee, please."

Della reached for her purse, wondering why they both spoke English when they were Russian. She stood up and walked by the seat occupied by the woman. She glanced at her and their eyes met.

They smiled at each other.

While following the server to the next car, Della remembered she'd first seen the woman sitting in the crowded train station in St. Petersburg before boarding. She stood out because of the large red, straw hat and of course the polka-dot dress. White, scuffed high heels and a white handbag topped off the attention-getting outfit, so unusual for a typical Russian woman to be wearing. Della had also noticed that her dress was wrinkled and she seemed wilted, as if she'd been traveling for a couple of days. The woman had seemed self-conscious and conspicuous in her attire that was so different from the rest of the passengers.

Della thought of Leslie Caron in the film *Lili,* although this woman would be an older version of Caron, and stouter, but with the same dark hair and pixie haircut and those same endearing big brown eyes.

Della could smell the woman's flowery perfume as she walked the length of the car. It had a hint of citrus in its aroma, a welcoming scent that camouflaged the otherwise musty, mildew smells of the aging passenger car.

In the forward car where the waiter was turning in orders, Della caught up with him and asked for a bottle of champagne and two glasses, told him that she wanted to share it with the woman in the red hat. Asked if it would be all right.

The waiter was overjoyed to accommodate her. He seemed to reflect her own thoughts that the woman either couldn't afford a bottle of champagne, or she didn't want to drink more than one glass.

"That is very nice of you to do," he said. "I will bring it to you." He watched the American woman return to her seat, mass of wild, curly, coppery hair fanning out and behind her as she moved. She was dressed in a black tunic and leggings, quite a contrast to the other passengers.

Della leaned back in her seat, thinking she could drink a bottle of bubbly by herself, sometimes two, a carryover from college days and her Irish heritage, if the rumor was true about the Irish. But these days over-drinking was something she tried to avoid, so sharing a bottle was a good thing. *And a good deed*, she thought to herself.

The train was slowing at a village station where more matchbox houses dotted the landscape. Many of the houses lined the tracks, others were scattered back across the flat land, with a bit of acreage between them. Then to Della's delight, a huge lake appeared out of nowhere beyond the dwellings. She remembered it from the last time she'd traveled between the two cities, but couldn't remember the name of it. Maybe she'd look it up, maybe she wouldn't. It didn't matter. She just loved looking at it.

The lake stretched for miles and was unexpectedly beautiful. Tall trees bordered the railway, blocking the view in spots, but what she could see was wonderful and inviting.

Yea, I could live a nice, quiet, simple life here. She leaned her head back against the seat, her ample spiral curls spreading out over the headrest and dropping behind, and she watched the continual changing landscape through the window.

Although every house was different from its neighbor, they all seemed to be about the same size, but with assorted trim of different materials. From the train they looked like little decorated boxes when in reality they probably were about thirty by thirty feet square, or forty, or maybe larger, maybe smaller.

She'd never been much of an estimator of the size or distance of anything. She was okay with guessing a three- to five-foot distance, but nothing more than that. And she didn't really care if she could or not. It wasn't that important. She noticed as she grew older she was less and less interested in details, definitely not conducive to running a publishing company.

At that moment, she was thinking she would give anything to see the inside of one of the houses along the tracks. Maybe the woman in the red hat was from one of the villages. Maybe she was on her way home from a visit to St. Petersburg.

One thing Della had noticed about the working people in St. Pete was they wore monochromatic colors. Nothing bright. Della's black clothing blended well with the general female Russian populace, as well as her stature, for most females were short and stout. Della wasn't extremely short and stout, just an inch or two above short and a few pounds shy of stout. But her Irish red hair and freckles were a far cry from the usual in Russia and were a dead give-away that she wasn't one of them. As well as the bright orange lipstick and nail polish being a dead give-away.

For the most part Soviet women were fashionable, but didn't wear colorful garments. Definitely not red hats or red and white polka dot dresses. So Della was curious about the woman sitting across the aisle one row ahead of her on the train.

The waiter brought the champagne and set one glass in front of Della and one in front of the woman. He spoke in Russian to the woman and nodded toward Della.

When the woman looked back, Della smiled and motioned for her to join her.

The waiter translated.

So the woman moved to Della's table and sat across from her.

"Thank you very much," the Leslie Caron look-alike said with a thick English-Russian accent.

"You're welcome," Della replied. "Do you live in one of these villages?"

The waiter poured the champagne.

"In a village, yes."

"You speak good English." Della lifted her glass and the woman did the same.

"*Za vashe zdorovye!*" the Russian said.

"Cheers to you too!" Della replied, figuring she'd just given a Russian toast.

"You are English?" the Russian woman asked.

"American."

"I would love to live in America."

"I guess we all want what we don't have," Della said with a smile, amused that she wanted to live in Russia and the woman wanted to live in America. Maybe they could change places, she was up for it.

The woman took a sip of her champagne. "I was in Paris to visit my sister."

Della raised a brow that disappeared up under the curls that covered her forehead and sprung out over her ears and fell to her shoulders. "No kidding?"

"You are going to Moscow, no?"

"Yea. But I'd rather spend time in one of these villages instead of Moscow. I've been to Moscow before." She took a sip. "Just spent a few weeks in St. Pete."

"We are a poor people. Not as it appears in Petersburg."

Della nodded. "I figured that out. I walked back away from the usual touristy areas – the city façade. It reminded me of Mexico when I was in Puerto Vallarta and went two blocks off the beaten track. Poverty-stricken. Same as in St. Petersburg."

The woman nodded. "Yes, it is like that in all of Russia."

"But it's getting better, right? You're able to come and go freely and can afford to travel?"

"It took me five years to save money to go to my sister in Paris. But yes, some things are better. Yes." The woman gulped the rest of her champagne.

Della poured more in both their glasses. She could see the sadness in the woman's eyes as she had attempted to convince Della that life was better. But Della knew what the average wages were; she had talked to several people in St. Petersburg about it. It was ahead of the Ukraine and Afghanistan, though, with around $220 per person per month. The monthly wage was barely $25 in Afghanistan. So she knew already what the woman probably made a month, at the most, and being from a small village, unless she worked in a factory near or in the city, she probably made even less. Maybe she didn't work at all. Maybe her husband brought home the bacon.

And here Della had been thinking that she could finally wear her full-length white mink coat in the winter if she lived in Russia. Now she was thinking that it probably wouldn't be gracious to wear it in one of these small poor villages. No, no mink coat. Anyway, the activists were crusading to get all the Russian women to shed their fur coats for man-made fur, same as in the States. Years of being the fur capital of the world was now on the brink of change in Russia.

Della wondered what this woman would do with the money she had spent on her mink. She thought of Julie Christie and the wonderful fur coats in *Doctor Zhivago*. She loved that movie. Ingrid Bergman in *Anastasia* was her favorite since she'd been a teenager. Chekov's stories were fascinating. She'd read all of Dostoyevsky and Tolstoy.

"What is your name?" she asked the woman.

"Anastasia."

Della's big eyes grew bigger, "You're kidding me, right?"

Anastasia looked at Della curiously, wondering why she questioned her.

"I mean, well, I'm thinking of the Czar Nicholas and Caterina. Their daughter Anastasia—"

"Oh yes. A fable. Yes."

"You don't think she escaped?"

She shook her head. "No. She was executed with her family."

"Dammit! I prefer to believe she lived. Please say she did!"

Anastasia giggled, thinking, *crazy, gullible American.* She took a sip of champagne and then asked, "What is your name?"

"Della Doheny. I'm Irish. Or rather my grandparents were from Ireland, both sides. So I guess that makes me Irish, although I was born in the U.S., in Oklahoma, am an Okie at heart. But I've lived in New York for years." She took another sip of the bubbly. "Where do you live?"

"In a small village near Rybinsk. You know Rybinsk?"

"No, I've never been there. Where is it?"

"North of Moscow. I will take a train from Moscow to go to my village. My brother lives in the next town, ahead. Klin. I will visit him before I go home."

"So you have a sister in Paris and a brother near Moscow."

"Two brothers near Moscow. My oldest brother lives both in Moscow and Brussels. He is in Brussels now."

"Such nice places to visit, yes?"

"Paris and Switzerland are nice," she said quietly. She began sipping her drink again, not commenting on Moscow or Brussels. She looked out of the window, her thoughts seeming to drift.

Maybe it was the Russian way, but Anastasia offered no more information than what was asked, Della noticed. "Do your brothers have big families?" Della asked.

"No."

"What about your sister? Any kids?"

"No, no children."

Della poured more champagne for both of them. "The brother where you are going, is he younger than you?"

"He is older." Anastasia said.

"How many brothers and sisters do you have?"

"One sister, three brothers. My youngest brother lives in Switzerland." Anastasia seemed to loosen up a little and went on to tell Della about her family, how her mother and father had been killed when terrorists blew up a bus in the Ukraine, how her husband had been killed in the war in Afghanistan, and how she was glad she didn't have children. She told about her oldest brother and how he took care of the family business and was prosperous in Moscow.

Della liked Anastasia. She was a shy, sweet person and showed no animosity or anger over life's obstacles that had been thrown her way. She said she was a seamstress in her small village, did piecework for a sewing factory in Rybinsk. She had designed the dress she was wearing and had been to Paris to show her designs to the owner of the retail designer shop her sister was managing. She said she felt that the meeting had been successful, and although no deals had been made, she felt sure that something would come of it. She talked about how her oldest brother was helping her start her own design business.

Della thought Anastasia's tenacity and positive outlook were amazing. Traveling all that way to Paris by train had to have been utterly exhausting, and here she was as cheerful as one could be. Della had to hand it to her; she didn't know that she would have been as cheerful after such a long train trip.

"Would you care to join us for a meal before you go on to Moscow?" Anastasia asked. "My brother is preparing the food and I am certain there will be enough. Other village people will be there to welcome me."

Della leaned forward in excitement. "Do you think that would be alright? I mean, I wouldn't want to intrude on your private time with your brother."

"I am sure he will be pleased if you come."

"Oh, this is so exciting! You have no idea. Thank you so much. A real Russian village? Oh my God! A dream come true."

Anastasia laughed as she watched Della's excitement. "Yes, a real Russian village. Like the one we passed a few moments ago."

Della reached into her purse for a wide tortoise barrette to fasten her flying hair to the nape of her neck, and then put on more lipstick. She was ready for whatever came next.

Chapter 11

Stepping off the train, Della reached back for her bags she'd placed near the door. Another passenger was already lifting them down to the platform for her with ease.

"Thank you so much," she said as the courteous passenger stepped back on the train to retrieve his own bags.

One thing Della had noticed about the people in Russia was that they were polite and helpful, especially in the train stations. Didn't matter if they spoke English or not. With a smile on their faces they were more than eager to be of assistance.

She nodded her thanks to the gentleman, and then turned to see Anastasia hugging the Marlboro man.

Oh my God! This is her brother? Della felt like she had stood there forever with her mouth hanging open, staring at the rugged and handsome hunk. Finally, they came towards her.

"Della, this is my brother, Valentin."

"Hello," was Della's whispery reply, it was all she could muster. She was speechless for the first time in her life.

"I am most happy to meet you, Della," he said in a deep, pleasant voice. "Anastasia tells me you are to stay for the meal today." His eyes shone ebony through long, dark lashes and his sexy smile revealed perfect teeth in a scruffy, unshaven face.

"I—I hope I am not inconveniencing you," Della managed to sputter.

"Of course not, you are most welcome. Come, I will take the bags. Go with Anastasia."

Anastasia took Della's arm and led her toward the opposite platform where the car was parked beyond.

"Oh my God, Anastasia! Why didn't you tell me your brother is so gorgeous. I'm embarrassed at my blushing and my tongue hanging out when I slobbered all over him."

Anastasia laughed. "Everyone reacts that way when they first see Valentin."

"I can't imagine why he has never married. He looks like a Marlboro man."

"Marlboro?"

"Cigarettes. You know, the guy with tons of sex appeal that is usually sitting on a horse in American cigarette advertisements. Oh, maybe you didn't get them over here. So how old is he?"

"He is forty-seven."

"And you say he's never married? Why? What's wrong with him? Is he gay?"

Anastasia laughed. "No, he is not gay. Valentin has not met a woman he wants to marry, and he is such a busy man. You call it workaholic, yes?"

"Yea, I know what you mean," Della chuckled, remembering Miley calling her a workaholic before leaving New York. Della had never married, so she understood how that could happen. She wasn't gay either. Here she was forty years old and still single. But she had her own reasons for not marrying. The most recent attempt at a relationship had been disastrous. She had allowed a younger man to worm his way into her life, right into her house, and after several times telling him literally to "get out," he still hadn't left. She'd been staying in Manhattan in her townhouse the past six months while he was entrenched in her country house refusing to leave. She knew there was definitely something wrong with that picture.

Before she left on the trip, Miley told her not to worry that she and her husband would handle it and would make sure he was out of there before Della returned. So that's where she left it, in Miley's hands. Everything about her Manhattan life was in Miley's hands.

As it turned out, Kaman the homesteader was a con man from the get-go. A suave, good-looking Latin with a hell of a phony story, said he had been a personal trainer to the stars, travelled a lot, said his family had been Spanish royalty when he was a child, and that he was now an entrepreneur—bought and sold real estate to amass his fortune. Della had fallen for it all . . . hook, line, and sinker. None of it was true.

As Miley had written in an email the day before Della left St. Petersburg, it took the police to get him off her country estate. During the process it was discovered there were three felony arrest warrants out on him for assault and battery, burglary, and possession of a controlled substance. So they arrested him.

After all the years of being wise and careful, Della had fallen for the jerkosaur's malarkey. She'd known for years that handsome men had serious flaws to be wary of. This one skated by her.

And now she had just met the most handsome man ever.

God save me! "What does Valentin do? What kind of work? He does work, doesn't he?" she whispered to Anastasia.

But before Anastasia could answer, Valentin had caught up with them.

It was incredible how much luggage one man could carry. Valentin had two bags hanging on one shoulder, one on the other, and one in each hand. The weight alone would have flattened any other guy to the ground.

"Oh my God, give me one of those, Valentin. That's way too much for you." Della held out her hands.

"Thank you, no. There is the car. Please, go to the car."

His words, although polite in front of a smile, had an unmistakable finality to them. She suspected that no one ever contradicted or challenged this man. Neither would she.

Chapter 12

Mealtime in the Ballenchine household was something to behold. The great room was situated next to the kitchen where a huge hand-hewn timber table sat with benches along each side. At each end were two gigantic armchairs that also appeared to have been carved and handmade. The table easily sat the fourteen people that were now sitting around it. Two of Valentin's neighbor women were serving, though they weren't servants. They were friends who had offered to help with the early afternoon dinner he had planned for his sister's homecoming.

At one time, Anastasia and her three siblings all lived in Klin together, all in Valentin's house - all but the oldest brother, Maxim. Maxim was married and lived in Moscow, but the rest of them lived with Valentin. This was after their parents had died. One by one they scattered off into different directions - to school, to marriage, to work in a different city. Now only Valentin remained.

Anastasia sat at one end of the table, Valentin at the other. Della was sitting to the right of Anastasia.

As Della took in every nuance and every cheerful sound of the villagers around her, she didn't want it to end. Maybe it was because it was reminiscent of the Oklahoma ranching days when she was a little girl - her parents and grandparents and all the ranch hands, dining together at the huge oak table in the bunkhouse on special occasions. God, she missed that!

She watched Valentin connect in a friendly manner with every person at the table over the next two hours. He left no one out of the conversation. He was truly a wonderful host. He made her feel as if she was one of them. She was thinking that her desire of disappearing in Russia was becoming stronger and stronger as she sat there soaking it all up.

She began to wonder how she could arrange her defection. Would she be called a defector? Nah, she thought she might be called an ex-pat. She wasn't sure, though. She'd look it up. Where would she live? She needed a home base. What would the legal process be? And if it came down to it, could she leave everything behind in the States? Her publishing company might be a concern. She would just have to sell it, or appoint someone to run it for her. All she knew was that she wanted to live in Russia, and she mentally made the decision to do it at that very moment as food was being passed to her.

"Della, how do you like the Galushki?" Valentin's voice broke into Della's reverie and was easy to hear over the din of conversation.

"It's—it's fabulous. I love it. Normally I don't eat veal, you know, the baby calves and all. But in this case, I'm enjoying it. Thank you."

"I cooked it myself," he said as he grinned from ear to ear.

"No way Jose! You're kidding me." She couldn't believe he had made the delicious dish. She figured one of the village women had prepared it. "Did he really make it, Anastasia? Tell me the truth."

"Yes. He cooked most of the food we are eating. The fish Tolcheniki which are the fish balls, Nalystniki, the potato

81

pancakes. Wait till you taste the Knydli, plum balls. Yes, he is a cook."

Della leaned toward her and whispered, "My God, a good cook *and* good-looking. There must be something wrong with him. What is it, Anastasia? Tell me."

They both giggled like schoolgirls and gave each other raised eyebrow glances.

"He snores while he sleeps. That's all I can think of," Anastasia finally replied.

"A set of earplugs would take care of that little problem," Della said as she took another bite of the Galushki.

Anastasia laughed heartily into her napkin. "For him or for the other person?"

"The other person, girlfriend."

After dinner and an assortment of pastries and desserts had been served, the table was cleared as everybody stretched their legs outdoors on the patio where Valentin had built a fire in a round rock-lined pit. Although the weather was cool, not cold, the heat felt good. It was just enough to keep the chill at bay.

Della walked around the outside of the house looking at the plants and flowers and the outbuildings. It was very homey. So were the neighboring houses, all had gardens and sheds. Clotheslines; she hadn't seen clotheslines in ages. The houses were more like the smaller tract houses in the States, minus the attached garages, and were spaced an acre or so apart. Chicken and pig pens were of the norm as well as vegetable gardens. Some even had goats, a horse or two, a cow.

It reminded her of what she had seen in rural Oklahoma when she had visited her parents' birthplaces the year before. She missed her mom and dad whose tragic deaths had devastated Della when she was seventeen. They were returning from a 30-day European cruise when their plane crashed near Minneapolis. No survivors. Della never understood why they took the trip in the first place since they hadn't been speaking in years. Nothing made any sense. Their deaths didn't make any sense. They shouldn't have been together on that trip.

But they say—whoever *they* are—that you feel most comfortable in the surroundings of your heritage, and that you're most likely to return to your roots in your later years. Well, her ancestors had lived a long time in a rural environment, and she still had aunts and uncles there, but she had no intention of ever returning to ranch life in Oklahoma. She had almost lost the nasal Midwestern accent, due to her years in the east – graduate degree from Mount Holyoke College in Maine, then an MBA from Harvard Business School in Boston, a PhD from Notre Dame in Indiana, then immediately to New York City to work for Simon & Schuster. She had been a brilliant student and was snapped up by S & S before she graduated. It had been quite a transition from an Oklahoma cattle-ranching, horse-riding, gun-toting maiden to the major global center of the publishing world. And although now she was a New Yorker, through and through, she missed her growing up years, the homey environment, and the family closeness.

She reached for a flower she didn't recognize and bent to smell it.

"You like Russia?" Valentin startled her with his question.

"Oh! I didn't see you behind me. Yea, I do, as a matter of fact. Very much." She felt nervous alone with him in front of the house, away from everyone else.

"How long will you stay?" he asked.

"Where? You mean in Russia? How long will I stay in Russia?"

"Yes. That is what I mean. In Russia." His deep, mellow voice, broad smile, and sultry eyes made her even more nervous.

"Well, I'm not sure. I'd like to stay longer. Maybe forever. I'd love to live in a village like this and find out how the real people live. That's something I've always wanted to do."

"You have been to Russia before?"

"Yea. this is my fourth trip. And each time the visit is too short. I want to go further inland and see how people live there, too. Experience the natives, so to speak. But I have always had to get back to my work in New York. God, how I hate that."

She gazed across the expanse of land to a train that was on its way to Moscow. *If I were smart, I'd be on that train right now.*

"You can stay here," he offered. "I have room."

She jerked her gaze back to Valentin and looked into a face that clearly reflected sincerity.

"My sister will be here a few days longer; you will be good company for her. I must leave tomorrow."

"Well, I—I don't know."

"There is time to decide. Come have glass of wine. I am opening very special bottle; and would like to share with you."

He reached for her arm and led her back around the house to the patio where the other guests were laughing and talking.

After all the guests departed, Anastasia excused herself and retired for the evening, even though it was early. It took several days to travel by train from Paris, and she was exhausted to the point of incoherence.

So Della helped Valentin tidy up the kitchen, the two of them acting as if they'd known each other forever.

"So, will you be leaving early in the morning?" she asked.

"Yes, very early. But I am not yet ready to retire this evening. We will sit and talk, yes?" he asked.

"Absolutely!" she said as she hung the damp cloth on a hook near two round stainless steel kitchen sinks. She turned and reached for her wine glass.

"Please, rest on the *tania*, divan you call it. Sofa?" He picked up his glass and the wine bottle and followed her into the seating alcove.

"I haven't heard a sofa called divan since I was a little girl on the ranch. My folks called it that," she laughed. "Sure brings back memories." She sat at one end of the sofa, Valentin sat in the adjacent leather club chair.

"You grew up on a ranch?"

"Yes, we raised cattle and oil wells."

"That is a unique combination."

"In Oklahoma it wasn't. Most ranchers had both. I rode horses and drove pick up trucks in those days. And you were raised where?"

"In Kopeisk near the Ural Mountain range, southeast of Moscow. When Maxim and I were young boys we worked in the coal mines, as did all young boys in that region."

"Oh no. I've read about the kids in England working the mines, but didn't realize Russian kids did the same thing." She held out her glass for a refill.

Valentin filled up hers and topped off his. "Oh yes. We went everyday before sunlight with our father. And when he died, we continued working till my brother Maxim got us out."

"How did he do that?" she asked.

"He found work elsewhere and the rest of the family followed. Maxim has led since he was fifteen."

"So, are you now doing what you want to do? Are you fulfilling your own dreams?" Della reached for a pretzel in the dish on the table in front of the sofa.

"I have been thinking I would like to do something else. I am grateful to Maxim for building the Ballenchine Brothers empire, and I have been in charge of the amber division, he the diamond division, which is all we do now. At the beginning when we were Ballenchine Brothers Mercantile, we handled many products, but that has all changed. Now we do only mining of amber and diamonds, and marketing and selling them."

"But you would like to do something else?"

"Yes."

Della waited, but he didn't expound on the subject, didn't offer up any information, nothing was forthcoming.

After a few more moments of silence, Valentin said, "And you want to make changes, you said earlier. You want to live in Russia?"

"Oh my god, yes! When I'm here I feel so much better and I feel excitement. Excitement for living. You know what I mean?"

"Yes, and that is because you are free to do whatever you want to do. When you have a passion and you step out to live that passion, that's when the excitement begins. I do know what you mean." He looked down at the glass he was holding with both hands on his lap, and stared at it for a few seconds. Then he added, "Soon I will step out to live my passion."

When he looked up, Della saw a faint glistening of tears in his eyes.

Chapter 13

Valentin left the next morning for Siberia. He didn't want to go and leave the women, but it was a business trip he had to make and he would be away for at least a week.

He convinced Della to stay the few days Anastasia would be there, and he asked her to promise to leave a phone number where she could be reached in Moscow after she left Klin.

Three days later when Anastasia left for Moscow en route to her home, Della remained. Anastasia's insistence and the daily phone calls from Valentin helped her to make the decision.

But Della was sad to see Anastasia go, and promised her the next time she came back to Russia she would come to visit Anastasia too. And she invited Anastasia to the U.S. to spend time with her in New York City, said she would work it out for her. Anastasia was excited about the possibility.

Over the next few days, Della settled into the simple little house in the simple little village. She didn't want to go to Moscow at all; she didn't want to go home either. The village women were kind and she had begun to feel comfortable walking through the settlement each day, stopping to talk with those who spoke in broken English. She made a few friends and learned a few Russian words she found on an Internet site that gave the audio pronunciation of Russian phrases - which came in handy.

She emailed Miley on Valentin's computer, to let her know what she was doing, her change in plans. No WiFi connection for her laptop computer.

Miley was thrilled and wanted to know all about Valentin. Of course Della had nothing to tell her other than what little she knew.

She told Miley that he was in the amber business, traveled all over Russia, but mostly to the major Amber mine in Kaliningrad, and occasionally the diamond mines in Siberia. Anastasia told Della he went to Kaliningrad more than any other place, though, but his office was in Moscow with his brother. And that was it, that's all Della knew about him. Except that he was a big man, and strong, and reminded her of her father.

Miley assured her that everything would be all right in New York, she'd handle everything and Della needn't worry, told her to stay as long as she wanted.

It was a perfect morning for Della to cut fresh flowers and place a bouquet on the center of the dining table and one on the table in front of the leather sofa. She opened all the windows in the house to let the cool breezes flow through.

Then she took her cup of coffee to the porch and sat in a painted Adirondack-type wooden chair. She could tell it had been hand-hewn.

It was a sunny summer day, but the breeze was cool and nippy. Valentin was due to return home that afternoon after being away for three weeks. She hoped he wouldn't mind her being there all this time, he said he didn't. He had phoned her almost daily to make sure she was all right, that she had everything she needed, and he hadn't sounded as if he didn't want her there. But she'd told him two days before, the last she'd talked to him, she was leaving, she had to go. But here she was, still in his house.

She felt like a bride waiting for a groom to come home from work. She had been pretending and enjoying every minute of the imaginary relationship with anticipation. In fact she laughed out loud at herself and the ridiculous fairy tale she was weaving, but it wasn't harming anyone, she was just playing a solitary game. She certainly was glad none of her friends could see her; they would think she had totally lost her mind.

Here she was . . . one of the most up and coming brilliant independent publishers in New York City. She'd begun with ten book titles and had built the business into a three-imprint company publishing hard covers as well as trade and mass paper back and eBooks—over 500 titles now, and still counting. She went from a two-employee company working out of her apartment to three floors in a skyscraper in the middle of Manhattan - one floor was her apartment. No one would believe where she was at that very moment in Russia, and how she was living. She could hardly believe it herself.

Valentin arrived at noon. He drove up the drive and stopped the car.

Della stood up and waved at him from the porch. His look of surprise puzzled her, for she wasn't sure if it was a pleasantly surprised look or a *what-the-hell-is-she-doing-here* look.

He left the car door open and hurried to the stoop where she was standing. He stared at her for a moment and then suddenly scooped her up in his arms and hugged her tightly.

"What a surprise that you are still here," he said as he set her down. "I am happy to see you."

She pulled her shirt down and nervously straightened her collar. "I'm happy to see you, too. You don't mind, do you? I hoped you wouldn't mind."

"Of course I do not mind. Excuse me; I must bring my things into the house." He hurried back toward the car.

Della immediately tried to calm herself and willed the flush from her face and the speedy beating of her heart to subside.

She held open the door for him as he walked through with packages and luggage, as usual hanging and dangling from him.

He took the bags to his bedroom that was off the kitchen and great room, and then returned with a huge grin. "I have something for you." He handed her a flat, blue velvet box.

She stared at it, speechless and not moving.

"Please, I give it to you. You take it."

She reluctantly reached for it, and then opened the snap that held the lid down. It was a beautiful box trimmed in gold, a lovely gift in itself.

"Oh my God!" Inside was a stunning amber necklace. "This is spectacular! It's prettier than anything I've seen in all the jewelry stores in St. Petersburg. It's Hermitage quality. I can't take this from you. It's too valuable! You must sell it to your customers. Don't give it to me."

"I do give it to you. It is yours. Please."

Della couldn't believe it. "Oh my God, I love amber. In fact I have a small collection of it. But this is the grandest of all. Oh my God! Thank you so much."

She stepped in front of a small mirror hanging on the wall, lifted the multi-strand filigree necklace with its large oval pendant from the case.

Valentin took the case from her and placed it on the table.

She opened the clasp.

He took the necklace from her to place it around her neck.

She lifted her hair and he fastened the necklace.

Then he rested his huge hands on her shoulders, still standing behind her.

Her heart stopped at his touch. She felt dizzy.

He bent down and kissed where her shoulder met her neck.

Goosebumps covered her entire body. She turned and looked up at him.

Their eyes and lips met at the same time. It was the softest, most thrilling kiss that Della experienced in her entire life.

He didn't push further, didn't do the tongue trick.

Thank god! She hated that.

He just gently caressed her lips with his and then slowly leaned back to look at her as if for the first time.

"You are beautiful in amber," he whispered. "It is same color as your hair and spots."

"My freckles," she said as she giggled.

She turned and again looked into the gilded-framed mirror. "Look at that, it does match my hair, doesn't it?"

Moving close behind her, he wrapped his arms around her waist, clasping his hands against her body. "How long will you stay with me? I do not want you to go."

Chapter 14

"Della, where are you!"

"In the bedroom, Valentin. Be right there." Della looked forward to his arrival from work every day, especially after he'd been away two or three days, like this time. She was still thrilled at the sight of Valentin Ballenchine after living in his house for two months. He was the most loving, attentive and adorable man she'd ever known, she was thinking maybe *the man of her dreams*—cliché or not.

This time she believed she was truly out of her element and had cooked the first dinner for him, which made her very nervous since he was the chef of the house, the food expert. But back in New York she was known for her successful dinner parties in Manhattan. Even still, she hesitated to prepare the meal, for fear of disappointing him and embarrassing herself. What if it didn't taste right? It was different in Russia. She had to make do with different oils and ingredients, which could be critical.

"The aroma is good, what is it you are cooking?" Valentin asked as Della walked into the kitchen from the bedroom.

"I made a pot roast with vegetables, American style, and a salad, American style. I love Russian food, the way you prepare it, but I've a craving for some good ol' American food. I hope you don't mind." She paused for his response, hoping he wouldn't feel slighted. The Russians were a proud people— proud of their culture, their heritage, and that included their tried and true, age-old epicurean delights.

Valentin grabbed her. "I like American pot roast and salads. When I was in New York two years ago, I was pleasured to have sampled it at the hotel where my brother and I were staying. It makes me happy you want to cook your American food for me."

He pulled her to him, swaying with her in his arms as he spoke. "Are you happy, my little *golubushka*? You will not leave me?" He held her out at arm's length for a moment, looking down into her eyes and then pulled her back to him again. "No, you cannot leave me. I will not let you."

But as much as she wanted to stay, Della knew she had to make some decisions soon. There was so much to consider—the publishing company, her property, a visa and maybe emigration, and of course this relationship with Valentin. Where was it going . . . marriage, maybe? Or maybe not?

She had avoided thinking of the future, trying to stay in the moment and savoring it as it happened, her new love. But the time was coming, she knew it. She had stalled as long as she could. She'd given herself till the First of August to discuss it with Valentin. They would have been together almost three months by then, which was two weeks away.

He kissed her on the forehead and loosened his grip. "Go, woman. I have a bear's appetite. When do we eat?"

Della giggled. "In about thirty minutes. So freshen up you big teddy bear, and I'll pour you a drink. Found some American wine, too, today, when I was in Moscow."

"You went to Moscow alone?" he frowned.

"Yea, I took the train this morning and did some shopping. Wait till you see what I bought to wear later." She gave him a sexy smile and a wiggle before she turned to check on the dinner.

"You must be careful when you go to Moscow without me. I would rather you not do that."

"Why the hell not? I've been to Moscow before. I've been all over the world by myself. I'm not afraid." She lifted the lid on the pot roast and spoon-tasted the liquid.

Valentin was amused at Della's use of American curse words. He hadn't met a woman who spoke so freely and openly. He went into the bedroom and stood near the bed for a moment, before taking off his shirt and tie. But he did worry about Della and her independence. He knew she wasn't aware of the dangers in Moscow, in all of Russia. She was an American and didn't know any better.

He was going to have to warn her; he had wanted to spare her from the precariousness of his position as long as he could. But now, he would have to attach bodyguards to her, especially after tonight. She wasn't aware of how many bodyguards flanked and covered him every place he went. The few times they'd had dinner in Moscow, he had given orders for most of them to conceal themselves. She hadn't noticed.

After the pot-roast dinner, a happy full-to-the-brim Valentin reached for Della's hand and lifted his wine glass with the other. "To *milaya* and the delicious American food she prepares for me . . . I give you all my love."

A blushing Della squeezed his hand and said, "I love being here with you. Thank you so much for allowing me to learn more about your people and how you live."

They both sipped, both in admiration of the other.

"So is it this month when your brother is coming to visit?" Della asked.

"I do not know. He phoned today to say his Katarina has been hospitalized."

"What happened?"

"I have told you she is quite a drinker, yes? Well, she took a fall, has concussion. This is three times she has fallen this year and been taken to hospital. But she will be all right, he said. Maxim will come to Moscow when she is situated once again at home with her nurses."

"They have a strange relationship, don't they?"

Valentin hesitated before answering. "Yes, it is different. I am not so sure I would do the same under the circumstances. I believe a man should be with his wife, no matter what happens."

"Why haven't you ever married?"

He leaned on the table toward her and grinned as he gently placed his gigantic hand around the back of her neck. "Because I had not yet met my pretty little Della."

"Oh," was all she could muster as she leaned toward him. She loved it when he called her *little*. Of course compared to him, one could say she was little. But standing at five-foot-seven and weighing in at 145 pounds, she didn't feel very pretty or little. She had always felt plain and plump . . . until she met Valentin Ballenchine.

"I should ask, why you have not married?" he grinned back at her.

"Oh, too busy pursuing a career, I guess. Doing all the things I wanted to do. Getting married has never entered my mind. Besides nobody ever asked me."

The truth was that she had a history of being beleaguered and conned by men who were after her money and the estate that was left to her by her cattle and oil baron father. Three such gold-diggers over the years had made her gun shy, and she had just shed the fourth one . . . or rather Miley had done it for her.

"And now, would you marry if you were asked?" Valentin moved closer, running his hand from her neck down to the space between her shoulder blades, rubbing gently.

She closed her eyes. "Oh, that feels so good." She scooted her chair closer to his. "You keep that up and I'll have to marry you if you ask me." *Damn!* She couldn't believe she had blurted out those words. She wished she could take them back but it was too late. One thing she didn't want to do was to suggest in any way or push the point with Valentin. Besides she wasn't sure what she wanted. *Shit!* She wished she could roll back the moment and answer that question with something much more clever and elusive.

"Then I will ask. Will you be my wife, Miss Della Doheny?" He reached into his pocket and to Della's astonishment he pulled out a gorgeous amber and diamond ring. He was obviously waiting for just the right moment, and this must have been it. He had planned it.

"I— I—" She was speechless. "I wasn't hinting— I— you're not serious?" She stared at the ring. The square amber stone was flanked by a generous-sized diamond baguette on each of its four sides, in a gold setting.

"Yes, I am serious." Valentin slipped the ring on her left hand, fourth finger, and scooped her up from the chair, carrying her around the kitchen, spinning around, while grinning and kissing her at the same time.

Della held on with both arms around his neck, feeling escalating arousal with every kiss.

Finally Valentin sat on a chair, still holding her, both of them engrossed in a very erotic kiss.

Della turned, straddled him, and unbuttoned his shirt. She began kissing his neck and muscled, hairy chest, trailing her tongue across his nipples.

He lifted her shirt over her head and tossed it across the room, then fondled her braless ample breasts with his huge hands.

Della closed her eyes, leaning back as Valentin pulled and nibbled her nipples, going back and forth from one to the other. She moaned and lifted his face up to her mouth, smothering it with kisses, culminating in a deep, probing kiss that shot them both into oblivion, taking their breath away.

She quickly stood up. "Don't move, stay right there," she said as she removed her jeans. She slowly unzipped his pants, exposing and fondling his readiness. This time, a readiness she sat astride while together they sustained a long, thrill-evoking kiss till the movement of their bodies and increasing waves of pleasure inundated them both and Della cried out in ecstasy, "Yes! yes! My answer is yes!"

Chapter 15

Maxim Ballenchine arrived at his brother Valentin's house the middle of September. The temperature was still warm that time of year—60s to 70s Fahrenheit, beautiful weather, a pleasant breeze stirred the air, the sight and faint smell of blossoms were pleasing to the senses.

Maxim picked several of the chamomiles—Russia's national flower—that were in bloom along both sides of the front walkway—Della called them white daises. The chamomile's strong, fruity, apple aroma always soothed and relaxed Maxim, and he enjoyed the tea made from steeping the fragrant blossoms for just that purpose. As he climbed the steps leading to the front door, he also pinched off one of the climbing miniature red roses that had entwined the posts of the front stoop. It was wonderful to be back in Russia. Although Brussels was also his home, his heart and soul remained in his Russian homeland and he was always happy to return.

Valentin opened the door before Maxim had a chance to knock. "Da-*bro* pa-*zha*-la-vat, Maxim!" He gave Maxim a vibrant hug, lifting him off the ground.

"Ya tak silno skuchal pa tibe, Valentin!"

"I missed you as well, my brother, but we must speak English for my American friend." He reached for Della and pulled her into the doorway, placing his arm around her, holding her close. This is Della Doheny . . . soon to be Mrs. Della Ballenchine, my wife."

"Tti takaya krasivaya," Maxim said as he reached for her hand and kissed it enthusiastically.

"He says you are beautiful, and of course I agree. English, Maxim, English! Come in. Your room is ready and waiting. Della placed a huge bouquet of flowers in your window. But first we must have a drink to your arrival."

"I have blossoms for tea this evening." Maxim handed Della the flowers and she took them into the kitchen.

A half hour passed and Della hadn't been able to get in a word edgewise, but she was enjoying listening to the two men catch up on the business of the day—sometimes in English, sometimes in Russian—as she sipped the wine Valentin had poured for them.

She couldn't get over how handsome both men were. Valentin's brother was as much Cary-Grant-handsome as Valentin was Tom-Selleck-handsome. Even Valentin's sister Anastasia was a beautiful woman . . . resembling Leslie Caron. Such family genes. She wondered if she and Valentin would have had children as good looking as the rest of his family. Of course it was too late for children now, at her age. She was nearly past child-bearing years. In a way she was sad about that, but when she thought about the present-day world and the dangers the youth were exposed to, she was glad she wouldn't have to contend with it.

"Della, how did this happen with you and Valentin?" Maxim asked her, finally. Obviously man-talk was over and now it was woman's turn.

"I was on the train from Petersburg to Moscow when I met Anastasia and she invited me to join her welcome home luncheon. She was returning from Paris. I mentioned I wanted to see a real Russian village and meet the people, so she invited me. That's all it took. I haven't left, and that was nearly three months ago. Valentino is a pretty persuasive man." She grinned lovingly at Valentin over her wine glass.

Maxim raised his eyebrows at Valentin, "Valentino, Valentino, she calls you?"

"Yes. To her I am Valentino." He blushed.

"And you waste no time asking her to marry you." He chuckled.

"That is right. I have waited many years for Della, and I do not intend to let her get away." He poured more wine in the glasses. "So, what of the woman you said you were meeting in Moscow? Who is she?"

Maxim sipped his wine, remembering his recent visit with Rachel in Cornwall. "We met New Year's Eve in Brussels, at the square . . . a very attractive woman. She is a writer, an American like you, Della."

"Oh, really?" Della perked up. "What is her name? Maybe I know her, being a writer and an American to boot."

"Della is publisher of books, Maxim."

"How wonderful! Such professional women we have met, Valentin." He grinned widely. "Her name is Rachel O'Neill, she writes romantic novels."

"Oh my god! Of course I know of her. She's a west coast author, has an L.A. agent. Lives in England, I believe. Is that the one?" Della held up her glass for Valentin to refill.

"Yes, that is she. She lives in Cornwall in a most quaint little village." Maxim was pleased. The fact that Della knew of her gave more credence to Rachel. It wasn't that he doubted her; he was just skeptical where women were concerned. He'd had his share of them, and he hadn't taken the time to do a security check on Rachel, actually hadn't felt the necessity.

Valentin filled Della's glass. "Well! We shall have party when she arrives. Shall we? In Moscow, Maxim? We will present your Miss O'Neill to our friends and announce engagement to Della. Two birds with one stone. Yes?"

Della suddenly felt anxious with trepidations.

Maxim filled the silent gap, "Of course! We shall have a grand party!"

PART THREE

MOSCOW

Chapter 16

It was cloudy the last time Rachel had traveled by train through the Russian countryside. But this time, not a cloud in the sky in the middle of October.

Rachel was deep in thought as she stared out the window remembering the last time she made this train trip. That was before she found Cornwall, after her runaway trip to Idaho and Montana. When she was forty she ran away from life like a child runs away from home. Twice in her life she ran away. The first time she was sixteen. Her father had forbade her to be with the boy she loved – he was in college, she was in high school. She stayed away for three days that time, but as a forty-year-old she stayed away for three months. Progress possibly? Three months vs. three days?

A friend told her, after the three-month disappearance, that many times he had wanted to duck out of his life and leave all his obligations behind. He thought she was a brave soul to do what she did, gutsy. Said he didn't have guts. But some would say her actions were cowardly. To Rachel it didn't matter what others said, pro or con. She did what she had to do and she was glad of it. Both times. No regrets.

Rachel felt it was odd that she should be thinking about all that at this particular moment while the Russian sun was warming her nearly fifty-year-old face. She was on her way to do research for her novel and to reconnect with Maxim Ballenchine in Moscow. She shouldn't be thinking of some obscure incidents that happened so long ago. So much more had transpired since she was that lovesick teenager and that confused forty-year-old. She'd come a long way since then, and still no regrets.

She breathed in the cool fresh air coming through the open window of the coach. The train was slowing down for a village stop and she could smell the smoke from the chimneys of the peasant houses on each side of the tracks. There was something about the Russian countryside that seemed more than familiar to her, something other than it being her second trip to the region.

Her thoughts returned to the time she ran away at forty to the northern regions of the U.S., not knowing a soul up there, losing herself in the small towns of Idaho and Montana on her way to she knew not where, all the while being eerily drawn to the Black Foot Indian Reservation in northwestern Montana.

And then it happened. There on the reservation she found her mother, alive. After all that time thinking she was dead. Since Rachel was three years old she thought her mother had died. Her father had told everybody that Lily had run off with another man and was killed in a car accident and he didn't want to talk about it, ever.

Rachel had been traumatized by losing her mother literally over night. To her it was as if she had been yanked from the warmth and love of her mother's arms and thrust into the stand-offish, cold care of her father who found it difficult to show his love for anybody. No physical display of affection at all. The contrast was tragically confusing to little Rachel. Not until she reached the age of nine did she understand that her father was an alcoholic.

She had never learned anything about her mother's death in all those years growing up, so one can only imagine the shock it was to stumble upon her mother teaching school at the Blackfoot reservation in Montana - all those years later when Rachel was forty years old and a runaway. Haunting dreams had led her to the reservation, straight to her mother. It was uncanny.

The train jolted, shaking Rachel loose from her memories. It stopped at a village station along the route to Moscow.

In the past year Rachel had been feeling the draw to Russia again, same as when she was drawn to Montana and to Cornwall. And it seemed more than a coincidence that she had met Maxim in Brussels the year before and that he was from Moscow. It was Rachel's belief there had to be a reason for it. She believed everything happened for a reason, and it had always panned out to be that way.

All of a sudden Rachel felt tired. She leaned her head back against the head rest and closed her eyes.

The dream came quickly.

Rachel was pushing through crowds that were preventing her from getting to where she wanted to go. She felt the bodies blocking her, pressing against her, shoving her, suffocating her. She couldn't breathe. She cried out for help. No one heard her. She stumbled to the pavement, the people trampled her, not caring.

She heard gun shots. People were falling all around her, on top of her. She was buried under bodies falling. There were screams and cries. More shots fired. Then it was quiet. No more movement, no one left standing. All dead. She crawled from under the heap of bodies. Her mother and father were in the pile. Ethan and Pete were there. She sobbed as she stared at the pile of dead bodies.

107

Then she realized she was the only survivor. The only one alive. She turned and walked away.

Chapter 17

Maxim Ballenchine was eager to finish the last meeting of the day. It was a simple meeting, a regular staff meeting, and he was glad of that, nothing critical. It was Friday in Moscow, and staff just needed to go over the schedule for the following week.

Rachel had telephoned Maxim that morning saying she had arrived in Moscow and was staying at the Metropole near Red Square. Said she hoped they could meet for happy hour in the hotel Shalyapin bar. He happily agreed to meet her at six-thirty.

He glanced at his watch as his meeting ended and saw that it was five. Plenty of time to freshen up in his office apartment, change clothes, and drive to the Metropole. He had designed the apartment connecting to his office because sometimes his work would run far into the night, even into the wee morning hours. His country estate was twenty miles outside Moscow and it was easier to just stay overnight in town when he needed to. It was also handy, such as now, to be able to make a quick change and go to dinner with clients or, as in this case, with a lovely woman.

Valentin and Della were coming to town, too. Maxim telephoned them right after Rachel called and invited them to dinner at eight at the Metropole. Suggested they meet in the bar around half past seven. That would give him an hour with Rachel before they arrived. He figured it would make her feel more comfortable to have another American present, especially someone she could talk to who was familiar with her work. It was exciting to Maxim, too.

Rachel was dressed and ready by five-thirty. So she decided to go downstairs into the Shalyapin and watch people while she waited for Maxim to arrive. One of her favorite pastimes while traveling was people-watching. Sitting in bars observing others, in restaurants, airports, train stations, malls, it was all intriguing to her. And doing it in the Moscow Metropole was a special treat. She'd rather wait in a cafe or a bar than in her room, that was a given.

Here at the Metropole, people from all over the world cross paths, she wrote in her notebook after she snuggled into an oversized leather wing-back chair facing the rest of the lounge. Her view was of the carved wood bar flanked by the most beautiful peach and ivory marble columns she'd ever seen, and of other groups of tables and club chairs. It was an open bar area situated in the vestibule on the ground floor of the Metropole and seated thirty people who were served by waiters—no waitresses, all waiters.

The interior was marble—floors, walls—as it was through-out the hotel lobby and restaurant, stucco and wood molding on the high ceilings, with an abundance of chandeliers in the modernist style remaining intact since the hotel was built in the early 1900s. She was surprised it wasn't older than that.

Rachel had a view of the ornate elevators that seemed to move continuously. From where she sat she could watch who got on and off. And at that hour very interesting people were coming and going. Most were elegantly dressed for the evening, more women than men.

At a table with eight chairs across the room from her, near doors that led outside to a patio, Rachel noticed three women laughing and talking. One of the women was older, more like a mother to the other two who had to be models because they were so gorgeous - one a redhead, one a platinum blond with hair like silk. Rachel was drawn to them because they were very animated in their Russian conversation.

The mother figure was tweaking the hair of the redhead, pulling down a curl, pushing another back, telling her to put on more lipstick, handing her a mirror. The older woman's cell phone rang and she had a brief conversation, looked at her watch, and hung up. She seemed upset, pointing to the time and scolding the girls. Another girl finally arrived and hurried to their table. They all stood and hugged, the late arrival seeming to apologize for being late. She was a brunette, another beauty.

Rachel was becoming even more curious about who they were. It now seemed to take on another possibility. Maybe the 'mother' was an agent and the girls were at the hotel for a photo shoot.

The waiter came to Rachel's table and poured a second glass of champagne in her flute.

"Are those models here for a photo shoot?' she asked the waiter.

He seemed amused. Looked over at the table of noisy women and gave Rachel a grin and a *so-so* gesture with both hands and raised his eyebrows before he walked away.

Rachel wasn't sure what he meant, but she was beginning to see the light. *Hookers? Nah, they can't be hookers. But then again, they could be. Definitely expensive ones.*

Another girl arrived. The most stunning of all. Long, straight, coal black hair with bangs. Now every hair color and body type was represented. A complete assortment of Barbie dolls. Definitely not sisters, definitely not a mother. They were all primping each other. The noise level increased.

The 'mother's' cell phone rang again. She answered and this time only said a couple words and hung up. It appeared she was readying the girls for someone who was about to arrive.

And sure enough, here he came. He got off the elevator and walked to the table. Rachel watched the man. He was of middle-Eastern descent, wearing a keffiyeh headdress, elegantly dressed, wearing lots of jewelry. He handed the 'mother' an envelope then spoke to each girl as she was introduced. And then he motioned for the girls to follow him and they all went to the elevator, going up.

The 'mother' left through the side doors.

Yep, hookers.

After a few minutes, the same man came down the elevator again and walked into the bar, glancing at Rachel as he passed. He sat on a stool and ordered a drink. As he sipped his Brandy, he stood and took a step toward Rachel. Grinning widely, he gestured to her to come join him upstairs.

Yep, definitely hookers.

She shook her head, smiled and lifted her glass, toasting his kind consideration. Sure. Right.

He bowed and returned to his barstool, glancing over at her occasionally and smiling.

Chapter 18

Rachel shifted in her chair after sitting in the lounge nearly an hour, writing and watching. She was feeling more and more conspicuous and uncomfortable by the minute. Even though she didn't like to admit it, she was eager for Maxim to get there.

He arrived.

Thank god!

The months that had lapsed since Maxim was in Cornwall hadn't dulled her memory of him, but he was even more handsome now as she watched him coming towards her in his silk jacket, shirt, and pants – three shades of grey. His looks seemed to radiate cleanness, freshness, and sparkle. She could feel the blood rush to her face in a flaming blush.

Heads turned as Maxim entered the bar carrying an aluminum briefcase.

The man in the turban, still at the bar, looked at Rachel and nodded with approval at her choice in men when Maxim leaned to do the European kiss on each cheek.

"I'm so happy to see you, Maxim." She leaned back in her chair with a sigh of relief.

He sat in the chair angled beside her and signaled for the waiter. "You do not know how much I have longed for this moment," he said as he reached and grasped her hand. "May I buy you another champagne?"

"Well, I think I still have some left," she lifted the bottle from the ice bucket. "Would you like to share it with me?"

"Yes, and I'll order another."

The waiter came and Maxim ordered, requesting that the previous bottle be put on his tab also.

"So where is your brother?"

"He and his fiancé will be here soon. I wanted to spend time with you first." He squeezed her hand. "You are beautiful today. Green is your color."

"Well, I don't wear colors very often, but I saw this dress in St. Petersburg and just had to have it."

"Exquisite!" He kissed her hand. "Is your room adequate?"

"Oh my god, yes! More than adequate. I love it here. Like the Metropole in Brussels, no disappointments whatsoever. Are you staying in town?"

He reached for his glass and leaned back in the chair. "Tonight I will. Maybe you will think of coming to my chateau in the country while you are here? You can have your own rooms, there is much space. And of course the servants are there to tend to your every whim. Yes?" He gave a most convincing grin.

"Oh, I don't know. Maybe we can talk about that later, okay?" She nervously reached for her glass and tipped it over onto the table. "Oh dear. I'm so clumsy."

He quickly blotted the spill with his linen napkin. "Are you hungry? Shall I order some hors d' oeuvres?" he signaled the waiter again, letting go of her hand.

"That might be a good idea." She smiled at him. "I've been sitting her awhile, drinking maybe a bit too much."

Maxim asked the waiter for a bar menu and another napkin. The waiter also wiped the table and poured Rachel another drink.

Maxim looked at his watch. "Your perfume, what is this scent?"

Rachel was surprised he even noticed. She wasn't aware it was strong enough to be detected a few feet from her. "Flower by Kenzo. One of my favorites."

"Lovely. What are your other favorites?"

"Shalimar, Obsession, Addict, Emeraude . . . those are tops in my book. Oh, and believe it or not, I love White Shoulders. I guess I just love the sweet, flowery smells."

"I am not familiar with Emeraude and White Shoulders," he said as he lifted his glass to sip.

She laughed. "Well, that's probably because both are very inexpensive. You can buy them in any American drugstore or discount house. I still have the tastes of a young girl growing up in the Central Valley of California. Some things remain instilled in one's being regardless of what one becomes or where one goes. You can take the girl out of the country but you can't take the country out of the girl . . . or something like that, however it goes," she said.

"The price isn't the issue, the scent is most important," he said in a sexy whisper.

For a few moments they gazed into each other's eyes over the rims of the champagne flutes.

Finally, "How is your novel coming along? Were you able to find the inspiration you needed in St. Petersburg?" Maxim set his glass on the table.

"Yep. I even had some impromptu inspiration here this evening before you arrived." She giggled and glanced at the man at the bar.

"Here, in the bar?"

115

"Yep. Here, in the bar. There were four hookers and their madam congregated over there at that table, waiting to be summoned by someone upstairs. I'm pretty sure that's what was happening. I suspect the *john* is an Arabian prince or king or whatever. Some middle-eastern type. The guy in the turban over there at the bar is the procurer. He even asked me to join them." She laughed. "Can you imagine that? I didn't take offense, I felt complimented, actually."

Maxim glared at the man who after a few moments turned his back and began talking to the bartender.

"Would you excuse me a moment?"

"Please don't worry about him, Maxim. I can take care of myself. I told him no, there was no harm done. Really. Please."

"No no, it isn't that. I must make a quick call, I just remembered. I'll be back in a moment."

He took his briefcase and left the lounge, walked back into the lobby around the corner out of Rachel's sight-line. He spoke to two of his six bodyguards, handed off the case to one of them and gestured towards the bar.

His protectors were dressed in black with tell-tale ear wires and microphones and were watching everyone who entered the lounge area; two were outside the glass double doors leading to and from the lounge to a patio area.

Rachel folded her notebook and put it in her purse.

When Maxim returned he kissed her on the cheek.

"Why thank you," she said, blushing.

"Now, what shall we have?" lifting a menu from the table.

"You order, I don't feel like thinking. I've just emptied my mind."

"As you wish, mademoiselle."

This man is a dream come true, so charming, so suave, she thought to herself as she sipped, watching Maxim studying the menu.

116

Two of Maxim's bodyguards, one carrying the aluminum case, appeared at the elevator and nodded to the man at the bar.

The man downed his drink and joined them on the elevator.

It was half past seven and Valentin rounded the corner to see his brother sitting at a table with a pretty woman dressed in emerald green.

He reached for Della's hand. "There they are."

Maxim saw him immediately and stood. "Valentin!"

They gave each other bear hugs.

"Valentin . . . Della . . . this is my friend, Rachel O'Neill, the writer."

They greeted each other with grins and hellos.

Valentin spoke up as they were seated by the waiter. "You have heard of my Della Doheny, Rachel? She publishes books in New York." It was obvious how much he admired and adored Della.

"After Maxim told me about you, Della, I did a search on the Internet of your publishing company. Quite impressive."

Della laughed. "I did one of you, too. Although I had already heard of you through one of my editors, we were considering one of your books. This is incredible, I mean, what are the chances of this happening, meeting in Moscow? So are you living in England full time now?"

Rachel nodded as the waiter perched to pour her a glass of champagne on her approval. "Mostly. I go back to the States for one reason or another when I have to. I still have property there, my son lives in Denver. And of course my agent is in L.A., so I go there periodically. But most of the time I'm in Cornwall, my favorite place to be. Or Paris, I have a place there too."

"Paris? Oh my God, I'd love to hear more about that. Maybe at lunch next week? I'm coming into town on Monday."

Della squeezed Valentin's hand. "I'll be careful, don't worry," she said as she looked up at him.

Maxim darted a glance at Valentin, understanding his concern.

"I will send someone with you," Valentin said.

"No you won't, dammit! I'll be fine. I'm a big girl, or hadn't you noticed?" She grinned. "He's very over-protective, Rachel. My Valentino."

"Valentin-o?" Rachel was amused. "Not Valentin?"

"At least it is not Valentine. That would be worse." He was as amused as Rachel.

"Valentin-o, I would like to speak to you for a moment in private. Ladies, will you please excuse us?" Maxim stood.

Della was first to reply, "Go ahead. That'll give me time to get acquainted with Rachel. Take as long as you want, guys. In fact we'll meet you in the dining room at eight. Okay with you?"

The men agreed and left the lounge.

Forty-five minutes later the women were still discussing life.

"So you see, that's my dilemma. I think I could love Valentino more than I could have ever imagined. I'm obsessed with him, that's for sure. But I'm at a crossroads. Do I marry him, or do I go back to New York and my dreadful life there?"

"Dreadful? Methinks therein lies your answer," Rachel chuckled as she touched Della's hand. "We have to pay attention to how we're feeling." Rachel empathized with Della; she completely understood where she was coming from. "I've known quite a few professional women who come up against that same question. You can't imagine how many I know who have gone through this."

"And, what is the consensus of opinion?" Della asked as the waiter poured the last of the champagne. "Oh, waiter, please bring a large bottle of water and add it to the dinner tab. So, tell me, Rachel, what happened in most cases?"

"Well, in most cases, love won out. And in most cases the women were able to continue their work, but in a different configuration. For instance, my friend Shellie. We met in Paris, ended up rooming together with her friend Janet. Shellie's passion was jazz, she's a singer. She went to Paris from Los Angeles to work as a singer. All she ever wanted to do was sing, but she got a late start. And she got a terrific gig on a Paris river boat, but then she met Adrian, an artist. He wanted to go back home to live in a tiny village high up in the Swiss Alps. She fought it tooth and nail. But you know what? She got pregnant, married Adrian, and now they have another child and are living happily ever after in the Alps. She calls it a fairy tale marriage. She sings at a local hofbrau down the mountain on weekends. Everybody's happy. So I think it depends on what is most important to you. We sometimes have to be creative to have what we really want." She sighed heavily. "Of course we have to know what we want."

"My problem is my publishing business. I'm not necessarily keen on it anymore; it wouldn't hurt my feelings to be out of all that crap."

"Then I would say you don't have a problem. Get rid of it, sell it."

Della reached for her glass and held it in her lap as she thought for a few moments.

Rachel continued. "What would you do if you weren't a publisher? Do you write?"

"I used to write when I was in college, published quite a few articles as a matter of fact, but wrote less and less the more I became involved in publishing. You can't do both, I've found that out."

119

Rachel saw herself in Della, recognized the inner struggles of taking on too much. "So, could you write or would you want to write if you sold the company and settled here in Russia?"

"I could, yea. I could. I'd certainly have plenty to write about here. I love the Russian people and the culture. Every time I come here I want to just drop out of my life in New York and stay. I'm serious."

"We have a lot in common. I used to have those thoughts everywhere I went. And I did drop out a few times, till I found where I belonged." Rachel laughed. "Looks like you're about to do the same."

"Yea, looks that way." Della sighed happily. "I suppose I could write articles and send them to magazines in the U.S., especially with all my contacts." She sat up straight. "You know, that's a damn good idea! A freelancer. I could do that. In fact, I could be a photo journalist. I love taking photos, too. Used to be my hobby when I was growing up and going through college. I even exhibited in a New York gallery once, before I got so busy with publishing. I forgot about that, how I felt about photography. I drove my parents crazy taking pictures all the time, around the ranch and every place we went. "

"There you go. There's your answer. You get the man you want, the life you want, the country you want, and the creative juices start to flow, and everybody's happy."

"Let's drink to that!"

They lifted their glasses in unison and reveled in the clinking sounds of their happy toast.

Chapter 19

Time seemed to pass quickly in Moscow for Rachel. It had been two weeks since she had arrived at the Metropole. Maxim was with her almost every day . . . taking her to lunches, to dinners, clubbing. Although at times it felt a bit tedious, having a man around so much.

She was thinking of renting an apartment, had decided against accepting Maxim's invitation to stay at his country estate. She couldn't do that for it would be suffocating, of that she was sure. So she told him it was more convenient for her to stay in the city where she could do her research as needed. Short term rentals were available, which would be perfect if she was to stay through the holidays.

It was noon in November, and Rachel was doing a rental search on her laptop at the Metropole corridor café, while waiting for her lunch date.

"Darling, you must come with me tonight to a dinner party at the Kremlin," Maxim said as he joined her. He leaned and kissed her on both cheeks before he sat and set his briefcase under the table.

121

"At the Kremlin? What is the occasion?" Rachel's eyes lit up. This could be good for her novel.

"It is a political get-together of the Federation's administrative division heads. I'll be representing the Sakha Republic," he said as he picked up the menu that was lying next to his plate. "It is at seven."

"Is it formal attire?"

"Yes, tuxedo and gown. You have a dress you can wear?" He looked across at her. "If not we can go to GUM. You know GUM, yes?"

"Yep, I do. It's a fabulous shopping center, and so close. I'll find something to wear, you needn't bother."

"It is not a bother to me. I want to buy you an evening gown . . . jewelry . . . shoes . . . and fur coat to wear tonight. It would give me pleasure to shop with you. I insist." He reached across and took her hand. "I want to please you."

Rachel was taken aback. No man had ever made that kind of offer to her. No man had ever been as rich as Maxim, either. It didn't seem right for some reason. She was flabbergasted, staring at him without saying a word.

The waiter arrived and all thoughts shifted to ordering lunch.

The interruption also gave Rachel time to gather her thoughts after the sudden shopping spree offer.

When the waiter left with the order, Rachel said, "Maxim, thank you for offering to accompany me to shop for tonight's event, but I must say no." She gave him an affectionate look, not wanting to appear to be ungrateful. She couldn't help thinking that possibly this was the manner of wealthy Russian men, and he probably missed doing things for his deceased wife. But then Rachel didn't want to open up that door. Her independence was ever more important to her now, and she certainly didn't want or need a sugar. The offer made her feel like a bimbo.

He frowned. "You do not want to go?"

"No, no, I don't mean I don't want to go the dinner. Yes, I'll go with you. Yes. I mean shopping. I'll go shopping for a dress, myself." She smiled.

He patted her hand. "As you wish. I was only wanting to be of some help." He quickly looked away as if he saw someone he knew. Then darted a look in the other direction. "Will you excuse me, please." Off he went without another word.

Rachel wondered if she had hurt his feelings. He'd left so abruptly. Maybe she should relax on the point. Maybe he needed to do it. What difference would it make to let him dote on her a little? What harm could it do? Maybe she should give her damn independence a rest, for god sakes. It could have been just a kind gesture on his part.

She buttered a piece of bread and munched slowly watching for Maxim to return from the direction he had gone.

At the exact moment the waiter brought the food, Maxim returned and apologized for rushing away as he had. It couldn't be helped he told her. Business.

She smiled up at him and told him not to worry. Said it had given her time to plan the afternoon and wondered when he could get away to go shopping with her.

He beamed a broad grin. Said she'd made him the happiest man in Moscow.

Rachel thought she saw a tear glisten in his eye.

Chapter 20

It was the day after the gala event at the Kremlin and Rachel was on the train to Klin to visit Della. She was still reeling from the excitement of the night before.

Maxim had picked her up for the gala that evening, but not before she had the chance to Google the event. She was taking the Internet printout to Della. It read:

"The roof top Ballroom of the Kremlin Palace Congress Centre will be the venue for this sit down gala dinner. Take the panoramic views of the flood-lit Kremlin and the golden domes of the Cathedral of the Assumption! Entertainment will showcase the rich cultural and musical heritage of Russia!

"Pre-reception cocktails will be served to the sounds of strolling Russian folk musicians. A formal sit down four course dinner will be served. The evening will showcase a variety of cultural music and entertainment . . ."

Della had telephoned early that morning and invited Rachel to come to Klin. She wanted to hear all about the dinner, what she wore, who was there. She and Valentin had been invited, too, but Valentin had to be in the Kaliningrad Oblast.

And since amber was his living, he had to go there to solve a problem that had arisen.

So Rachel threw some things together and hopped a train to Klin. Della was waiting at the station fifty miles northeast of Moscow.

Klin turned out to be more than a village contrary to what Della had originally thought. 100,000 people. When she first saw it from the train that day with Anastasia, and during the first couple of weeks of her stay, it appeared to be nothing more than another small village along the tracks, which was what had attracted her. But soon she discovered it not only held one of the major tourist attractions in the district, the Museum of Pyotr Ilyich Tchaikovsky, there were also grand churches, as well as a national hockey team housed at its Valery Kharlamov ice palace. She'd learned that Kharlamov was one of the best Russian hockey players, ever.

So it didn't take her long before she found out that a 15-minute ride on the bus would take her to the heart of Klin and the hustle bustle of the little city.

Although she had wanted to escape any visage of a city, Klin proper was far enough away to make her feel as if she lived in a village in the country. She was grateful Valentin's house was located in a settlement on the outskirts near one of the Klin train stations.

Now her excitement mounted as the train from Moscow carrying Rachel arrived.

Rachel stepped down onto the platform, carrying a weekender bag and a big grin of anticipation.

They both hurried toward each other and hugged.

"Oh, I am so glad you're here, I really am," Della said.

"Me, too. This is exciting, my first outing away from Moscow since I've been here. I've always wanted to see one of these little villages along the train tracks."

"Come, come. The car is over this way." Della took Rachel's arm and led her across the station to the parking lot. "Did you know that Klin was the last known residence of Tchaikovsky? I mean think about it, Tchaikovsky. Isn't that incredible?"

Working on a second bottle of wine that evening after dinner, the American transplants were laughing and talking about the current men in their lives. The *Ballenchine Boys* as they referred to them.

"Valentino says he wants to build a house for us, close to Maxim's country estate east of Moscow. Have you been there, yet? Has Maxim taken you there?"

"No, but he keeps talking about it. He said when he gets back from Brussels this time; he'd like me to spend a weekend. But I don't know—"

"What don't you know, girlfriend? What is there to know?" Della asked before taking another sip of wine.

"He is so good-looking; he scares the poop out of me. I might lose control. "

They both laughed.

"So really, why does he scare you? He's not a gremlin. Doesn't look like one."

Rachel's eyes widened, "Well, for one thing, I guess I'm afraid of me. I definitely don't need another man in my life. If I have sex with him and it's good, I'm a goner. So I don't want to get that close just yet. I need time to think about this before he's part of my life." She stood and walked to the window looking out onto the back garden.

"But he is in your life. So why not enjoy him? He certainly adores you. That's obvious. I can't believe you haven't made love, yet. Why not?"

Rachel turned and smiled at Della. "I was feeling close to it last night when we went back to the hotel, but no. We haven't." She turned back and gazed out the window at the neighboring houses with lights gleaming through their windows. "I don't think I ever will." A bit of silence prevailed. "But I'll tell you who adores *who* . . . Valentin is head over heels in love with you." Her countenance brightened as she went to Della and grasped her hands. "You are so lucky."

Della responded, "I know. But I'm not so sure about it. It's a bit overwhelming right now."

"What do you mean? I thought you were crazy about him."

Della reached for a pretzel from a dish of assorted nuts and tidbits sitting on the cocktail table. "I am. But I don't know. It's just that sometimes I wonder what the hell I'm doing. I mean— well, I do care for him, I do. But is it enough to last? I'm forty years old. Never been married. Is Valentino really the one, or am I feeling desperate in my old age? And then I think do I want to live in Russia for the rest of my life? He'll never want to live in the States. Of course I don't blame him, I don't either."

"Then where you live isn't a problem, is it? But that's a big issue with me. Living away from my Cornwall isn't a choice, I couldn't do it. I love my cottage in Newlyn. I wouldn't leave it for anybody, no matter how much I cared for him." Her thoughts immediately drifted to Paul and Belinda. She could visualize their faces, and made a mental note to call them when she returned to Moscow on Sunday.

Rachel continued: "But then, I'm not in love with Maxim. I like him. Yep. I like him very much, am attracted to him. Was from the first moment we met in Brussels last New Year's."

"Then what's the problem?" Della asked.

"I just don't want to be hurt again."

Della laughed. "None of us do, girl."

"Right."

"But you do care for him, you admit that."

Rachel looked at Della. "Yes, I do."

"But not enough to have sex with him?" Della asked.

"Right," Rachel lifted her glass gesturing a toast, then took a swig. "Hey, enough of this man-talk. What are we going to do tomorrow?"

"I'm going to show you the highlights of Klin and then we'll have lunch at a little place I know you'll love, then we'll go shopping. Valentino will be back tomorrow evening, so we have lots of time to talk and catch up on everything."

Chapter 21

It was Sunday afternoon and they'd just seen Rachel off to Moscow; Valentin's arm was stretched across Della's back, his hand grasping her waist.

Della frowned. "Do you think Maxim is going to tell her about his wife, soon? I mean, don't you think it's time?"

"He will tell her when he is ready, it is not our problem."

"But I don't like the fact he is not being up front and honest with Rachel. He better tell her before I do. I mean it."

Valentin frowned at Della and shook his head. They turned and walked to the black SUV with its motor running near the entrance to the train station, the driver holding open the door to the back seat.

"I just worry about her, that's all. She's had such heartbreak, you know? Her fiancé was killed in Brazil last year right before the Christmas wedding she'd dreamed of, and before him her previous fiancé was killed in a car wreck in Cornwall. Those are two huge heartbreaking tragedies, don't you think? I mean, how much can one girl take? Obviously she isn't very lucky in love, was divorced twice years ago from two jerkolas, and I don't think she can take much more of the disappointment. I suspect she's more fragile than she looks. She keeps up a good front."

Valentin helped her up into the SUV, shut the door, and got into the front seat with the driver. He looked back at Della who was still frowning and in a depressed mood. "My love, you need not worry, I will speak to Maxim." He reached back and reassured her with a squeeze of her knee. "He will not hurt her."

Della was grateful that Valentin was sensitive to her thoughts and moods. Never before had she experienced such a reaction from any other man and it was endearing to say the least.

At Valentin's little house on the outskirts of Klin the driver stopped the vehicle and one of the bodyguards checked out the inside of the house before ushering them inside.

There had been recent problems in Moscow when one of the Ballenchine business associates, another diamond dealer, had been assassinated. Valentin had explained the need for extra precaution to Della, but assured her that they were not in real danger.

After they were inside the house, Valentin said he would prepare the evening meal as he usually did. He loved to cook and Della didn't mind at all. It had never been her forte to whip up daily meals in a kitchen. Valentin took to it as flowers took to sunlight and water.

"You are a very rare find, do you know that?" Della said as she hugged him around the waist and gave him an extra squeeze before turning loose and heading for the coffee maker.

"I believe it is just the opposite. You are the rare find, a gem." He grinned as he began to pull food stuffs from the refrigerator. "I am truly a lucky man."

"Well, I don't know about that, but I do know how I feel about you."

"And how is that?" he stood with hands on his hips looking at her as she sat at the table pouring a cup of coffee.

She didn't expect the blunt question, and wasn't prepared to answer it in detail. Her comment had been more of a kidding, nonchalant response. But now he was asking her specifically, making her think.

"You know how I feel, Valentino."

"I am not sure," he said and turned back to the cupboard to reach for a pan. "Shall we have wine with our lunch?"

"Yea, I'll do the honors; you keep doing what you're doing." She went to the icebox on the back porch to get a bottle. They stored vodka, wines, and other liquors on the porch.

"I will have a glass while I am cooking, please." Valentin had three pans of oil and butter simmering on the stove, while he was cutting and chopping vegetables. "So tell me, *milaya moya,* how is it you feel about me?" He didn't look up.

Della was trying to figure out what *milaya moya* meant as she opened a bottle of white wine and poured two glasses. She handed one to Valentin and held her own glass as their eyes met.

"Valentino, I'm wondering if we're doing the right thing. I wonder if we love each other enough to withstand whatever problems we might have in the future. We both are of such different backgrounds and culture. What do you think?" She took a sip and moved to the table and sat facing Valentin's back as he stood at the stove.

He didn't say a word while he continued to prepare the meal. In a pan of melted butter he placed slices of black bread; in another pan of hot oil he put chopped potatoes and onions, in another thin slices of beef. Then he turned and leaned against the countertop, sipping his wine and gazing intently at Della. Still not saying anything.

She continued, "I mean, what if down the line we find we can't live with each other, that we're too different?" Della's facial expression was sincere and half-way sad.

"Do you feel we are too different?" he asked.

"No, not really. But what if I annoy you at one point? What if my American ways begin to irritate you, grind on you, piss the holy shit out of you? What then?"

He laughed. "Then we must discuss it at that point, if I irritate you, or if you irritate me." He looked directly into her eyes, "Is that not the way it is done in America? Do you not discuss your problems with one another? And do you not then fix the problems?"

He turned back to the stove and removed the pan of bread, placing a cloth over it and setting it in the oven to keep it warm. He stirred the vegetables, turned the meat, and then lowered the heat under both.

"Yes?" he asked, reaching for the wine and sitting at the head of the table, Della to his left, waiting for her reply.

"You know, I haven't said much about my parents, they died a long time ago, but I'll always remember one thing about them. During my early teen years in Oklahoma, they didn't get along. Many days would go by without them speaking to each other. And when they finally would, they'd argue. Sometimes to the point of violence. Violence in their voices, not their actions. They never got physical with each other, no hitting. They'd get so loud sometimes that I'd have to leave the house. I would saddle my horse and ride into the hills when I was younger, would hop in my pickup truck and drive into town when I was older. But it wasn't always like that. There was a time when they were madly in love, and then *poof!* one day they weren't. I never could figure out what happened to change them almost overnight. It just changed, though, for no reason at all."

Valentin reached across the corner of the table for Della's hand. "I would never treat you that way. I love you, my Della, *milaya moya*, my sweet. I would always love you, and I would never raise my voice to you. If we have disagreement, then we discuss disagreement. Do you not agree?"

Della took a gulp of her drink. "You know what? You're just too good to be true, Valentino Ballenchine. You are. I have finally hit the jackpot." She got up and stepped around the table and sat on his lap, her arms around his neck. She grinned up at him with teary eyes. "I love you too, and I will never raise my voice to you, I promise. Besides you're way too big and burly for anybody to even think about raising their voice to, if they had any smarts."

They both laughed and held each other in a loving embrace.

Chapter 22

Rachel woke up Monday morning in her hotel room thinking of Paul and Belinda. First she called room service and ordered a pot of coffee and toast, and then she opened her laptop to see if she had any messages from them. None. But as she was checking her other messages on AOL, an Instant Message popped up from Paul.

Rachel, are you there?

Her doorbell rang. *Hold on, Paul. Someone at the door. brb.*

"Set it on the table, please," she said to the waiter standing in the doorway.

The waiter did as he was told. She signed the bill and he thanked her for the tip, and left.

She poured a cup of coffee and returned to the messaging.

Okay, I'm back.

Have you decided when you're coming home?

She thought about the question, seriously, for the first time since she'd been there. *No, I haven't. Why? Something urgent?*

No, just miss you. The boys miss you. Belinda misses you.

She took a gulp of her first cup of coffee that morning then continued typing: *Well, to be honest with you, I'm missing you all, too. Was thinking of you yesterday when I was visiting Della in Klin. Do you know Klin?*

Paul replied, *No, don't know much about Russia. Have only been there once, Petersburg and Moscow, for a week. Not long enough.* He hesitated. *How are you and Maxim getting along? Is he sweeping you off your feet?*

Rachel took a deep breath and thought a few seconds about how she would answer his question.

Paul typed first, *I mean, are you in love yet?*

Hell, no! lol lol lol I'm not that far gone! She laughed out loud as she typed.

Good!

She stared at his one-word response. *You don't like him?*

A few moments passed.

It isn't that, it's just that I have a feeling about him. Something's amiss. Maybe it isn't anything, maybe I'm being over-protective, but . . . He stopped typing.

Rachel continued: *Yep, I know what you mean. I've got a feeling, too. And it isn't because of Pete. I believe I'm doing okay in that department. I know Pete is gone, and he would want me to carry on . . . as he would say. Lol lol lol But besides, it's too soon to get involved with another man. I like my life as is, you know? I love being able to do what I want, when I want, not having to report to anybody. I love Cornwall, being close to you and Belinda and the boys, love Newlyn. I wouldn't do anything to change any of that.*

Long hesitation. *That's good to hear.*

How is Belinda, by the way? Rachel leaned back in the chair and lifted her coffee cup, waiting for a full report.

A few more moments passed before Paul answered.

Well, sometimes it gets the best of her. She is too weak to work right now. But she's hanging in there. The treatments end next week. So we'll get the results at the end of next month when she's tested again. She tells me not to worry, that she isn't going to let it get her down. But I don't know, Rachel. I have such a feeling of dread and doom these days. It's almost too much to bear. If you were here . . . sorry!

Rachel set her cup on the table. *Should I come back, Paul?*

NO no no no no. I don't mean for you to come back till you're finished. I'm sorry, just a low morning for me. Let's change the subject. Actually, a customer just came in. We'll talk later.

Okay, I'll call tonight and talk to both of you, all right?

Yes, Belinda would love that, and so will I. Bye.

Rachel stared at the screen long after Paul signed off. She scrolled back up and re-read the sequence of posts they'd just exchanged.

Her heart felt heavy and sad.

Chapter 23

It had been two weeks since Maxim had left for Brussels on business. During that time Rachel found an apartment not far from the heart of things in Moscow, close to shopping and other conveniences. Everything was within walking distance – the Kremlin, the Metropole, cafes in GUM where she went quite often to have coffee or lunch, the Nautilus shopping center with its Loft Café, one of her favorites for cocktails and dinner. She was the inveterate people-watcher, so going to an assortment of cafes and bars was exciting to her.

She happened to be at the Loft having lunch when her cell phone rang.

"Hi, Rachel."

"Della, what's up?'

"Oh, I'm just getting nervous about the engagement party. Is Maxim back yet?"

"No, but he called and said he'd be back tomorrow in plenty of time. Said all the arrangements have been made. His social secretary and the house staff have taken care of everything. He said not to worry." Rachel signaled for the waiter and ordered another glass of wine.

"Oh good. I wasn't really worried about it, though. I know the party's in capable hands. He's so organized." She sighed and was quiet.

"What is it, Della?'

"Well, Valentino is going to meet me there. He called and said he couldn't get here today; he's flying in tomorrow, too. Suggested I come to Moscow and ride out with you. Is that all right? In fact, I'm thinking I could come right now and spend the night, if that wouldn't inconvenience you."

"Of course, please do. I could use the company. Definitely. Will you be driving?"

"Yea. I'm already on the road, in fact. Wanted to get there in time to do some shopping. We can drive out tomorrow early, surprise the guys. What do you think?"

"Terrific!" Rachel sat up straight as the waiter poured another glass for her. This was perfect. Tonight she and Della could have dinner somewhere where there was music. That would be fun. A pre-engagement party, just the two of them.

"Where are you now?" Della asked.

"I'm at the Loft Café, on the roof of the Nautilus shopping center. Just finished lunch. How far away are you?"

"Actually, I could be there in fifteen or twenty minutes. You want to wait there for me? I could use a drink. This whole engagement party business is stressing me out."

"Absolutely. I'll have a bottle of champagne chilled for us."

"Great! See you in a few. I feel a drunk coming on."

"I just love this place," Della said to Rachel as she rushed in and sat at Rachel's table.

They were sitting near the balustrade overlooking the street below.

"I do, too. I come here for the five o'clock tea a lot. It's perfect for an early supper with its snacks, sandwiches, and fresh pastries. To die for in fact. And it's just a short walk for me from my apartment."

"I can't wait to see your place." Della looked around at all the assorted types of people seated at the tables in the café.

"Spending afternoons here watching people is the best," Rachel commented.

"Yea, I bet it is. It's expensive, so that keeps the riff-raff out," she laughed. "Did you see all the bodyguards in the corridor? My God, they're all over the place."

"Yep. They are. Must be some high-rollers in here, today. In fact, I recognize that man over there; he was at the State dinner. Can't remember his name, but Maxim knows him. Look, those are his bodyguards sitting at the table next to him."

Della raised her eyebrows and reached for the glass of champagne the waiter poured for her. "You know, I have a feeling Valentino has set some extra bodyguards on me. I just feel it. He's so afraid something is going to happen to me."

"What makes you think that?" Rachel looked around to see if she could spot any that were assigned to Della.

Della turned and looked at the entrance to the roof café. "See that guy over there, looking through the doorway . . . I see him almost everywhere I go. Wouldn't you think that might be the first clue? I mean, do they think I'm stupid?" She laughed, again. "But I don't mind. Makes Valentino happy, although I can take care of myself. Always have. They don't know who they're dealing with, here." She chuckled then took a gulp of the champagne.

"What do you mean?"

Della looked across at Rachel. "Well, to start with I'm a gun-totin' mama."

"You carry a gun?"

"Always. One in my purse right now."

"Legally?"

"Is there a legal in Russia? But I do have a license to carry in the States. I don't know how it works here. Haven't told anyone about it. Might come in handy with whatever is going on with all the bodyguards, though."

Rachel frowned and leaned forward. "I wonder why he feels you need them? Has he said anything?"

"No, not really. Although he gets all uptight when I come to Moscow alone. Maybe he's just the overprotective type. Maxim has six or seven around him all the time. Haven't you noticed?"

Rachel thought for a moment. "No. But then I haven't paid much attention. Of course, everywhere we go there are tons around; you can't tell who is protecting who. It's comical in a way. More bodyguards than the people they're protecting." She lifted her glass and leaned back in her chair. "But I know it is serious business. There's so much going on behind the scenes in this country. The Russian Mafia is as big if not bigger than the Mafia in the States. Spooky. Not to mention the political machine."

"Valentino says it isn't safe in Moscow for anybody. We were reading in the paper last week about an American businessman who got a haircut at a barber shop one morning, left the shop, and nobody ever saw him again. He's missing. Gone. Valentino knew him, so I imagine Maxim did too. The guy had something to do with diamonds. I think our guys are in a dangerous business."

Rachel nodded as she shifted in her chair and looked out over the balcony at the view of the old KGB headquarters building, sipping her champagne. "A lot of intrigue and espionage in this city over the years. Has a thrilling historical undercurrent, don't you think?"

"Yea, it does, I feel it too," Della added.

"Oh, look at that!" Rachel said quietly. "Those people left that table next to the guy with all the bodyguards, and now another table of diners are leaving. They haven't even finished their meals, the food just came. Looks as if they're being ushered out. Oh look, more bodyguards have moved in. Something's going down."

The diner in the center of all the attention, was a small man, dressed elegantly, dark silks, designer sunglasses, shaved head same as his protectors, two beautiful women flanking him. He stood suddenly, looking in the direction of the doorway. Two men were being frisked and then allowed to continue on to the diner's table. They shook hands with him and seated themselves.

The group occupied one end of the café, half secluded by the decorative plants and trees. But Rachel and Della had a full view of them, and wondered why they hadn't been asked to leave as the other patrons had. Possibly it was because they were American women and no one felt they were a threat to what was going on.

One of the two newcomers was writing on a notepad. He tore off the slip of paper and handed it to the head guy who read it and appeared to be initialing it. The guy handed it back to the newcomer. Both men nodded, then stood and shook hands again, and off they went.

In came another subject, this one huge and intimidating. The same thing happened. It was as if the small guy was holding court.

"This is right out of a Godfather movie, isn't it?" Della blurted. "Exciting. Remember when Brando was taking all the requests from his subjects?"

"I need to be taking notes, do you mind?" Rachel reached for her note pad.

"Of course not. Go ahead. You know I've seen a lot of this in New York. And not just Italians. Jews, Russians, Asians, they all have their own Mafia. In fact one of the most deadly are

141

the Mafia Jews, would you believe it? Speaking of diamonds, the Jews are up to their necks with racketeering and smuggling diamonds. I've learned so much since I've been here. Valentino tells me a lot, and I've done a bit of research about it myself."

"Maybe we should compare notes." Rachel didn't look up, kept writing in her notebook.

"I'd love to, would give me something to do. I was a good researcher in college. Loved it."

Rachel stopped and thought for a moment. She looked across the table at Della who was beaming . . . her brilliant coppery hair glistening in the late day sun, orange-frost lipstick contrasting with her white perfect teeth. She was absolutely ravishing, Rachel noticed.

"You know, I could use a researcher." Rachel felt a surge of energy as she did when her story ideas would appear out of nowhere.

"Well, here I am. At your service. I mean it."

"That's terrific, Della. And we can even exchange information if I've done research on one of your topics."

"Perfect!"

Chapter 24

Maxim and Valentin arrived at Moscow airport within thirty minutes of each other; Maxim flying in from Belgium, Valentin from Kaliningrad near Poland. As previously arranged, they met, and then Maxim's driver and security guards were waiting to take them to the country estate where the engagement party was to take place that evening.

But the main reason they were meeting early, before the festivities, was to discuss a telephone call Maxim had received the day before.

"Please arrange for some sandwiches and tea to be served in my study," Maxim said to his valet when he entered his bedroom at the estate.

Valentin had gone directly to his usual guestroom on the second floor where he was freshening up before their meeting in twenty minutes.

The country estate had been designed and built by Maxim. The rooms were very large and furnished sparsely – three floors. Ground floor contained a ballroom, a parlor, a billiard room, a library, an industrial-size kitchen, and several restrooms to accommodate visitors. Seven guestrooms including

Maxim's bedroom were on the first floor above ground level. His contemporary taste was evident throughout - sleek leather, modern wood and metal mostly, pristine, built-in furniture and walls of shelving containing artifacts, walls of priceless paintings by contemporary world-renown artists. It was the complete opposite to his home in Brussels which was chock full of French frou-frou and gild, more his wife's preference than his. His was more tailored and masculine.

It was almost as if he was in protest of his life in Belgium, which could very well be true. When his wife Katarina visited after it was first built, she didn't like it. It was cold, she said, had no style or flair. So she never set foot in it again.

Katarina was content to stay in Brussels which was home to her now. Besides she didn't have any reasons to be in Moscow. Her family had left years ago; a younger sister lived in South Africa, an older brother in the U.S. The ancestor strata above and below the three of them was nonexistent, no parents, no aunts and uncles, no children, no nieces and nephews. And since her alcoholism had taken its toll in her debilitation, she no longer traveled anywhere. It was all she could do to get out of bed in the morning; her social life was non-existent, with no change in sight. She was happy with her birds and animals.

Maxim had long given up hope that she would ever recover from her afflictions, and had made the decision to go his own way, but to continue to provide for her and make her as comfortable as possible. She had a staff of caretakers, a beautiful mansion, and had her aviary and small zoo.

In turn, Maxim had a life in Moscow in his own country estate and had a thriving diamond and amber business, with occasionally a woman in the picture, but never for very long.

Maxim reached to remove a painting that was hanging between two of the floor to ceiling windows. It was their wedding portrait.

He still loved Katarina, remembering how she was in the early days; she had been a gorgeous woman, petite and blond. He remembered how tragic it was when she miscarried several pregnancies in the first two years they were married. She never got over the fact that she was not destined to have children.

He couldn't bring himself to divorce her. That wasn't an option. So he usually had his guard up with other women, never let them get too close, although he'd enjoy them from time to time. That is, until he met Rachel on New Year's Eve in Brussels. Rachel was different. He let his guard down.

Maxim placed the wedding bportrait in a storage closet in the hallway on his way upstairs to meet with Valentin.

The entire top floor was Maxim's private area, another library, office, conference room, and gym. The entire floor surrounded with mitered windows that produced the most magnificent 360-degree view of the countryside. An iron-railed balcony ran the periphery of the third floor, with a metal escape ladder that could be lowered to the garden, as well as a hidden elevator through a pantry that went to the ground floor and to the two levels below ground - the safe rooms.

In the center of the top floor space were a pantry/bar and a bathroom. The overall design was similar to that of a revolving restaurant on the top floor of a hotel, with the services and the entry walled off in the middle of the space, elevator going down from the middle, although this room didn't revolve, it was rectangular. Moscow could be seen in the distance and at night the lights were breathtaking.

Valentin was already seated at the conference table on the north side of the floor. Maxim signaled the cook to serve as he passed the pantry.

"Ah! Such a lovely view, Maxim. I envy you," Valentin said as he sipped a cocktail. File folders and a laptop were open on the table in front of him.

"Which is one of the topics I wish to discuss." Maxim sat at the end of the table on Valentin's left. "I would prefer that you live in one of the guest houses, Valentin, here on the estate. I've given orders to refurbish that one," he pointed to a large cottage about a half mile north of his house, near the north gate. "It would be more convenient for our business meetings and for another reason. When you are married, Della will have the protection she'll need, here. I have already begun the renovation."

Valentin stared at his older brother, wondering what was going through his mind. "You have decided without conferring with me on the matter?"

There were times when Valentin wished he could separate himself from his older brother. Sure he appreciated him, but he had spent his whole life in his brother's shadow, going along with whatever he wanted, and always being there for him, always being part of the Ballenchine Brothers businesses. Lately he had wanted something else.

"I didn't have time to confer with you, Valentin. And that brings me to the telephone call I received yesterday in Brussels. But first, let us have some lunch, shall we?"

The waiter was wheeling a double-decker cart with enough food for six people. The aroma preceded it and started to work the saliva glands of the two brothers. One thing they had in common, they loved their food.

First there was Salad Olivier: potatoes, carrots, hardboiled eggs, onion, dill pickles, peas, bologna, and mayonnaise and lettuce leaf. Each man had a huge helping of the salad with a glass of red wine.

Next came a bowl of Borscht - a beet and cabbage soup. The smells of garlic, beets and cabbage were enough to captivate a person who wasn't even hungry, it was so delicious.

Finally a plate of sliced Riga Rye bread was put before them, along with a platter of smoked salmon & sturgeon, and all the condiments.

More wine was poured and after an hour of feasting, both men leaned back in their chairs to enjoy the landscape view.

The waiter cleared the table and brought a pot of tea, then left them to fend for themselves.

Valentin poured the tea. "What is this telephone call that has caused you concern?"

"We are in danger, my brother. I have increased the number of guards for this evening."

"We will cancel!" Valentin reacted immediately, leaning forward in his chair and reaching for his cell phone. "I cannot risk my Della being harmed."

"No no, everything's under control."

"What is the danger?"

"Nicholas Madov is angry because I will not deal with him. He has formed a company, has invested in the Kochenko mine, and now insists we share the diamond market with him as a separate entity. I told him that it is not my decision. He argued that my influence could sway the others. I said, no. I would not. I don't trust him. I believe he is behind the recent killing of our associate." Maxim gazed across the grounds to the cottage. "It's known what he does to those who will not agree with him. So I feel it is necessary we combine forces, Valentin, until I can solve this problem. It would be safer if you and Della live in the cottage for protection."

Valentin stared silently at the cottage at the end of the graveled lane on the north end of his brother's property. He sipped his tea slowly. He wondered how Della would react to Maxim's proposition; she loved where they lived now, the village life. He was worried.

"Do not mention this to Della tonight, please. I will tell her when we return to Klin tomorrow."

Chapter 25

When she saw Maxim Ballenchine's mansion looming ahead at the end of the winding drive, Rachel felt the same passion DuMaurier's character in *Rebecca* felt when she first saw *Mandalay*.

"Will you look at that house?" Rachel leaned forward and clutched the dashboard. "Why didn't you tell me about this— this castle he lives in?"

Della grinned. "So you like it, do you?"

"Well, whether I like it or not, doesn't matter, does it? It's overwhelming. And what do you make of all the armed guards? God, they're everywhere. Look at them!"

Della responded, "Maxim probably wants to make sure everybody is safe, tonight. There are quite a few big-wigs coming, so I'm sure that's why he's put on extra to be on the safe side."

As the massive, heavy iron gates opened before them, two armed guards waved Della through.

Rachel turned and watched the gates close behind them. "Must cost him a fortune to hire all these men. How many does Valentin usually have around your place?"

"I don't know, but three or four I would imagine when he travels. I never see them, except for one that drives us on occasion and a couple hanging around the house lately. Most of them are just a front anyway, don't you think? Just someone to scare off the bad guys. I don't think it's because of any real danger. More of a status symbol." But as she spoke, Della wondered about the increase of guards. There seemed to be something afoot, more than usual. She felt it.

Rachel pointed beyond the house to the north end of the property, "Will you look at that cottage back there? Isn't that a beauty? It's huge. Wow! I'd like to have a look at that while we're here. Do you think we can?"

"I don't see why not. No one lives in it. It is lovely, isn't it?" Della stopped the car in front of the mansion's west portico, the main entrance. "Okay, here we are. Behold, the Ballenchine mansion!"

Two young men dressed in white opened the car doors and assisted the women from the car and up the entry steps. Two more gathered their luggage and their gowns for the evening swathed in clear plastic on hangers.

Rachel darted glances to the right and left, and whispered, "Will you look at this, Della? They're all over the place and they've all got guns."

They both turned and scanned the grounds as far as they could see, as well as the gardens leading back to the gate. In every nook and cranny were security agents and guards, clothed in black, with their tell-tale Bluetooth-like units attached to their faces.

Maxim startled the ladies with his booming voice from inside the foyer, while Valentin scurried down the expansive staircase behind him.

"Welcome, Ladies. It is good to have you here. Come, come." He gave a slight bow as they entered, sweeping his hand towards the inside of the mansion. "Would you like something to

149

eat, to drink?" He didn't wait for an answer. "Valentin, look at our beautiful American women! How did this happen?"

They all laughed, hugged, and kissed their greetings.

Valentin took one of Della's hands in his, "Come with me to the kitchen, my darling. I want to show you something." They took off, hand in hand, down the corridor leading to the north wing.

Maxim stood in front of Rachel, grasping both her hands. "You look lovely today." He was appreciative of Rachel's conservative attire, always simple and casual. Today she was wearing shades of brown: slacks, long-sleeved blouse, sweater vest, and bronze alligator shoes. "Was it a pleasant drive from Moscow?"

"Loved it. And your place is absolutely gorgeous! My goodness, it's huge. And the gardens . . . wow! You know I'm a garden person. It's beautiful, Maxim." She quickly glanced around the grand entry at the flagstone floors and walls. "I never would have dreamed you lived in such a place." She looked up at the giant, contemporary chandelier hanging from a steel girder that was at least sixty feet above them.

"A man's castle is his home, or is it the other way around? A man's home is his castle. You're the writer, which is it?" He put both arms around her waist, locking his hands in the small of her back, and drew her to him.

"I believe it's a man's home is his castle." She blushed at the intimacy she was feeling, and pulled away gently. She moved to the metal and wood staircase that wound up to the first and second floors circling the circumference of the foyer. "How many floors do you have?"

"Five, counting those below. But there are a few half floors and secret spaces in between."

"I love the use of the stone, wood, and metal. It's so different." Her gaze followed the winding staircase.

"Come, let us go into the sitting room." He reached for her hand and led her to a room off the grand foyer. Placed strategically were several sofas and chairs grouped for conversation creating cozy spaces throughout the expansive room.

"Shall we?" he motioned to one of the two sofas in front of the burning fireplace and then pushed a button on a nearby phone. He spoke into the receiver. "Please bring sherry and canapés for four in the front sitting room. Right away." He hung up the phone and leaned against the fireplace mantle, watching Rachel.

The contemporary décor of the room was completely opposite to Rachel's preference. Where she preferred flowery and multi-patterned fabrics and decor, he did not. But still he'd managed to make the room warm and cozy with striped fabric of browns, golds, and greens on the sofas, solid colors of the same on pillows and chairs.

"I created this sculpture in my youth. Do you like it?" He was pointing up to the seven- by seven-foot metal sculpture comprised of bits and pieces of copper, brass, pewter, and bronze that hung over the mantle. The fireplace was copper faced with brass adornments.

Rachel immediately stood up and faced the sculpture. "You did that? Such detail and so much work you put into it. Maxim, you could make a living at that. Or have you already?"

He laughed. "No, no. That was, as I said, during my youth. When I was desperate to make money."

"It's beautiful! Do you have others? I would love to have one for my cottage in Cornwall. I know just where I would put it. Maybe something a bit smaller, though." She grinned.

"I may have something that would suit you."

Two housemen entered with the sherry and food and began to arrange it on a long, teak buffet table against the wall near the doorway. Maxim immediately began checking to see that the food was placed as he wished.

Rachel walked over to the windows. The man definitely knew how to spend money, she could see that. The row of picture windows – ten feet high and six feet wide, each framed with wood and decorative metal – opened the room to the front garden adding plenty of light to the interior.

She watched an imposing olive green Humvee speed past on the driveway in front of the windows. Suddenly four armed guards ran past on foot, and then two more behind them. Shouts could be heard.

Gunshots!

"Maxim—?"

Before she could say anything else, Maxim grabbed Rachel's arm and pulled her from the windows.

"To the safe rooms, sir!" Maxim's head of security instantly appeared in the doorway with other guards.

The guards rushed Maxim and Rachel across the foyer and through a hidden door that led down a stairwell to an underground level. Once through the steel reinforced door at the bottom of the stairwell, Rachel couldn't believe her eyes. It was another world down there. Another house. All underground.

Valentin and Della were coming towards them from a hallway leading in from another direction flanked with more armed guards.

Both women huddled together on a sofa in an alcove situated in the main room, both speechless and wide-eyed.

The guards spread throughout the safe rooms, checking that everybody and everything was secure. There was plenty of space for the entire house staff as well as any number of guests, and the various rooms were well stocked and well appointed. There was a huge kitchen and two dining rooms, bathrooms, sitting rooms and bedrooms. Televisions, sound systems, exercise equipment, anything anyone would want for any length of time.

A computer center with all the latest security monitors and equipment money could buy was adjacent to the main room where the women were sitting. Maxim and Valentin rushed to the technicians who were manning the surveillance equipment.

"There!" one of the techies said pointing to a security monitor. Gun fire was taking place between Maxim's security guards and two black SUVs that were inching slowly up the drive towards the house. Two more SUVs were coming up behind them blocking the gate, surrounded by more armed shooters firing at Maxim's guards in the gardens.

"The north gate! What is happening there?" Maxim was standing with his fists on his hips, staring at the monitors.

"Nothing, yet," the techie said. He pointed to the monitor showing a full view of the north gate which was near the large cottage. Two other monitors were scanning the entire estate's northern section. The iron fence was closed and Maxim's guards were positioned every sixty feet on the fifteen-foot high stone wall. "The electric current is on. No one will get through."

"The east gate?"

"Safe."

Three gates, only one was compromised.

"What is going on?" Rachel whispered to Della.

"I don't know, but I don't think it's good."

"Might make a good story, huh?" Rachel tried to smile.

Della frowned with a slight smile. "Yea, right. A great story. We just have to survive it to write it."

Rachel held on to Della's arm, "We'll be alright. Look at those two strapping Russian protectors we have. And my god, they have an entire army at their disposal. Can you believe it? Are we ever lucky or not?"

"Yea, right."

Maxim and Valentin reentered the main room, both on cell phones walking towards the women.

"I want the Ka-50s at the west gate immediately. There are four black SUVs with armed gunman. Take them out. My men are in green Hummers and stay clear of the house." Maxim closed his phone. He rushed to Rachel. "I am so sorry you have to go through this. Would you care for a drink?" He walked to a bar that was set up near the sofa and began pouring drinks as if everything was normal. And everything was under control in his mind. "Ladies, a drink?"

"I believe I will," Rachel answered.

"Yes, I'll have one, too. Uh, Maxim," Della said, "the Ka-50s are helicopters, right?"

Maxim was surprised at her question. "Yes, they're known as *Black Sharks*. Manufactured here in Russia by Kamov in Arsenyev, a town in the Primorsky Krai in the Russian Far East. How do you know about them?"

"I published a novel written by a pilot who flew in Vietnam, it was quite fascinating. So do you rent them or own them or what?"

"I own two of them," he said as he handed Rachel a glass of wine, then one to Della.

"And how much did that cost you, if you don't mind me asking?"

Maxim poured himself a drink. "A mere $15 million."

"For both of them?'

"Each of them."

"Rubles?"

"Dollars."

"Oh." Della raised her eyebrows at Rachel who was taking it all in.

Valentin was still speaking on his cell phone. "Radio the men, tell them when they hear birds, pull back. They are coming.

How many vehicles outside wall? Be careful." He kept the phone to his ear and walked to the bar to pour himself a drink.

At that moment Della saw someone open a door from the inside of another room next to the computer room.

"Oh my God! Will you look at that?" she whispered to Rachel, pointing towards the door. She recognized dozens of assault weapons in glass cases on the walls inside the room.

Della's father had taught her all about the different types of guns, but she'd never seen so many in one place before, outside of a gun store. She recognized several sub-machine guns and assault weapons - the AK-47s and 74s, AR-15s and M-16s, all sorts of guns, but some she didn't recognize. She remembered that Mikhail Kalashnikov had developed most of the assault weapons used in the military around the world. She was thinking she could write a series of articles about Kalashnikov and Russian guns. Maybe Maxim would let her check out his gun stash.

Maxim sat in a chair across from Rachel, trying to hide his trepidations, for although he felt everything was under control, his men were still out there combating the assailants.

Rachel attempted to distract him from his thoughts, she could see his concern. "So, what about these helicopters, are they like our Cobra and Apache aircraft?"

Maxim cocked his head and looked at Rachel. "You know about the Cobra and Apache?"

"I've watched a lot of Sylvester Stallone movies." She smiled and Maxim smiled back.

"Well, they are not exactly like those. The Ka-50 is smaller, although fast and agile enough to handle support in Special Forces as well as situations such as this one. One difference is it has a one-pilot cockpit and can dive at 217 mph and do 196 mph in level flight."

Della chimed in, "So what does it have in the way of fire-power?"

"I am amazed you know about such things as this."

"Oh but I do, quite a bit," Della said as she smiled. "You'd be surprised."

"You American women do surprise me. I am not accustomed to this." He grinned. "But in answer to your question, it is armed with a cannon - 460 rounds, four under-wing gun pods - 240 rounds each, and two missile racks able to accommodate missiles, rockets, or bombs."

"Yikes!" Della said.

Valentin put his hand on Della's shoulder, she looked up at him.

He was listening on the cell phone with a heavy frown. "I'm afraid we must cancel the engagement party, my darling. I am sorry."

Chapter 26

In spite of what turned out to be a bloody assault on the Ballenchine estate - the helicopter pilots shot and killed nine perpetrators on the grounds and four of Maxim's men were wounded - a week later Rachel and Della were having lunch in the Klin house.

The attack seemed to have been just a figment of their imagination. The only reminder was that in Klin they were heavily protected by armed guards, more guards than they knew. There were the obvious ones posted outside, but inside two of the neighboring houses, one on each side of Valentin's, there were more.

It still wasn't safe enough in Valentin's opinion; he worried constantly for Della's safety and was eager to move into Maxim's compound which was scheduled in two weeks.

"Would you like another lemonade, Rachel? Della asked as she lifted the pitcher before sitting at the table in the kitchen.

"Yep, that would be nice. Valentin is coming, isn't he?"

"He called and said there was a delay, but he'll be here within the hour. We keep each other informed as to where we are now, since last week." Della poured a glass for herself. "You know, he wants us to move into that cottage at the mansion, that one you wanted to see. Although I wouldn't call it a cottage, it's more like a country manor, if you ask me." She laughed. "It has safe rooms like Maxim's. So it'll be like having two houses, one above ground, one under. What do you think?"

Rachel brightened. "Jump at it, Della! I wouldn't hesitate for a moment. I agree with Valentin, you're too exposed here in this village. Definitely do it. As soon as you can. Is that what he's suggesting?"

"Yea, in a couple of weeks. It should be finished by the end of the month. He was so sweet about telling me. He was afraid I'd miss this village and was reluctant to tell me, can you imagine? But I assured him our safety is more important than living in a village. And it's a lovely house, don't you think?"

"You better believe it. I'd move into it in the blink of an eye, never mind the safety features." Rachel picked up a sandwich. "I love these. You've changed the whole concept of a tuna fish sandwich."

"It's the minced apples and green onions that make it."

Rachel added, "And the nuts and raisins, not to mention the avocado, lettuce and tomato that tops it off nicely. Really yummy."

"Well, I started to add cheese, but I thought I'd put enough on them already, they're thick enough as it is, hard to bite into," Della laughed.

"Hasn't stopped me, I've already eaten more than I should, but they're so good! Will there be enough for Valentin, do you think?"

"Oh, he's already had lunch. This is all for us."

"I'm surprised there is avocado in Russia," Rachel said as she took another bite.

"Actually, they're imported from Israel. Did you know that Israel has almost all of the European avocado business? Speaking of the devil, here's Valentino. I hear the car." Della stood and went to the back door to greet him as she always did when he arrived at home.

Rachel thought it was adorable for such a high-powered professional lady as Della to give her full attention to her man. She admired Della for it and was thinking that that's the way it should be in relationships – always mutual admiration and feeling for each other regardless of the circumstances. She had a few regrets along that line.

"My darling Della, you look lovely," Valentin said as he lifted her off her feet in an embrace. "I love you." He kissed her and then greeted Rachel. "Ah, Rachel, it is a pleasure to have you dine in our home. How are you? I trust you have survived our little skirmish last week?" He went to her and exchanged cheek kisses as she remained seated.

"Yep, I survived. That was quite a new experience for me, one that I'd prefer not to repeat again." She smiled. "Della tells me that you will be moving onto the estate into that beautiful cottage. Great choice!"

"Yes, we feel it is right thing to do during this power struggle that has been thrust upon our family. This is not new to us, we have been through it before, and we will survive again. No need to worry. But we must be cautious while we deal with Nicholas Madov," Valentin said as he poured himself a cup of coffee and sat at the table.

"Della and I agree that this would be the perfect topic for an article to submit to the New Yorker Magazine - the struggle for control over the Russian market share in the diamond industry." Rachel took a sip of wine. "She wouldn't have to name names, just do a clever piece with an angle. She could use a pseudonym, which would protect both of you. You might want to do that anyway, Della, on all your articles originating in Russia."

Della nodded.

"Yes, that is good." Valentin said, averting his attention to Della.

Della touched his arm and rubbed it gently. "I wouldn't want to do anything that would jeopardize you and Maxim, but I would like to take a stab at writing articles. Rachel and I have been discussing it and I believe it's the right time for me. All my contacts in New York publishing would definitely come in handy." She beamed at Valentin, then at Rachel.

"Then, you must do it!" Valentin said as he grinned with enthusiasm. "I approve!"

Della clapped her hands together in excitement.

"Rachel," Valentin said, "would you like to visit amber mines after we move to cottage? Both you and Della, of course."

"Oh my god, of course I would love to do that," Rachel quickly answered.

"Perhaps, Della, you would like to do a story about amber, and famous Amber Room in Petersburg?" he said.

"Yea, I would. Good idea, Valentino! Rachel did you know that the existing Amber Room isn't the original? It was stolen and then recreated?"

Rachel's eyes brightened. "You're kidding! It was stolen and then recreated?

"Yes, that's right."

"So when do we go?" Rachel said.

"First we will go to mines in Kaliningrad after the move; the staff will have everything in order by then. I must be in Kaliningrad City for business. We will stay two nights then return Saturday."

"Will Maxim be joining us?" Della asked.

"No, he will be in Brussels."

Rachel didn't notice the frowns Della and Valentin exchanged. She was absorbed in her thoughts of going to Kaliningrad with these two lovely, newfound friends. At that moment she wasn't thinking of Maxim.

Chapter 27

After seeing Rachel off at the train station, Della decided to do some shopping in Klin. She called Valentin on the cell phone to let him know she'd be late getting back to the house.

He was busy doing financial reports, so he told her not to hurry, but to be careful, and said the guards were watching over her.

Della was also carrying a weapon, a concealed weapon. She'd promised Valentin she would carry it until the "war" with Madov was over, if that would ever be the case. She wondered. But regardless, it didn't take her long to learn how to use the Russian MR-444 Bagira which was similar to the western pistols Glock and Beretta, but was lighter in weight. She wasn't carrying her own Beretta as she usually did, Valentin had insisted she carry the Bagira.

Since she wasn't new to guns, not by a long shot, it was rather simple to learn how to handle the Bagira. She had an underarm/waistband holster, could be used as either, but today she carried the gun in her purse, since she would be trying on clothing as she shopped.

As she drove she thought about when her father had received the Cabella North American 29 Trophy of big game hunting and had been competing for the Safari Club's International Grand Slam Trophy before he was killed. The North American 29 requires the hunter to visit eight dissimilar regions across North America and slay 29 different big-game animals to earn the trophy. She'd gone with her dad on a few of the hunts, knew how to use shotguns, rifles, and even used a bow on several occasions. She was a daddy's girl if ever there was one. If her New York City animal-activist friends knew about that side of her, she'd be shit-canned, she was certain of it. But it was a way of life in Oklahoma, where she came from, and she had no regrets.

Today was a beautiful day in Klin, clear blue sky, although a bit on the cold side. But weather never deterred Della, she just dressed accordingly. She parked across the street from the dress shop.

Damn those guards are good, I don't see them at all, she thought to herself as she got out of the car, hesitated, looked around, and headed for the most exclusive dress shop in Klin where Anastasia had placed some of her dresses.

The Russian designer Dasha Gauser owned the boutique in Klin and had hired a manager to run it. Her main store was in Moscow. New designers not yet recognized were encouraged to bring in garments that would be displayed on racks in a special "introducing new designers" section. Anastasia had gone to school with the manager, so she was a shoe-in.

When Anastasia had left Della that day to go home to Rybinsk, she had gone to the Klin boutique to visit her old school chum Danella. And since she had some samples with her from the Paris excursion, she showed them to her friend. It was quickly agreed that Anastasia would send more dresses to Danella when she got home, which she did. Della hadn't seen the dresses yet. So the shopping trip was two-fold: seeing

Anastasia's new designs and buying a dress for an upcoming State dinner in Moscow.

Bam! Out of nowhere, two men grabbed Della.

Without thinking twice she kicked and jabbed, twirled and crouched, reaching quickly into her purse for her gun during the quick movements. "You fuckin' assholes, what the hell do you think you're doing?"

The moment the men saw the gun and were confronted by that unexpected deep, loud voice emanating from Della, they backed off, stunned.

"Get the fuck out of here or I'll shoot your god-damned nuts off!" she growled.

It wasn't more than three seconds before a herd of bodyguards descended upon the two men and rushed them off to a black van that screeched to a halt at the curb. The two perpetrators were stuffed into the van that sped off immediately.

Three guards surrounded Della, concerned, but looking at her with a newfound respect. She had thwarted the attack single-handedly. And there was no doubt in anyone's mind that she would have shot the abductors. She had an mean, wild, merciless look in her eyes.

Della finally heaved a sigh, stuck her gun back into her purse, tucked her disheveled scarf back into the front of her leather jacket, smiled and said, "I'm all right. You can go back to wherever you were. I'm going shopping," and she walked briskly toward the shop as if nothing had happened.

The men stared wide-eyed at each other, grinned, shook their heads, and went back to their posts in cars and across the street. But already two other guards were inside the shop, and two were flanking the door, grinning with a nod, as she entered.

Chapter 28

Valentin Ballenchine was now convinced that the move had to be immediate. He was swift with his decision after Della's foiled kidnapping and wasted no time that afternoon, putting everything into motion for the move from Klin to begin.

Trucks arrived the following morning with movers geared to do it all in one day. And they did do it in one day. By evening Valentin was at the cottage on the estate directing the last of the furniture movers in placing the furniture.

Della was spending the day at Rachel's apartment surrounded with security guards.

It was decided that Rachel would occupy a wing in the Ballenchine cottage since her connection with Valentin, Della and Maxim had become common knowledge. It was too risky to leave her out there on a limb, so she'd been convinced it was the best thing to do till Madov was less of a threat.

Della stood on Rachel's apartment balcony in Moscow overlooking the square and the Kremlin beyond. "This is becoming more complicated than I would have ever thought, you know? I mean, what is this about? What the hell am I doing here, Rachel?"

164

"Don't ask me. Makes my quiet, peaceful little life in Cornwall look more and more compelling by the moment," Rachel said as she sipped her coffee.

"Makes New York City seem quiet and peaceful, too." Della laughed.

"I still can't believe how you handled yourself yesterday. That was amazing! You've astounded the guards; they can't stop talking about it. It shows on their faces when they look at you."

Della turned and faced Rachel, "Comes from being raised on a ranch in Oklahoma and hanging out with the wild bunch. We used to do target practice for fun in the river bottom a mile from the ranch house. Just me and the guys. I remember the first time I used a shotgun; my shoulder was bruised for a week afterwards. But I learned how to shoot it. My dad was a stickler about that. He believed that since I was around so many of his guns that I should at least know how to use them and to be safe about it." She grinned as she returned to the sofa and reached for her cup. "I didn't think twice about what I did yesterday, seemed like second nature actually, defending myself. Yea, all that hanging out with my dad and his pals taught me a lot about guns and self defense. Sure came in handy this time."

They both nodded and grabbed a halved Piroshki from the platter on the cocktail table. Maxim sent lunch to them earlier - salad and Piroshki, which was a deep-fried yeast pastry, filled with mixtures of beef, cabbage, cheese and dill leaves, served with a tomato relish—similar to Mexican salsa.

"This is so good," Rachel commented. "Reminds me of Cornish pasties. Very tasty."

"Valentino makes these all the time. He loves to cook," Della said in-between bites. "I'm really hungry today. Must be post traumatic syndrome."

"I wonder what's going to happen with all this Madov business. It can't go on indefinitely, can it? I mean, how can one live like this for any length of time. I'd go mad. Yum, the salsa is delicious. Would you like some champagne with lunch, Della?"

"Sounds good to me." She reached for a spoon of the tomato relish. "I don't think it's going to last much longer. I have a feeling Madov is going to disappear off the face of the earth. Just a feeling." She looked up at Rachel widening her eyes. "You know what I mean?"

Rachel stared at Della. "Oh boy. And here we are in the middle of it. You especially, 'cause I can always get the hell out of Dodge!"

They both laughed.

"Well, so can I, if I want," Della added.

"Really? You would do that?"

"If I had to, I would."

Rachel looked quizzically at Della. "You could come to Cornwall. I'd love the company. And we could help each other with research. Do a bit of traveling."

"Thanks for the invite. I don't particularly want to go back to New York. Life is much more exciting over here, especially not having to punch a clock and shouldering all the responsibility of running a damn publishing company. Of course that isn't an option anymore, anyway."

"Oh?" Rachel said while pouring champagne.

"Yea. Life is too short. I already let everybody know in an email last night. My senior editor was quick on the draw, is buying me out, which is perfect. She'll also arrange the sale of my house in the country and my townhouse in Manhattan."

"Lock, stock, and barrel?" Rachel was amused at her friend's decisiveness.

"Yea. Done deal. When I make a decision, I make it. No ifs, ands, or buts. My daddy always said 'if you hesitate, you lose.'"

"I've often thought I should sell the house my father left me in L.A. I'm hardly ever there, and when I do have to go on business, I could stay at a hotel. Plus the cabin in Montana my mother left me, I never go there. Seems a waste of money to hang onto both of those houses. I wish I could let go like you."

"Just do it. If they're just sitting there empty, and you never use them, sell them. Or lease them out. I just didn't want to deal with all the rental stuff and taxes, it's too mind-boggling for me, clutters my life," Della reached for the champagne bottle.

"I think you're right. I should do that. I'll be going to California for Christmas, so I plan to discuss it with my son and step-mom Lee. And I have an attorney and a business manager who handles my dad's investments, so that's not a problem. I get a quarterly check. Easy enough." Rachel leaned forward for her glass. " I'll have some more of that too, Della."

Della poured. "Then let's make a toast to safe and clutter-free lives, whatever and wherever they will be!"

They lifted their glasses in unison and took a gulp.

"So I think we should cook a turkey for Thanksgiving. What do you think?" Della grinned at Rachel mischievously. "We can have our own little celebration while the guys are off doing their own thing on Thursday and Friday."

"Sounds good to me. I make a fabulous candied sweet potato dish. Let's do it all. Cranberry sauce, green beans, corn, salad, dressing, the whole works."

"Mustn't forget pumpkin pie," Della said.

Rachel reached for paper and pen to make a shopping list. "Of course we'll have to make do with Russian ingredients."

Chapter 29

"Ninety percent of the world's amber deposits are mined in Kaliningrad," Valentin said. "Do you know how amber is formed, Rachel?"

Two weeks had passed since the move to Maxim's estate and they had just settled into their seats and buckled up on a private plane to Kaliningrad. Della was sitting at the window, Rachel on the aisle, Valentin across the aisle from Rachel.

"Well, I do know that amber is actually tree resin, and that about does it for the extent of my information. I've done some research, but not much. But I wanted to witness it first hand, so I'm depending on you, Valentin." Rachel squeezed Della's hand. "I love flying; I'm so excited about this trip, Della."

Della mirrored Rachel's excitement. "And it's only a three-hour flight, so it'll be a breeze."

"Actually, it's fossilized tree resin, right?" Rachel asked Valentin, sensing he wanted to tell her more about it.

"Yes, fossilized from recent times all the way back to 300 million years ago. In its fresh form it collects insects or leaves, due to the stickiness – you'll see that in some of the jewelry. In fact there's an insect in the pendant I gave Della. You have seen it, yes?"

Rachel brightened, "I sure have. It's a beautiful piece, Valentin." She patted Della's arm. "You're so lucky."

"I am the lucky one." He leaned forward and winked at Della, and then continued with his explanation. "Baltic amber, which is what we mine in the Kaliningrad Oblast, oozed out 35 to 50 million years ago from a forest of conifers in the region now covered by the Baltic Sea. It hardened into clear lumps that glaciers and rivers moved around as far away as England and Holland."

Rachel looked over at Valentin and asked, "And Oblast means province or region, right?"

"Yes, that is true. Oblast is an administrative division. In your country it would be considered a state, such as California or Texas. And although Kaliningrad is completely separated from the Federation, it is still governed by Russia, like your Hawaii. There are 86 such subdivisions of the Russian Federation – 46 are Oblasts, 9 are Krais - same as territories in your United States. 21 are republics. Republics have their own constitution and are not necessarily inhabited by the Russian people. I could go on but I would not want to bore you."

Della spoke up, "Valentino's hobby is world history, Rachel. So anything you want to know about Russia, he's your man."

Chapter 30

Kaliningrad Oblast was situated between Poland and Lithuania on the Baltic Sea, the region was German and consisted of the northern half of historic East Prussia. It had been renamed Kaliningrad a few years after WWII, so it had only been part of Russia since 1945.

Rachel was surprised to find that many charming towns were on the Baltic Sea coast with beautiful sandy beaches as well as ruins of old castles and forts. She hadn't expected that. She and Della were typical tourists while Valentin was engrossed in business meetings and dealings.

But he did take the time to show the women amber fishing, the crude collecting of amber with nets on long poles along the sea edge where it had washed up in clumps, tangled in seaweed, or had been deposited between the rocks and boulders, for Baltic Amber normally washed up on the seashore. They also visited a site where divers would go out to loosen amber from the ocean floor with small shovels or spades.

And there were more modernized sites that used digging machinery—backhoes and cranes—where drops or blocks of

Baltic amber were mined from open pits of 40 to 60 million-year-old glauconite sand, or blue-earth as it was called.

The visit was too short in Rachel's opinion; she wanted to return at a later date to delve more into the people aspect as she usually did in her travels.

When they returned to Moscow on Saturday, they settled even more into their new habitat on Maxim's palatial estate. All the remodeling of the north cottage was complete and now they could enjoy their surroundings, safely.

The cottage was exquisite. Rachel's rooms were beyond expectations. Maxim had remodeled a writing room for her facing his country manor with the beautiful park and gardens filling in the space between the two residences. She had a sitting room equipped with all the latest electronics, a garden room with a bistro table and two chairs exiting to a veranda, and an elegantly furnished bedroom and bath suite. It was like an apartment all for her.

Valentin schooled Della and Rachel on the security system and the safe rooms underground, so now they were ensconced and were easing back into a daily routine, although now sharing the same house.

Della also had an office where she had already begun her new vocation. She'd made email lists of contacts, magazines, and e-zines and was considering the first topics to cover. It was an exciting time for her, especially with Rachel nearby. But she knew that wouldn't last forever, Rachel would be leaving soon.

"Della! Where are you? Come here, look at this!" Rachel was shouting and running down the corridor on the opposite side of the house from her set of rooms.

Della stepped into the hallway. "What is it, Rachel? I'm here, in my office."

"Hurry, come see this."

171

They both rushed back to Rachel's sitting room where CNN television was broadcasting. One of Rachel's habits was to run CNN while she worked … the background noise comforted her. Plus, that way she felt she was always abreast of the news of the day. And in this case, she definitely was.

A London reporter for CNN was announcing in a clipped, frantic voice:

"It is confirmed, diamond mogul Nicholas Madov is dead! Two of his bodyguards were shot and killed and seven pedestrians are wounded. Madov was attending a jewelry store opening when machine gun fire sprayed the event, targeting Madov. However it has been determined he was killed by sniper's bullets shot from a long-range rifle positioned on the roof of the building across from the event. The machine gun bombardment was subterfuge . . ."

"Oh, my God!" Della said as she looked at Rachel. "Do you think— do you think Maxim and Valentino had anything to do with it?"

Rachel plopped down on the sofa. "Dear God, I hope not. Jeez! I hope this doesn't turn out like in the old days in Chicago and New York, sparking an all-out war between the mafia factions. Maybe I should hightail it back to Cornwall while I can. And maybe you should come with me."

"Oh boy. What a mess!" Della pushed the button for the kitchen on the nearby phone. "Would you please bring a pot of coffee to Ms. O'Neill's sitting room? Two cups. Yea, that would be nice. Some cheese sandwiches, too. Thank you." Then she pushed the button allocated to security. "Have you seen the news, Stas? Should we worry? We're in Rachel's suite. Okay." She hung up and sat on the sofa next to Rachel. "He said to sit tight."

"Do you know where Valentin is?" Rachel asked her.

Della sat across from Rachel. "He said he'd be in Moscow till tonight. Maxim is there, too."

"Oh my God!" Rachel sat up straight and glanced out the windows.

"Well, we're safe here, that's for sure. I mean, there's an entire army surrounding us," Della laughed awkwardly. "Would you have ever thought you'd be smack dab in the middle of a situation like this?"

"Hell no!" Rachel laughed too. "I mean, look at us. Two American writers in the middle of a diamond tug of war. No one would believe us."

The phone rang.

Della took the call. "Hello? Oh good! We'll meet them at the door. Thank you."

Rachel stood before Della had a chance to hang up the phone. "They're here?"

"Yea, let's go."

They both hurried from Rachel's rooms and down the corridor to the main part of the house.

Four SUVs were pulling up outside the front entrance. Armed guards were already surrounding the vehicles as the doors were opened and Maxim stepped out of the second one, Valentin was in the third one. They had traveled in separate vehicles.

Valentin rushed to Della and held her tightly.

Maxim was more reserved, talked a few moments to Stas, his head of security and then headed up the steps and reached for Rachel's hand. "I understand you heard," he said to her.

"Saw it on CNN. Are you all right?"

"Of course. Such an unfortunate occurrence. One that I would not wish upon my worst enemies. Not even Madov. It has ruffled the feathers of our organization, but I suspect all will be calm very soon and business will be as usual. Shall we go inside? How do you like your rooms?"

173

Maxim didn't seem nonplussed at all, Rachel noted. She didn't know how to interpret his reaction to the killing. He was so . . . so . . . nonchalant.

Finally Rachel said: "I love my rooms, but I'm thinking I should go home till all this blows over."

Maxim put his arm around her waist as they walked through the doors into the foyer. "You are not in danger; you can be assured of that, my darling. But if you feel you must leave, then you must. But before you go, I want to spend an evening with you alone, something we have not done lately. Come to my house tomorrow evening for dinner, will you?"

"I would love to."

He kissed her lightly on the lips. "Good. And if you decide you want to leave, I'll make the arrangements for you on Friday. But now I must have a meeting with Valentin and Stas. Is there anything else I can do for you?"

"No, I'm fine. Thank you."

After Maxim joined Valentin in his office, Rachel waited for Della who was walking towards her.

"I don't know about this," Rachel whispered to her friend Della.

"I don't either."

Chapter 31

Rachel walked the long gravel pathway through the expansive gardens from the cottage to the elaborate mansion of Maxim's on the southern portion of the property. The sun was just beginning to set, casting shadows and heightening the vivid colors of the roses within Rachel's view. At this time of year the sun set around four in the afternoon. The shortest day of the year being in December when the length of daylight was only seven hours.

Regardless of the dangers surrounding Maxim and Valentin, something had to be said about the magnificent grounds and the painstaking creativity and care that Maxim's wealth exemplified throughout. Take away the dangers and a beautiful world remained, laid out at Rachel's feet.

As she strolled, stopping periodically to reach for a flower to gaze upon and smell, questioning thoughts prevailed.

Could I ever feel safe with Maxim? Am I attracted to his money, the excitement, or to him? Would I even be considering him if he didn't have this gorgeous garden and spectacular home? Could I live here without my independence and my

175

precious Cornwall cottage? What about Paul . . . and Belinda? And the boys? My freedom?

Not easy, there was so much to think about. She could imagine how difficult it must be for Della to be making her own decisions in the midst of all the chaos, although Della was unquestionably in love with Valentin and didn't miss New York and all it encompassed. That lessened the gap in Della's case.

Rachel wasn't sure how she felt about Maxim, or even if he wanted her, perhaps her assumptions of his feelings about her were way off base.

Before she realized it, she had arrived at Maxim's front entrance. A posted guard opened the front door.

She stepped over the threshold and was promptly greeted by Maxim, as if he had been standing there, on the other side of the door, waiting. But of course he had been notified in advance as she left the cottage and had made the half-mile journey through the property. Guards were heralding her progression to him, no doubt . . . step by step.

"Greetings, my darling. You are lovely this evening," Maxim said as he gave her the European cheek to cheek, both sides, kiss-kiss, and then took her hand to lead her into the sitting room.

The butler was pouring champagne from the sideboard. A silver ice bucket and flutes were flanked by massive Bird-of-Paradise floral arrangements. The reds, oranges, and purple blossoms looked too perfect to be real, but they were real.

"This is beautiful, Maxim. I just love this . . . and the flowers. I feel I'm in a fairyland, a bit of a contrast to the chaos we last experienced here." She grinned and accepted the champagne handed to her.

"I am so sorry you had to witness that. You can be assured it will never happen again." He took her arm and walked with her to a camel-colored leather sofa, where they both sat.

"How can you be so sure it will not happen again?" she asked.

"The matter has been remedied." He touched her knee and lifted his glass. "Shall we make a toast to this evening?"

"Of course."

"To our happiness, wherever it takes us. That is all I can ask." He leaned across and softly kissed her on the lips.

"I'll drink to that." She was relieved that the subject of love hadn't been broached, and why should it? Maybe she was too sensitive about it. Besides, it was a bit early after all, she surmised. Regardless, her fears were somewhat alleviated.

Maxim took a sip. "Now, shall we get to know each other a little better? Tell me about your childhood, if you please. Then I will tell you of mine."

Rachel gladly told the story of her childhood, how her mother Lily had disappeared when she was three years old, how her father had told her that Lily was dead, how it had traumatized her at such a young age.

She told Maxim about living her young life with an alcoholic, quarrelsome father who was a barkeep. How she lived without the love of a mother to soothe her feelings and make her feel secure. If it hadn't been for the housekeeper's gentle care during those formative years, she wouldn't have known kindness at all. Her father, Neal, usually in a drunken stupor, finally married the housekeeper, Lee, for Rachel, not for love.

Then a strange phenomenon took place. Her father grew to love Lee and through her gentle guidance, he stopped drinking. It was then that his career and financial investments blossomed, and life became easier for Rachel.

But that only lasted till Rachel was in her teens when Neal began to dally with other women. Lee left him, and that was that. He took a third wife, a real estate broker, who wasn't interested in mothering Rachel or even having her around.

Rachel told Maxim she left home when she was sixteen, married early, had a child, the husband ran off with another woman. Then she met and married a physically abusive husband.

"I went straight from the frying pan into the fire," she said.

"Oh my dear, I am so sorry you experienced such hard times, and so young," Maxim took her hand and kissed it.

"Well, I survived it all, raised my son by myself, he turned out great. Is now living in Denver with his wife, and my dear stepmother Lee is still alive and lives in California. I've kept in touch with her; she was so good to me. That's the first stepmother, not the real estate broker." Rachel smiled at Maxim, moved by his caring and genteel behavior. "I'm definitely a survivor. So tell me about your childhood."

"First let me pour more wine. Would you like something to eat?" he asked as he stood. "Dinner will be at eight, so we have a while yet to wait."

"No, I'm not hungry, thank you. I had a late lunch. These olives are enough." It was the custom in Russian to serve a dish of olives with pre-dinner drinks.

Maxim kept his promise and told Rachel about his childhood, although somewhat different to hers.

He was born to a coal miner and a domestic. Both his parents were menial laborers, working long hours to support their four sons and two daughters living in a poor neighborhood of Kopeisk near the southern Ural Mountain range in the Chelyabinsk Oblast – southeast of Moscow.

When he told Rachel about his father dying in a mine collapse, she told him the story of Belinda's father dying in a mine of southeastern England when she was a young child. Said she understood the impact that could have on a child.

Maxim went on to say that he and his three brothers worked in the mines, as their father had done, beginning when they were old enough – seven and eight. It was a hard life for them.

Then one day, when Maxim was fifteen years old, being the oldest, he jumped at the opportunity to go to work for a local merchant, delivering goods from his general store in Kopeisk to the outlying farms and mines. The owner of the store had a daughter who was attracted to Maxim and long story short; they married when they were both sixteen. Her name was Katarina.

There was a two-story, three-bedroom, shack behind the store where Katarina's grandmother had lived before she died. It was in need of dire repair, but Maxim and his bride moved into it without hesitation. He was industrious, working on the house during his off hours, making the upstairs suitable for his own mother and siblings. His own family moved in with them three months after Maxim and Katarina were married.

By the time he was eighteen, Maxim had brought in additional lines of merchandise to the mercantile. In addition to grocery and dry goods he added leather goods, toiletries, jewelry, vodka and wine. He managed the high-end sections and eventually hired his brothers to help with the rest of the operation. His father-in-law welcomed the help of Maxim's family because his store had fast become one of the busiest and most successful of its type in Kopeisk, due to Maxim's industriousness.

"After my father-in-law died, I took over and renamed the department store *Ballenchine Brothers Mercantile*. And that was the beginning of what was to come," Maxim ended his story with a sigh. "Of course there is more, we eventually became diamond and amber merchants. But that is enough for one night. Do you agree?"

"Yep, I think we've covered our basic beginnings well enough. Thank you, Maxim; I feel I know you much better, hearing about your early life." She stood and stretched for a moment. "Will you excuse me while I go to the ladies room?"

"Of course, my darling. I'll put on some music. Do you mind?"

"Not at all." She walked into the long corridor and headed towards the kitchen. She knew there was a restroom there. She could hear the classical music begin, and felt safe and comfortable in Maxim's gigantic home as she entered the servants' lavatory and shut the door.

Maybe she would stay in Russia a little longer.

Chapter 32

"Rachel, are you ready?' Della was standing in the foyer, a packed weekender sitting next to her feet.

"I'm coming, I'm coming," Rachel shouted from out of sight. "Just getting off the phone."

The front door of the cottage was standing open, the driver and a guard waiting at the SUV. They were going to the train station for their trip to visit Valentin's sister Anastasia in her village near Rybinsk.

A guard carried Della's bag and put it in a black SUV. Three other SUVs were lined up at the gate. Two would follow and one would lead the vehicle in which they would be riding.

Della was excited about the trip; she had been wanting to go to Anastasia's home for weeks. But it hadn't been deemed safe enough till the prevailing threat was removed - Madov killed. However, Maxim and Valentin felt that precautions still had to be taken, hence the added security. Four security agents would be traveling with them on the train and would be joined by others in waiting vehicles at their debarkation.

"Okay, I'm ready, Della. Only taking one bag, right? Where's yours?" Rachel looked around the foyer.

"It's already in the car. Come on, go. I am so excited about this trip. I haven't been anywhere in months it seems. I need some breathing space."

They both laughed and hurried through the doorway; Rachel carried her lightweight bag with her.

"I'll take that, Miss," the driver said as he reached towards Rachel.

"Thank you," Rachel said and followed Della into the back seat of the SUV.

The trip to the station and the journey on the train was uneventful, no sign of trouble. The plan was to spend the first night in Yaroslavl, 155 miles from Moscow. The women traveled in a first-class car, entire car reserved by Maxim, with only their security and the two of them occupying it.

Watching the countryside through the windows was a treat, since both women were avid train travelers. They planned to stay in Yaroslavl so that they wouldn't be traveling during the dark hours on the last leg of the ten-hour trip, since the day-light hours were shortened this time of year. They wanted to be able to see every village and sight along the route.

After arriving they checked into their hotel - The Ring Premier Hotel, which was close to the station. Maxim had reserved a deluxe apartment with three bedrooms, so the guards could stay inside with them.

Since they would only be there one afternoon and night, they immediately took in the sights of the eleventh century city, at one time the largest city in Russia in the seventeenth century. They toured the Volkov Theatre built in 1750 - the oldest theater in Russia - with its pale yellow exterior and white ornate pillars and trim.

"I'd love to do an article on this theatre, and maybe all the major theatres of Russia. Wouldn't you think that would be of interest to the readers of the New York and London mags?" Della's voice and eyes were full of excitement.

"What a great idea!" Rachel said as she squeezed Della's arm. "You're getting into the swing of it, you really are."

"I believe I am. I'm almost convinced how wonderful life could be, here with Valentino. Not to mention I love the socks off the man. He is the sexiest man I've ever met."

They both giggled, looking around to see if security had overheard their conversation.

Of course they had. The guards were grinning at each other.

"I don't know if I'll ever get used to having body-guards, though," Della said

Rachel put her arm across Della's shoulders as they headed towards shopping on Kirov Ulitsa, a popular Yaroslavl Street. They planned to stroll along the Volga after a mid-afternoon snack and coffee in a café along the way. Then back to the hotel to rest and relax before having a late dinner in the hotel's Sobinov Restaurant.

"What a wonderful day we've had," Rachel exclaimed at dinner. "And Maxim sure knows how to pick the hotels."

"Wealth isn't all that bad, is it?" Della laughed heartily before she took a sip of the white wine. "I think I could get used to being taken care of by my man."

"Well, you have your own money, too. You could easily take care of yourself. I think that gives us an edge, don't you? Having our own money. We could do this on our own, you know." Rachel smiled at her dear friend, Della, feeling a strong connection to her.

"And without the body-guards, of course," Della added with a grin.

Rachel sighed. "Yep, without the body-guards."

"So what are you thinking? Are you feeling any different about Maxim now that the crisis is over?"

"Crisis meaning the life threat?" Rachel lifted her glass and gulped her champagne instead of sipping. She wasn't sure if that was what she was talking about or about the night she'd just spent with Maxim - which hadn't been mentioned.

"Yea. Do you think you could handle a life of luxury with him?"

Rachel laughed. "I'm still mulling it over. You know I do have a great life back in Cornwall. I have Paul and Belinda, they're my dear friends. Their boys. My friend Margaret, and mustn't forget my friends Shellie and Adrian in Switzerland and, of course, Mandy and Richard in Brussels."

"Well, Maxim has business in Brussels, you know." Della hesitated for a moment, wondering if she should tell Rachel about his wife. But she decided against it. "I do understand how you feel, though. I have no one back home. So staying here works for me. And now I have you, my newest and only friend besides Valentino. But we wouldn't be far from each other, even if you do go back to England. And we're going to work together on projects, right?"

"I hope so." Rachel reached across and touched Della's hand that was resting on the table. "I hope so."

"By the way, you never told me whether or not you and Maxim did the—I mean—" she giggled. "You know what I mean. Did you?"

"I'll tell you later, when there aren't so many ears straining to hear my every word."

She was glad Della didn't push the point. She really didn't want to talk about it. She felt guilty. Felt like she had cheated on Pete. She'd been wooed by a gorgeous man, a beautiful evening, heartwarming stories, and had succumbed to the mood.

Was it love? That was the question hammering her mind.

She thought back to the moment when the evening with Maxim had changed from casual friendliness to torrid

184

lovemaking. She never would have dreamt a man at his age would be able to follow through with the actual fornication, or lovemaking as it was. Although the word fornication came to mind being the proper description of a man and woman who are not married performing the deed - she grinned at calling the event 'the deed' – she preferred the term *making love.* She also grinned at the thoughts of his prowess and surprising moves and adeptness, his ability to make her feel like a sexy woman, adored and loved. Even though it was rather awkward for her, first times were always embarrassingly awkward. But the memory was making her feel warm and cozy all over again.

"Something's making you smile, what is it?" Della asked as she watched Rachel. "You are thinking of Maxim, aren't you?'

"Yep, I am, as a matter of fact." She laughed aloud.

"C'mon, tell me."

"Later," she continued to giggle.

"You did do it, didn't you?" Della grinned widely. "Just say yes or no."

"Yes."

"How was it?"

Rachel raised her eyebrows and whispered, "Great. And that's all I'm going to say about it." She blushed as she signaled for the waiter.

Chapter 33

When Rachel awoke for the last time the next morning, exhausted from a toss-and-turning fitful sleep, she glanced over at Della who was sipping coffee, dressed and ready to go.

"You're up and at 'em early, aren't you?" she said as she sat up in bed.

"Like you, I had a restless night. Boy, you were wildly restless all night. Nightmares?"

"Not exactly," she said as she grinned and jumped out of bed. "It won't take me long to get dressed since I'm wearing the same thing I had on yesterday."

"Your idea was great, not unpacking our bags, just wearing the same clothes." Della stood and stretched, feeling a bit weary. "You know, I was thinking—"

"Uh oh!"

"No, no, it's good, trust me." She laughed and primped, looking in the mirror. "I'm thinking that before I actually marry Valentino, I'd like to take a holiday, maybe come stay a week or two with you in Cornwall. What do you think?"

"I think that's the best idea you've had today." Rachel came out of the bathroom, brushing her hair straight back off her face. "So, we'll plan it. I'm not sure when I'm going home, but it'll be before your wedding."

"Terrific! Then it's settled. A holiday in England before I marry Valentino. Just in case."

Rachel shot a glance at Della. "Just in case what?"

"Well, you know, it'll be a breather. I've been with him the entire time. I think I need a test to see if he's really the one I want. I need to get away from him for a while to make sure it isn't one of those relationships that's just feeling comfortable and rolling along at break-neck speed, building momentum."

"But isn't that the kind of relationship most people want? With a bit of passion thrown in?" Rachel chuckled as she thought of her own situation.

"Yea, but I just need to know I haven't fallen into a routine and it's just become second nature. It's feeling that way, you know?"

Rachel sat on the bed to put on her boots. "Yep, I know. It's easy to slip into a routine pretty quickly if you're living together, and then before you know it, everything becomes dull and boring. Is that it? Are you bored?"

"No, no, I'm not bored. How could I be bored around Valentino and Maxim? God no! Just the opposite. I guess it just boils down to wanting to be sure I'm making the right decision."

"Well, I certainly understand that. But if you're thinking of testing your feelings on someone else in Cornwall, you'll be shit out of luck! There are absolutely no men there that you'd be interested in. Believe me, I've combed the woods. Been there, done that."

They both giggled and laughed and gathered their bags and coats.

The drive to Rybinsk was short and easy. Anastasia's town of 4000, Volkova, was a short distance across the Volga River and up the west side of the Rybinsk Reservoir. Her house was easy to find, exactly as she had instructed.

She lived in a neighborhood of houses that looked alike, flanked by their gardens and animal pens, like those in Valentin's village of Klin.

When the three vehicles pulled into the driveway, Anastasia came rushing out the doorway to greet them. She immediately hugged and kissed Della, not wanting to let go.

"Anastasia, this is my friend Rachel," Della said with her arm still around her.

"Hello, hello, Rachel," Anastasia greeted. "I am so happy to meet you at last. Valentin has told me all about you, as has my brother Maxim. We speak on the phone every week."

"I am happy to finally meet you, too." Rachel was impressed at the cheerful countenance and beautiful face of yet another good looking Ballenchine family member. The woman was utterly captivating in her red belted, black and white polka-dotted dress and red shoes. She even wore a red headband in her hair. She reminded Rachel of someone, but she couldn't pinpoint it.

"Don't you think she looks like Leslie Caron?" Della offered as she kissed Anastasia on the cheek again.

"That's it! I was just trying to figure that out. Leslie Caron, of course."

"You are too kind, both of you. Come, come. Your rooms are ready." Anastasia hesitated. "But I do not have room for the bodyguards."

Stas stepped forward and assured her they had already made provisions, and she was not to worry. He also told her they would be near, so everybody would be safe.

The women went into the house, Stas followed with their bags.

After a full afternoon of sharing experiences of heartbreak and dreams, the three women decided they should go into Rybinsk for a night on the town. Della and Rachel had talked about treating Anastasia, knowing that she probably didn't go out often, so they insisted. The only problem was there wasn't a proper place to go for a night out in Rybinsk.

So Della telephoned Valentin and asked him for a suggestion, and he said he'd call her back, to just sit tight.

"Well, actually Yaroslavl isn't too far away," Anastasia said on her way to open another bottle of wine. "Or we can just stay at home and I'll prepare fish for you."

"No, no, no. Valentin will think of something." Della's cell phone rang almost before Della finished her sentence. "Hello? Did you think of something? No kidding. That sounds like fun. How did you manage that? You're right. I should have known. Okay, luv. You'll call Stas, then? Okay. Miss you, too. Bye now."

She laid the phone on the table next to her chair and grinned widely at the two women. "You aren't going to believe this. We're going to a private river cruise ship that is docked in Rybinsk. We can go aboard and take part of whatever we want - dinner, cocktails, music, dancing. Maxim's making the arrangements. It'll be there overnight and we can stay on the boat if we want. But I think we should come back here, don't you?"

"Yes, oh yes." Anastasia couldn't believe her ears. "That Maxim! He can practically walk on water."

Rachel laughed and held out her glass to Anastasia for more wine. "So, when are we going to the ship?"

"We'll leave here at eight. Valentin is telling Stas the plans. So we have lots of time to visit before we dress up for the occasion. Okay?" Della was elated.

"Unbelievable!" Rachel leaned back into the sofa and took a sip. Once more the charming man she'd met the year before in Brussels was astounding her.

189

Chapter 34

When they arrived at the ship, the party had already begun. As they got out of the vehicles, they could hear music echoing through the night air, mixing with laughter and chattering voices. Groups of passengers were on the decks with drinks in hand, couples were embracing along the railing.

Rachel saw him first. Maxim was standing at the top of the gangplank. He was grinning from ear to ear, Valentin beside him.

Anastasia screamed. "Look! It's Maxim and Valentin! Oh, this is too good to be true! Look, Della. They're both here!"

All three women were ushered to the ship by the guards in a tight group. Several guards were already flanking Maxim and Valentin.

"Anastasia . . . you look beautiful tonight!" Maxim said as he hugged and kissed his sister.

Valentin immediately reached for her too, adding more hugs and kisses. "I have much to tell you, my dear sister."

"I am so happy to see you, Valentine," she teased.

"No no, not Valentine!" He laughed and squeezed her face lovingly between his two gigantic hands.

Della reached them next. Valentin pushed by Maxim. "Ah, my darling Della. Maxim, you must go to Rachel, I will tend to Della." He grinned mischievously as he swept Della and Anastasia along the deck towards the bar area. "Come my angels, we have drinking to do."

Rachel stood in front of Maxim, beaming. She was staring at the picture-perfect man before her. He was dressed in grey slacks, same color as his hair, and a black turtle-neck sweater. A black leather sports coat was draped over his shoulders. The most sophisticated, handsome man she knew.

Maxim held out his hand to Rachel, thinking what a glorious vision stood before him, dressed in her black woolen pants and sparkly sweater. His lady in black. He loved her understated way of presenting herself - most times in black, conservative, expensive looking. Her face was glowing as the ship's mini-lights reflected on her skin.

"May I have this dance?' he asked as she stepped on deck. He whisked her away in a waltz towards the direction of the music and where the others had gone.

Chapter 35

They decided to stay on the boat for the evening, after all. Maxim made all the arrangements with the vessel owner, who was an old friend and just happened to be onboard with his mistress. There was plenty of room for them for it was a special charter, and was not the usual river cruising tour group, so half the boat was empty.

But there were plenty of party-goers to make the night a fun-filled, merry-making event well after two in the morning.

Around three, Maxim escorted Rachel to her stateroom. He unlocked the door for her and stood in the doorway, holding the door open.

"May I come in?" he asked, his sexy eyes looking directly into hers. I can call for coffee or tea, or more champagne if you wish."

Rachel hesitated.

"I would like to be with you alone, Rachel. And it is such a beautiful night with the music and the moon. Come, let us go to the balcony." He closed the door behind him and with his arm around her waist he led her across the stateroom to its balcony facing the opposite bank of the river. Diaphanous curtains fluttered in the cool breeze behind them as they leaned on the outside railing. The moon was skimming the rippling water, meeting the lights of the villas near the river's edge. Distant voices and laughter could be heard echoing in the night. It seemed no one slept in this part of the world, at least not this particular night.

Rachel leaned back against Maxim, his arms wrapped around her holding her close. She placed her hands on top of his.

"What a lovely night."

He turned her to face him, without releasing his strong hold on her, and then they tenderly kissed. One long soft kiss. Then a more heated kiss. Then a backing up towards the bed kiss. Then a rolling on the bed kiss.

Finally, Rachel spoke first. "What about that champagne? Do you mind?"

"Of course not, my lovely."

They both rose to a sitting position, straightening their sweaters, as if embarrassed.

"I shall be right back with the bottle and flutes myself. Maybe you would like to make yourself more comfortable?"

"But I didn't bring anything with me, silly. Nothing. Not even a toothbrush."

"Check the wardrobe and the toilet. You'll find everything you need." Out the door he went.

And sure enough, there was a new daytime outfit for her to wear the next day, rust color, matching shoes and all, as well as a fur coat. There were several sleepwear choices on hangers: pink satin pajamas and matching robe, a short sexy red nightie, and a long black lace and silk see-through designer night gown like an old-fashioned, gorgeous peignoir set. Maxim had thought of everything. Of course she selected the latter. It was perfect for her. And she was feeling sexy and loving. *Bring on the champagne!*

Maxim returned to a candlelit stateroom.

Rachel was standing on the balcony and turned when she heard him close the door.

He stood still, champagne in one hand, two glasses in the other. "Oh my darling . . . you are the most gorgeous woman in my life." He quickly freed his hands and rushed to hold Rachel in his arms. "My darling, my darling," he purred as he stroked her hair while kissing her.

It took a few moments before they both gained their composure and broke away for the bubbly.

"Are you happy, my Rachel? Are you happy with me?" he asked as he poured the drinks.

"Well . . . I think you are the most amazing man I've ever known. You are the most charming, the most handsome, the most creative, the most attentive . . . I don't believe I've ever met anyone quite like you." She took a sip and curled up on the sofa.

He sat next to her. "But are you happy with me? Do you think you could love me?"

"I—I— " She looked away from his eyes. "I don't know, Maxim. I mean, well, I'm very fond of you."

Both were silent as they continued to immerse themselves in Dom Perignon.

Rachel broke the silence. "Maxim, I do care for you, I do." She touched his knee. "I am very much attracted to you. You make me feel feminine and sexy, and I love that about you. It hasn't been easy for me through the years to feel that way. And only one man has ever done that for me, before you. That was my Pete Bell. And now he's gone. And I'm still getting over him. It's hard for me to say the word *love*; it's too soon for me. Can you understand what I'm saying?"

"Yes, of course, my darling. I understand. I can only hope that when you have finally laid him to rest you will come to me. I am here when you want me."

His obvious sadness overwhelmed Rachel. She set her drink on the table and stood up.

"Oh, Maxim." She faced her sensual suitor, and dropped the outer layer of the peignoir set, leaving only the see-through black gown covering her body. "I want you now. I truly do."

Maxim threw the glass, champagne and all, over the back of the sofa and nearly leapt over the table to get to Rachel. His eager strength almost knocked her off her feet, but he swept her up in his arms just in time and carried her to the bed.

"I can use the word freely, and I will. I love you, Rachel. I loved you the first moment I saw you at Mont des Arts in Brussels at midnight. I have thought of no other since then." His voice softened to a whisper, "I love you, my darling. I hope that does not offend you."

Rachel's answer came in the form of a captivating, deep, penetrating series of kisses that led to a breathless, exotic, hour of lovemaking.

They both seemed to know what pleased the other. Maxim's touch was thrilling to Rachel, hers to him. They explored each other's body with hands, fingers, lips and tongues. It went beyond anything either of them had ever experienced. The passion was incredible.

The ultimate came when Maxim raised himself above her and gently parted her legs and slipped his hardened cock inside her. Rachel's movements and moans heightened his sexual sensitivity and at the exact same explosive moment they both gasped and grasped each other in utter rapture.

They lay tightly in each other's arms, afraid to move for several minutes before either of them spoke. It felt as if movement or words might spoil the precious moments, so they waited for the vibrating thrills and sexual rush to abate.

Maxim thought his heart would explode. He could hear it beating wildly and could feel the rampant beat of Rachel's pressed against his chest.

Rachel couldn't believe what she was feeling. Never before had she had such sexual fulfillment. How could she not love Maxim? They fit so perfectly. In most everything. How could she not love him?

Chapter 36

After saying their good-byes to Maxim and Valentin on the dock after breakfast, Rachel, Della, and Anastasia returned to the village of Volkova. Anastasia had prearranged a luncheon for the visiting women at her associate's home.

"This is Salinka, my new sales partner," she said as Salinka opened the door. "Salinka, this is Della, and this is Rachel. Are the others here?"

"Yes, yes, welcome, we are ready for you." Salinka stepped aside and ushered them down the wide corridor that led from the front of the house all the way to the back door.

As they walked, Rachel and Della glanced in the sparsely furnished rooms along the corridor; vases of fresh flowers were in every room, floors sparkled, oriental rugs also in every room. There was a study, a sitting room, a larger living room, a music room with a piano, a kitchen, a library. Small rooms, but impressive. It was obvious that Salinka was financially comfortable.

When they reached the garden room, seated at a long table filled with salads, cheeses, breads, and fruit, were six other women of all ages.

Salinka made the introductions, poured the wine then they all lifted their glasses for a toast.

Anastasia stood as she spoke; her glass held high, "This is to all of you, my dear friends. To my wonderful seamstresses and helpers, to Salinka my new sales representative, and to my new American friends. Now I will repeat for you who do not speak English. *Moim zamechatel'nym shveyam i pomoschnikam, k Salinka, moyemu novomu predstavitel'u prodazh, i moim novym amerikanskim druz"am.*"

They all said in unison – *Budem!*

The chatter began around the table as trays of food were passed from one to the other.

Della touched Anastasia's arm in affection, "I am so happy for you, that your line of clothing is taking off."

"Thank you. And thanks to Maxim for making it possible for me to have the sewing rooms and equipment," Anastasia said.

Della smiled. "I took Rachel to the shop in Klin to see your dresses."

"And I just love them," Rachel added. "I have a friend in Brussels who is a designer. In fact she has two shops and is planning to open another. Maybe you could sell some of your dresses there. I'd be happy to put you in touch with her."

"I would love that, yes. Do you hear, Salinka? Maybe we go to Brussels to take my dresses?" Anastasia was beaming.

Rachel glanced at Della. "And I would love to see more of what you have, maybe something for New Year's Eve?"

Della chimed in. "I need a gown, too. You know we're all going to the Metropole for New Year's Eve, right? And Red Square. You're invited, too. Did Maxim tell you?"

"Yes, and I am happy to come. After we finish here, we must go to the workroom and decide on your gowns. I have ideas already on the table."

"This is exciting, isn't it?" Della squeezed Rachel's arm. "Can you believe that we're in Russia, with a fabulous dress designer, and in love with two handsome, prosperous Russian men who mine diamonds and amber? I can't stand it!"

The women around the table were gleeful at Della's exuberance and lifted their glasses once again, saying, "*Budem!*"

Rachel quietly sipped; she was stuck on Della's words about being in love.

Chapter 37

On December 22, the shortest day of the year in Moscow, Rachel boarded a plane at Moscow airport for the United States. It would arrive in New York City and then connect two hours later for a plane to Los Angeles, total trip seventeen hours.

It had been a difficult decision to make because Rachel was torn between wanting to stay in Moscow with the Ballenchines for Christmas, going home to Cornwall to be with Belinda and Paul and friends, or to her son in the States.

Being with her own family at Christmas, however, her only son, won the tug of war. Besides, her step-mom Lee had turned eighty in October and hadn't been feeling well, according to Devin. So it was time to make the trip before it was too late. She'd always felt guilty at not visiting her own mother more often before she died.

Rachel's son Devin and his wife were to pick her up at LAX when she arrived at 8:35 p.m. Devin and Kellie had been in California two weeks already, from Denver. Kellie loved the beach, so they took a three-week vacation to soak up sun and sea. In southern California the temperatures could reach into the

90s during December, so they were taking full advantage of it. It wasn't unheard of to go to the beach on a hot, sunny Christmas day. Rachel had done it many times when she lived in Santa Monica those many years before. She remembered one special Christmas when she and her second husband sailed on their Hunter sailboat with two other couples to Catalina for Christmas – cooked Christmas dinner in the galley on the boat.

It hadn't been all bad with her husbands; she had good memories too. But the two marriages had been short-lived. The husbands' major complaints were that she wasn't able to show love; she wasn't affectionate and sexual enough. They both said her focus was elsewhere, she was more interested in her own career than theirs. Then when Rachel would begin to make the final pull away from each of them, the result was either physical abuse or indiscretions on their parts, and the gaps grew wider till divorce was imminent.

But most of her memories of the L.A. area were good. In her father's last years in Brentwood, after her mother Lily had forgiven him and he had made amends, Rachel and her father had formed a special father-daughter relationship, loving and gentle.

On this trip the plan was to spend a couple of days at the Brentwood estate, and then drive up to Cambria on the Central Coast to spend Christmas with Lee. It was during the two days in Brentwood that Rachel was scheduled to meet with her attorney and the property manager to discuss the properties. She wanted to work out something to benefit Devin. Her life was changing and she didn't feel a connection to L.A. anymore, so she wanted to make sure Devin was well-versed and situated with his inheritance.

The flight to New York was uneventful, long, but quiet. There weren't any crying babies and unruly children in the section where Rachel was sitting. Maxim had insisted she fly First Class, had made the arrangements for her. Very few times had she flown First Class, usually it was business class, most times coach, depending on when she booked or could get an upgrade.

She changed planes in New York and settled in quickly after boarding. The excitement was building. She hadn't seen her son in a few months, and hadn't seen him since his promotion.

At 28 years of age, Devin was a talented construction superintendent, the level attained by quickly working his way up the ranks in major, international, commercial building firms. Rachel was proud of her son. He'd survived an abusive, alcoholic step-father, Rachel's second husband. And until Devin was nineteen, he suffered the repercussions of that despicable union . . . struggled with alcohol and drug addictions himself, had low self-esteem and depression. Then almost overnight, after his grandmother Lily resurfaced with spiritual words of love and wisdom, and with continual encouragement from his mother and grandfather, Devin quit his addictions cold turkey. And his life turned around.

Now he regularly was offered positions by competing companies. Headhunters telephoned him out of the blue continuously. He always considered the offers, but said he wouldn't make changes strictly for the money, he would take everything into consideration: the relationship with fellow workers, how he felt about the company, the location, the benefits, bonuses, etc. He'd been in Denver for three years now, and was feeling a pull towards the Los Angeles area. So while he was in L.A., he'd been doing his homework and had been sent out by headhunters for interviews. He was taking a good look at the possibilities.

You're a chip off the old block, Rachel had written in an email when he told her what he was doing. She was filled with gypsy blood too, she told him. But his hadn't taken him to other countries yet.

"Is your destination Los Angeles, or are you going on?" asked the young man sitting next to Rachel on the plane.

"Los Angeles till Tuesday, then on up to the Central Coast . . . Cambria to be exact. Do you know where that is?"

"Yes, of course. South of Hearst Castle, San Simeon. Been through there many times on my way to San Francisco. Highway One. Beautiful drive." He shut off his Kindle reader and gave Rachel a closer look.

She continued talking. "I used to live in the area. My step-mom lives in Cambria now. So I'm meeting my son and daughter-in-law in L.A. and we're driving up together for Christmas. I'm getting more excited by the minute." Rachel's wide grin and sparkling eyes exuded her joy. "You have business in L.A.?" she asked.

"Yes, I split my time between L.A. and New York."

"One of my best friends is a New Yorker. I just left her in Moscow where she's living now. We're spending New Year's Eve in Moscow together, so I'll be heading back after Christmas. She owned a publishing company in Manhattan, just sold it."

His interest piqued. "What's her name?"

"Della Doheny."

"You're kidding me. Della's in Russia? When did she do that?"

"You know her?" Rachel couldn't believe that of all the people she would be sitting beside on a plane it would be someone who knew Della.

"Yes, I do! We used to work together. Or rather I worked for her. Four years ago. I'm an editor with Hearst Publishing now. I guess I sort of lost track of her. The publishing business changes faces literally every day. So is she publishing in Russia?" He was half turning in his seat looking at Rachel.

"No, she just picked up and moved lock, stock, and barrel because she loves it there. Met a handsome Russian and they're getting married. A true love story."

"I don't believe it. I can't believe it! She never gave anyone a second look in the city. I even tried to get her attention. But no. She didn't have time for romance. A true work-horse, dedicated and focused. I always wondered about her." He raised his eyebrows and gestured with his hand, "You know what I mean?"

Rachel laughed. "Well, she definitely loves a man. And she's going to do some freelance writing. Has no interest whatsoever in starting up another publishing house."

"Unbelievable! Wow!" He reached into his shirt pocket and pulled out a couple of business cards. "Please give one of these to her when you get back, will you? And the other one is for you when you're in town, here or there. We'll have to do lunch."

"Thank you, I will."

Chapter 38

The time was passing too quickly for Rachel. She wished she had made arrangements to stay longer in West L.A. and Santa Monica. Spending time with her son brought back a lot of memories between the two of them, Devin's childhood, and memories of her father Neal, Devin's grandfather.

Neal's English Tudor mansion in Brentwood was still beautiful; the caretakers had groomed it to perfection. Rachel was surprised at the lack of wear and tear it had shown. Of course, no one lived there, it was only Rachel's stopping off place when she was in the States, and she hadn't made many trips back since her father died.

At her request, the family attorney, Tony Parker, was scheduled to meet with her and the management company rep in Brentwood at the estate on Monday morning.

Before they arrived she and Devin waited in the study.

"So what do you think of Brentwood? You like this house?" Rachel asked her son.

"Well, it's pretty big, mom. But I love it. I like this room, grandpa's study. It's something I'd have in my own home. The leather sofa and club chairs. The desk, paneled walls, bookcases. Pretty neat."

"Yep, it is pretty cozy, isn't it? A bit on the masculine side for me. Totally opposite of my house. Pete used to call my cottage my cotton candy world."

Devin chuckled then became quiet before asking, "So, Mom, how are you doing? You haven't mentioned anything . . . I mean . . . you know . . . Pete. Are you doing all right now?"

"Well, I've accepted the fact that he's gone, if that's what you mean. I try not to dwell on him anymore, what good does it do? It's like grandpa and grandma, they're gone too, you know?"

Devin put his arm around his mother. "But we love them just the same. And we think of them all the time. And that's okay to do. They were part of our lives, it's okay to remember them."

"Listen to you, ye old wise one." Rachel looked up and grinned at her son. "It is good that we can remember them, isn't it?"

"Works for me," Devin said. He hugged his mom.

The doorbell rang.

"Oh, that's got to be Tony," Rachel said.

"I'll get him," Devin said and left the room.

After saying their greetings and being served a cup of coffee, they sat at the conference table. Tony set copies of the document in front of Rachel and one in front of Devin.

"I've drawn up the new trust agreement per your instructions, Miss O'Neill, making Devin an equal partner and trustee and insuring that survivor gets all. The list of properties is attached, as you see. And I've drawn checks for you individually, as you requested, the same amount will be paid every six months." He placed more documents in front of them. "Here are the first ones, along with the accompanying financials. If at any time you wish to sell any of the properties," he glanced at Devin, and then back to Rachel, "we will need both signatures of approval." He reached for his coffee and took a big gulp. "I think you'll find everything satisfactory. If not you can give me a call tonight and we'll discuss any changes you would like to make. I can have it all finalized and filed before you return to the UK."

Rachel flipped through the pages, looked over the property list, then glanced at Devin. "So what do you think, Devin? Do you see anything that you don't agree with?" She smiled, knowing full well that he was in shock. She hadn't told him what she was doing. He hadn't a clue what the estate was worth.

Devin stared at the six-figure check. "You make this much money on property rentals?"

Tony spoke up. "No, no. The stock dividends are also included in that total. You'll see when you take a look at the financial breakdown. It's all there."

"I had no idea granpa was so loaded." He grinned at his mother.

Rachel chuckled. "And so are you, sweetheart."

Devin whispered, "I can't wrap my brain around this."

"Well, there's one more thing I wanted to talk about today. And I wanted Tony to be here to advise us. Devin, what I'm thinking is . . . well, you know I'm making good money with book sales and movie rights and so forth, and I need to invest it pretty quickly or Uncle Sam is going to get most of it. So, what I'm thinking is this . . . I'd like to invest in you … maybe you can start your own construction company out here. Live here in grandpa's house, I'm sure Kellie will love that; she'd be near the beach. Tony can advise you financially, can set you up with our accountant; we've got a terrific accounting firm. All you'd have to do is use your expertise and drum up the clients? What do you think?"

Devin stared at his mother in disbelief. "Are you serious?"

"Sure am. I'll be spending all my time in England and Europe mostly, and I'd like to be able to help you by starting up our own company. I'm dead serious. You certainly have the experience in building, that's been your whole life; you're the best superintendent ever, right?"

Devin laughed, "I think my mom is prejudiced, Tony."

Tony smiled and said, "Works for me, Devin. Besides I've done some checking around and your mom is right on the button, you are one of the best. I think we can work something out for you; I have a few projects in mind. What do you think?"

"When is all this supposed to take place?" Devin stood up and began pacing with his hands on his hips, obviously excited.

"Right away is okay with me. When we return from Cambria at the end of the week," Rachel said.

"I'd have to get my contractor's license."

Tony handed a file to Devin. "All the information is in here, the schools, and class schedules. I'll cut a check for the tuition when you decide when and where you want to study and take the exams."

"I'll need to go back to Denver and settle things there, first. Can't leave them in a lurch."

"Yep." Rachel went to the bar and poured a glass of water. "We figured you would say that." She took a sip. "So my dear, it's all up to you. When you're ready, you have a home here in Brentwood, you have the school locations and all that, and finding vacant property for building will be your next step. That is, if you want to build houses. Maybe you'd rather go commercial? Take whatever direction you want. But let's talk about all that later. Let's take care of this trust right now and then we can plan our trip to Cambria. Okay, luv?"

Devin walked over to his mom and gave her a bear hug. "I'll make you and grandma and grandpa proud, mom."

"I'm already proud of you, and so are they."

PART FOUR

Rebecca Buckley

Chapter 39

It was four in the afternoon on New Year's Eve in Moscow. Rachel had been anticipating this night for weeks, for months. One more extraordinary New Year's Eve in another romantic, historic, capital city - this time in Russia, the largest country in the world. And of its nearly 142 million people, over 8 million of them lived in the Moscow area.

As Della and Rachel dressed in the hotel suite Maxim had reserved for them at the Metropole, Rachel wondered about the millions of Muscovites, wondered how they would be celebrating the gala event that night.

"That gown looks fabulous on you, Rachel," Della marveled as she entered from the third bedroom of the suite. "Wow!"

Rachel turned and registered a look of admiration as she took in the flowing, green silk gown that Della was wearing. "Look at you! My god, I'm jealous!" She grinned as she moved towards Della and held her at arms' length. "I just love Anastasia's signature straight strapless neckline, and the ruched crossover front. It shows off your gorgeous back and bust line. Beautiful!"

"And what about yours, I'm envious of your olive skin peeking through that peach lace. Hey, I'm a lime and you're a peach tonight," Della teased. "Two of my favorite fruit.'

They both giggled.

"I wonder how the guys will like us?" Rachel posed as she glanced at her reflection in the gilded mirror over an ornate dresser.

Della leaned forward and fluffed her copper-colored tresses. Her full spiral tresses were bigger than ever tonight, as broad as her shoulders. "I think we've got these guys. They're ours. No one else is going to turn their heads. I'd bet on it." She giggled and headed for the bar in the living area. "How about a champagne?"

"I thought you'd never ask." Rachel did a final check in the mirror of her own hair that was pulled straight back to the nape of her neck, held by a pearl-studded clasp, and then she followed Della into the other room.

Della was already pouring the champagne. "Anastasia is so talented, isn't she? I can't believe she designed these gowns. We're lucky to have her in the family, aren't we?" She handed a glass to Rachel.

Rachel lifted her glass, "I'll drink to that. I thought she'd be here by now. Wasn't she going to dress with us?"

"She decided to go to her friend's place and dress there. She's bringing her to the party. Another dress designer, I think." Della walked to the doors of the balcony perched above the square.

Rachel followed. "I'm surrounded by dress designers. You know I have a friend and partner in Brussels who is a designer; I told you that didn't I?"

"Yea, you did. In fact you said we could meet there sometime. I'm interested in doing some research in Antwerp for some articles about diamonds. And my god, Brussels is the capital of the European Union, can't let that go to waste. Have to

214

see it all." She laughed and took a sip of her drink. "And I'm eager to meet Mandy and Richard. You say they live in a castle?"

"Yep, another castle in the family. Seems we're surrounded by castles and dress designers."

They both had a hearty laugh again.

"It was just a year ago tonight we were celebrating in the Grand Place. I was feeling pretty lonely and sad as it got closer to midnight. Was thinking about Pete mostly. Then I wandered off at midnight and met Maxim and he whisked me back to the Brussels Metropole where my friends were waiting. I'll never forget that night and the see-saw moods I had been having all that week. From the bottom of the pit to the highest peak—"

"And now? Which is it? The bottom of the pit or the highest peak?"

"I am definitely at the highest peak!" Rachel twirled in jubilation. "I am, I am, I am! I admit it. Silly, but Maxim makes me feel like a princess. You know?"

Della winced, knowing exactly how Rachel felt. She opened the glass doors and stepped out onto the balcony to a blast of cold, winter air and sounds of the city below. She was frowning and feeling guilty for not telling Rachel that Maxim was married. She had to do it if he didn't tell her soon.

Maybe he'll tell her tonight. Yea, of course he will. He's got to.

Chapter 40

The phone rang, it was Valentin. He said he and Maxim were waiting in the lounge for their women and asked if they were ready to come down.

A few minutes later Rachel and Della stepped off the elevator to the two eager faces of the most luscious Russian men in the hotel. No one compared according to the two Irish-American women facing them.

Valentin and Maxim felt exactly the same about their dates. They outshone every other female in the hotel. Maxim held his arm out for Rachel and escorted her into the lounge. Valentin and Della followed.

Just as they were seated at a round table set for six, Anastasia arrived with her new friend Maya. Both women were dressed in avant-garde finery befitting of contemporary dress designers. The designs were over-the-top spectacular. They both had combined bright colors, sequins, jewels, multi-length pieces of fabric and head gear as part of their costumes—a perfect description, costumery right off a Paris runway. They appeared hand in hand, laughing and carrying glasses of champagne.

"Hello, everybody!" Anastasia said as they stood at the table. It was remarkable how she had transformed from a shy, quiet-spoken sewing-room seamstress to the vibrant, self assured flamboyant dress designer standing before them at that moment.

Maxim and Valentin stood up immediately to pull out the chairs between Della and Maxim for the newcomers. Anastasia introduced Maya and then they all sat down again.

"Sorry we are late, we were in the cafe eating with our friends. Oh Della, stand up please. And you too, Rachel. I want to see your dresses."

Standing and doing pirouettes, Rachel and Della performed.

"Stunning, both of you. Perfect. Are you happy?"

They chimed in together, "Yes!", and then giggled as they sat again.

Della continued, "It's the most wonderful gown I've every worn, Anastasia. You surpass all others with your designs."

"And I must agree," Rachel added. "Mine is the ultimate, I love it. The fit of this strapless, straight neckline is incredible. Normally I wouldn't even attempt to wear such a garment. And I love the way the lace bolero falls loosely to a V in the back, because I'd feel a bit bare and self-conscious if it didn't. The gown goes down pretty low in the back. And I must hand it to you for putting me in a pastel; I hardly ever wear anything but black."

"You are lovely in whatever color you wear, my dear." Maxim smiled at Rachel and then leaned towards his sister and whispered, "You've already eaten? We were going to order food."

"Yes, but you must eat. We are drinking now, yes, Maya?" She giggled.

Maya lifted her glass, "We've had all the food we can hold . . . till maybe later?"

Valentin chimed in, "You are both stylish tonight too, and you design your dresses, yes?"

"I designed Maya's, she designed mine. We decided to surprise each other and this is what we created. We design much alike, no?" They were both grinning widely at each other, still holding hands.

Rachel noted they were like a couple of giddy school girls. She was glad Anastasia had found such a good friend.

A few moments later Anastasia and Maya shared a light, lingering kiss on the lips.

Rachel darted a glance at Della and their raised-eyebrow expressions revealed they were possibly thinking the same thing. The two designers were definitely a couple, in every sense of the word.

Anastasia blurted out, "So, what is the plan tonight?'

"Leisurely cocktails with appetizers," Maxim said. "Then we will go to the dining room for a late meal and dancing. After that we could stroll to the square and observe the midnight fireworks and activity, or we could go to the roof and observe the fireworks and all of Moscow. But we can decide later. For now, we must enjoy ourselves."

What an exciting time with such exciting people in such an exciting place! Rachel thought as she looked around the table and beyond at the magnificent creatures streaming through the lobby, heading for their New Year's Eve parties of choice.

Nothing thrilled Rachel more than a New Year's Eve, no matter where it was, no matter who was around. But tonight it seemed to be the crème de la crème of New Year's Eves in her memory. She was never happier. It was fabulous!

Chapter 41

The evening was full of surprises.

First Anastasia announced the merger of the two design houses - hers and Mayas - calling their label *Anamaya Designs*. At the table Maya handed Maxim a check to pay off the loan he'd given his sister, and told of their plan to open a shop in Moscow first and then one in Paris and one in London.

The brothers Ballenchine were ecstatic for their sister Anastasia. It had been a long haul for her; she had worked hard to get to where she was now going.

Della and Rachel joined in the congratulations and assured both women of their devoted patronage, said they would always order special gowns from them and would help spread the word.

Then came the announcement from Maxim that he would be officially retiring from the family business within six months. Valentin added news of his impending retirement as well, announcing his plans to open a restaurant in Moscow, something he'd always wanted to do.

Although not entirely new to Della, she was surprised that he had made the final decision to bow out of the diamond and amber business, and she was thrilled.

Rachel had tears in her eyes; she was absorbing the genuine joy of the Ballenchine family engulfing the table. What a way to start a new year - new horizons, new challenges, much happiness.

"Della, you have news to share, yes?" Anastasia knowingly prodded.

"Yea, I am writing again, I will be sending out submissions to magazines by the end of January, and soon I hope to be known as a published writer." She beamed up at Valentin who was grinning with a radiant pride. He placed his hands on each side of her face and planted a kiss on her lips.

"And Rachel, my love, what are your plans for the coming year?" Maxim asked.

She blinked her eyes, taken aback at the sudden question. "Well, I—I'm still working on my novel that is set in Russia, involving the diamond industry, but after that I'm not sure. I usually take a couple months rest when I complete a novel. At some point I'll be going back to England to regroup and decide on the next book, I suppose—" The heat from Maxim's penetrating stare stopped her dead in her tracks.

He leaned towards her and lifted her chin, "We will discuss your plans later this evening." He too planted a kiss on his woman's lips.

Valentin lifted his glass, "To the Ballenchines, and to a successful new year, and may we have more to come!"

They all lifted their glasses in unison and gave a cheer.

Rather than go to the square at midnight where hundreds of people would be congregated in the snow and coldness, the Ballenchine group went to the roof of the Metropole where

Maxim had arranged for a table to be set up for them, their own personal waiters attending. Portable heaters had been placed to keep them warm. If they needed more warmth, their fur coats were nearby. Even the men wore furs in Russia in the wintertime. Maxim had also arranged for a jazz combo to play American music after the fireworks.

Red Square separated the Kremlin from the town. On the four sides of the 400 x 150 metre square, actually a rectangle, stood the Kremlin, GUM Department Store, State Historical Museum, and the famous St. Basil's Cathedral in all its grandeur at the far end. The fireworks display, presenting a brilliant background for the church, began at the stroke of midnight and the couples throughout Moscow were undoubtedly enjoying the traditional New Year's Eve kiss and embrace. The view from the roof of the Metropole was spectacular.

After the fireworks Maxim said to Rachel, "I hope this evening pleases you," as they settled into their chairs around the table once again. The combo music began. "The music is just for you, as last year in Brussels, the music at the Metropole," he added.

"It's wonderful, Maxim. Nothing suits me more than listening to a combo playing jazz in a romantic setting. And this tops it all. Thank you so much. I'm the happiest I've ever been." And she meant it.

The evening of dancing and drinking lasted well into the early morning hours. Della and Valentin were the first to excuse themselves to their hotel suite.

Rachel stood and faced Maxim, "I'm really tired, Maxim. Would you mind if we call it a night? It's been a whirlwind day for me too."

"Of course, my love. We will go." Maxim was quick to fetch their coats and escort Rachel to the rooftop elevator door after saying goodnight to Anastasia and Maya.

After a final glass of champagne and making love in a romantic bubbly bath, lying entwined in an embrace in the giant four-poster bed was how Rachel and Maxim fell asleep early in the morning of the first day of the new year.

It was indeed a happy time for everybody.

Chapter 42

New Year's Day was always a time of reflection for Rachel, in addition to *rolling with the tide* - one of her favorite expressions, and not making decisions, being open to whatever the moment produced. Not letting anything serious enter her mind, starting with a clean slate. She referred to it as her day of renewal.

But New Year's Day or not, holiday or not, Maxim and Valentin were already at a meeting in one of the conference rooms.

Rachel met up with Della that morning at eight o'clock for coffee in the Metropole coffee shop.

"Here she is. And how was your evening, young lady?" Della asked with a teasing twinkle in her eyes.

"Wonderful. Just wonderful!" Rachel's smile and glow alone revealed how she felt. "It was an amazing New Year's Eve, wasn't it?"

"It certainly was for me. Valentin never ceases to amaze me, no matter what. Look at what he gave me in our hotel room." She held up her right hand adorned by a diamond and sapphire ring. "Can you believe it? He knows I loved Lady Di's ring, I've talked about it enough. It's exactly like it."

Rachel held Della's hand as she marveled at the beauty of the ring. "Wow! It is fabulous, isn't it? Rumor is that Prince Charles will give Prince William his mother's ring when he's old enough to marry."

"I know. Keeps the legacy going, you know?"

"Better still, it helps to be the fiancé of a jewel dealer, if you love jewels." Rachel laughed.

"Of course it helps even more to be madly in love with the jewel dealer," Della replied.

"No more doubts?" Rachel raised her eyebrows.

"Nope. We've worked it all out. No doubts at all. Signed, sealed, delivered!"

"Well, I have a bit of news for you this morning. Maxim asked me to move in with him. I don't know if I will, mind you. My heart is still in Cornwall, but we're talking about it. I suppose we can go back and forth."

Della reached for the carafe to pour a cup of coffee for Rachel. She was silent, a frown crossing her brow.

"What's wrong?" Rachel asked as she reached for her filled cup. "You got quiet all of a sudden. Why are you frowning?"

Della hesitated, as if she was searching for the right words. Finally, she looked Rachel straight in the eyes and said, "There's only one way to tell you this. Uh, Maxim is married. He isn't a widower. His wife isn't dead. She lives in their home in Brussels. He's married!"

The words hit Rachel like a giant wallop to the head. She was stunned. She just stared at Della.

"Rachel?"

"He—he's talking about living with me and he's married?" Rachel looked to her left at the doors that led off the patio. "I've got to get out of here." She stood up and grabbed her purse.

"Wait, wait! What are you going to do?" Della was frantic; she wished she hadn't told her.

"I'm getting out of here, that's what I'm going to do. I can't stay here, knowing this. Tell him I had an emergency call. Tell him anything you want. I'm taking a taxi to the airport. So if you'll just hang on to the rest of my stuff at your house, I'll make arrangements to get them. I have everything I really need here at the hotel with me. Bye." She headed for the elevator with Della on her heels.

"Rachel! Wait a minute, will you? Let's talk about this. Please!"

"Nothing to talk about. I was wavering anyway, and now I don't have to worry about it. It's over. He's a liar."

They stood silent together in the elevator.

Rachel gave a huge sigh and looked over at her dear, tearful friend. She hugged her, "It's alright, Della. I'm alright. I'll explain it to him after I get to England. But right now I can't face him. I can't guarantee what I'd say. So it's best to say nothing until I can collect my thoughts. Okay? I'll be out of here and at the airport before their meeting is over. It's better this way. And it gives me time to think without saying something I might regret. All right? You okay?"

Della pulled back and looked into Rachel's eyes, tears trailing down her cheeks. "I'm so sorry."

"Hey, it isn't your fault. It's that bastard's fault for not telling me sooner."

They smiled sadly at each other as the elevator doors opened.

"Now you go back down there, finish your coffee and I'll stop by on my way out. Okay?"

"Okay."

But Rachel didn't stop by, she took the service elevator and hurriedly left the hotel with bags in tow, making sure she wouldn't run into Maxim.

Chapter 43

Life will never be the same.

How many times had Rachel heard that phrase? How many times had she said it?

Life will never be the same. Of course it won't be, it never is. Life changes from one moment to the next. But this time it really was different. This time it was downright scary.

If she had learned anything at all in her lifetime, she had learned that changes are inevitable, and learning how to cope and roll with the changes, however drastic, was the ultimate trick and test.

She boarded the plane in Moscow without anyone seeing her off. She was going home to Cornwall.

She sent Della a text message as soon as she was in her seat on the plane, but didn't send one to Maxim. She needed more time to calm down before she said anything to him. She needed time to figure out her feelings.

All she wanted to do now was to get home to Belinda, Paul and the boys. She'd checked her email messages on her Blackberry and discovered that Paul had sent a text message at three that morning saying Belinda was back in the hospital and this time it was serious.

So everything was happening as it was supposed to happen. She was needed in Cornwall, and she was already on her way home when she got the message.

The direct flight from Moscow to London was uneventful, giving her time to make notes and collect her thoughts. She arrived in London just in time to catch a plane to Newquay, arriving there a little after eight in the evening.

After downing four Aleve tablets at the airport in Newquay, and after a cab ride to her Newlyn cottage, still with a throbbing headache she fell across her bed a split second after she dropped her bags beside it.

It had been a long and trying day. But after a few minutes she got her second wind, took a few deep breaths and turned on the bath water. It was so good to be home, diminishing headache and all.

She hadn't realized how much she'd missed her own cozy surroundings. But she did realize she hadn't eaten all day, which could be the reason for the headache. So while the bath was running, she opened a can of cold stewed tomatoes from the refrigerator, and gorged herself.

Should I call Paul? She had first called him when she arrived in London to tell him she was on her way, but would be getting in late. He told her not to worry, to get a good night's rest and he'd come by in the morning. They could go to the hospital together. So she decided not to call him at that late hour.

She felt better by the time she finished off the can of tomatoes and decided a big glass of wine in a tub of hot, frothy, scented bath water was just what the doctor ordered. What she had needed more than anything else was the comfort of her own home, surrounded by the familiar things she loved.

So she set the scene: soothing music, candles, heat thermostat set at a comfortable level, and a glass of the Zind Humbrecht Pinot Gris that she'd been saving.

Way too expensive to drink alone, she thought as she uncorked it, but she didn't care, it seemed the best choice under the circumstances. Maxim had brought it with him when he had visited, and it was damn expensive! $300 a bottle, she had looked it up on the Internet. So she was going to open it in spite of Maxim Ballenchine, *the liar and potential bigamist*.

She remembered what Maxim had told her about the wine, that it was a cousin of Pinot Grigio. 'Grigio is produced from grapes grown in Italy, Gris from grapes grown in France,' he had said.

"La tee da!" she said aloud. Maxim knew everything about everything. She wasn't aware of anything he didn't know. It was intimidating.

"And he out and out, bold-faced, lied to me!" she said as she took the glass, the silver wine bucket with ice, and the bottle of wine into her boudoir and set them on a mirrored table next to her claw-footed tub. Off went her clothing and she was in the oversized tub sipping wine in no time flat.

"Ahhh," she sighed. "This is the life. In my own house. In my own tub. With my own pretty things, my rosebud wallpaper. Listening to my own favorite music. Drinking elegant wine. This is the way I like it! This is the way I want it and I'm going to keep it! I certainly don't need a man hanging around gumming up the works. I do not need a man in my cotton-candy world!"

And as she relaxed in the tub, sipping the Pinot Gris, Shakespeare's '*Me thinks she doth protest too much*' came to mind

Chapter 44

"Have you talked to Maxim, yet?" Della asked over the phone.

Rachel tugged at a pillow to protect her bare feet from the early morning chill. She took a deep breath as she sank deeper into the over-stuffed sofa.

"I have nothing to say to him right now."

"I can imagine, I truly can." Della hesitated. "Rachel, I have to apologize, I'm so sorry I didn't tell you before. Will you ever forgive me?"

"It wasn't your responsibility, he should have told me."

"I know, but still, I feel bad. I could have said something before. I mean we girls have to stick together, right? If you knew something about Valentino that I should know, you'd tell me, wouldn't you?"

Rachel thought for a moment. "I would hope so."

"Well, I know you would."

"It isn't only that he's married, Della. I just don't see how I can even think of getting involved with anyone. Especially Maxim. I mean how could I anyway? The bastard is married!"

She took a deep breath, trying to calm herself, and reached for the cup of coffee on the cocktail table.

"Well, I'm just going to miss you, that's all. I hate it that this is happening."

"You can come visit me, Della. It takes only a few hours to get here. Well, nearly a day." She laughed. "About five hours to London, then almost five on the train to Penzance. Lots of scenery to see, though. Or you could take a coach from London, that's always fun. A bus. Not bad really. Or you could fly in to Newquay from London, and I'll pick you up at the airport. That's the best way, wouldn't take as long. Think about it." Rachel was already missing her, too.

"I will definitely do that before we're married, like we said. I promise. But in the meantime, please call Maxim. Valentino's upset with me for telling you. He was hoping the two of you would at least move in together. He says Maxim truly loves you and would have eventually told you. But I understand where you're coming from, he should've told you, so I don't blame you. It's just that men, well, they don't get it, you know?"

Rachel went into the kitchen. "Regardless, I can tell you now that I won't be moving in with Maxim. I won't for several reasons. I'll explain it in an email. I need to send you those edits anyway."

"Okay. And I'll try to explain it to Valentino. Don't worry; I'll leave it to you to tell Maxim, okay?"

Rachel sighed heavily. "Yep, I know I need to call him, that's the least I can do. Maybe I'll call him later today. Go ahead and tell Valentin that. Okay?"

"Great! Well, I must get off here and get some things done. We're going into Moscow tonight. It's that big dinner with clients, remember? So you take care, and again, I miss you, Rachel. I truly do."

"Miss you, too. Give my love to Valentin. Bye."

Rachel leaned against the kitchen counter and gazed out into the garden through the open French doors towards the magnolia tree and the table and chairs - the heart filigreed, white iron table and chairs that Pete had given to her as a housewarming present. She smiled, remembering, although the feelings attached to the memories seem faded somehow.

In the center of the glass covered tabletop the wrought iron formed a heart, and the backs of the chairs carried the same motif. Pete had said at the time that it signified him giving his heart to her. Said she could always look at the set and be reminded of his lasting love.

She remembered the morning when the two of them stood by the gate for the first time. It was after he'd picked her up at the airport in Newquay and brought her home to her lovely cottage for the first time. He'd found the house for her while she was in Montana at her mother's wake. He had helped arrange the purchase for her through her bank.

She smiled as she remembered how dreamy handsome he was and how stunning her cottage looked to her as they stood on the path in each other's arms.

"Okay now, that's enough. Knock it off." She turned to empty the remaining coffee dregs from her cup into the sink.

She had already decided it was time to let go and move on. In fact she was thinking of replacing the garden furniture with a set she'd seen in a magazine on the plane.

More changes.

The doorbell rang.

Chapter 45

"Paul, you're early." Rachel couldn't believe how ragged and drawn he looked.

"Well, I thought maybe we could talk and have some coffee before we go to the hospital, if you don't mind. I need to talk." He slumped into the chair next to the sofa, not looking at Rachel, staring at his fidgety hands clasped in his lap.

"I'll put a fresh pot on. It'll only take a sec." She hurried into the kitchen and filled the electric kettle, rinsed out the Cafetiere and added a scoop of coffee grounds, then returned to the living room and sat across from Paul. "Have you heard anything more since we talked?"

He dropped his head into his hands and began sobbing. "The doctor just called ... she's got maybe a week ... a day ... oh, Rachel ... how am I going to take care of the boys? . . . how am I going to live without Belinda? I can't do it!"

Rachel dropped to her knees in front of him, and reached her arms around his neck. "No, no, no. Don't give up on Belinda, Paul. Miracles happen, they do."

"Not this time. She wants us to let her go. She's in such pain. You'll see. But, I can't do it— no matter what she says." His sobbing increased.

"Paul, sweetheart," she didn't want to cry, she wanted to be strong for him. "Hang on, please hang on. You've got to. I can't bear seeing you like this." With her arms tight around his broad shoulders and his face buried into her neck, she was losing her own emotional battle.

Not dear, sweet, Belinda! Anybody but Belinda. "We have to be strong for her, Paul. She's counting on us. C'mon now. For the boys." That did it. Battle lost. Her emotions took over.

Paul lifted his head and it was as if they exchanged places, her face buried into his neck as she wept, him trying to console her.

"Rachel, please, don't cry. I'm so sorry I've dumped this on you. It's just that I'm not strong. I never have been; she's the strong one. She was the one who rescued me at the beginning, and I just can't stand the thought that I can't rescue her now . . . she might not ever— I might not—" He took a handkerchief from his pocket. "I'm so sorry; I'm so messed up. I can't talk to her mother, can't let her see me like this. Can't let the boys— the poor babies—" He broke off again, this time he stood up and rushed outside towards the magnolia tree.

Rachel wiped her eyes and nose with her shirt tail on the way to get the coffee. She didn't know how to make Paul feel better. She couldn't even make herself feel better. It seemed as if life was crumbling all around her again.

She grabbed a tray and took the coffee and the cups out to the tree under which Paul was sitting.

"Here we go," she said as she sniffed and blotted a tear from her cheek with her shoulder. She set the tray on the table and poured coffee into two china mugs. She couldn't think of anything to say.

Paul was staring out at the sea, "You know, when I sit here, I see a beautiful world out there. It is, isn't it?" He smiled sadly.

Rachel gripped his shoulder, handing a mug to him. "Yep, it's the only thing that is constant, Paul. The beauty of it all, it goes on and on regardless of what happens to us. I come out here and sit for hours, surrounded by all this," she sat near him, "trying to sort it all out. I've finally accepted the fact that Pete is gone and is never coming back— I mean—" she realized what she'd said. "Oh, I didn't mean to—"

"No, no, it's alright, it is. I've been thinking about my father the past few days, and my mother. You know, they were divorced years ago, when I was just a kid. A spoiled rich kid." He gave a weak laugh. "I grew up with a father who was an entrepreneur and a womanizer and had a questionable regard for women; I hardly ever saw my mother, she was busy opening one restaurant after another. I wonder what it would have been like if I would have had a caring and gentle mother like Belinda."

"And a father like you to teach his sons about love and life," Rachel whispered.

Paul took a good look at Rachel. He saw dark circles under her reddened eyes. "I can see I'm the one that should be sorry, for I haven't even asked you how you are. Something else is wrong, isn't it?"

Rachel sighed heavily, looking down at her cup. "Well, as a matter of fact everything is wrong. It turns out that Maxim is married. He isn't a widower like he said. He lied. He's married and has been for years. His wife lives in Brussels while he traipses all over the friggin' world. Who knows how many women he's got, not that it really matters, I mean, well, it matters, but then it doesn't." She covered her face with her hands, "Oh hell! Who am I kidding? It does matter. I don't know what ever possessed me to fall for Maxim." She looked up at

Paul with tired eyes, "I don't know what I'm doing anymore, Paul. I just don't know."

Paul got up out of his chair and raised Rachel from hers. He held her close to him, caressing her hair as she tightened the embrace and buried her face into his chest, crying.

He spoke first. "You know, it's like we're two lost souls out here on the edge of a beautiful world. You know?"

"Yep, I know."

They stood in each other's arms for a few moments, draining comfort from each other. Finally they both stepped apart awkwardly and reached for their coffee cups.

"We should probably go to the hospital now," Paul said.

Rachel nodded in agreement.

Chapter 46

It was horrid and heartbreaking sitting near Belinda who was unconscious, in heart failure, barely alive. She had developed cardiac lymphoma which had caused the latest death threat. In her case, there would be no return from cardiac lymphoma; the tumors were invasive to the extreme.

Paul and Belinda's mother had just made the decision to stop all life support, although a morphine drip was still in effect to relieve pain and make Belinda as comfortable as possible till her last breath.

Rachel was standing behind Paul and Belinda's mother, gripping their shoulders. Tears were streaming down her cheeks as she held back the sobs, trying to be respectful and brave for the two of them. She didn't think she could get through this, another death of a soulmate. *The numbers are piling up, too many too soon*, she thought to herself once again as she reached for a tissue from the box the nurse had supplied. But this time she knew she had to be stronger than ever, she couldn't let this pitch her back into the pit she had been slowly climbing out of; she had to hold on for their sakes as well as her own.

A nurse came into the room and checked Belinda's vital signs. "It won't be long now, she's slipping fast," she said softly in the quietness.

Paul got up from his chair and leaned over Belinda, kissing her forehead. He looked at the nurse, his face showing control he didn't think he could muster, "Can she hear me?" His voice cracked, control was surely slipping.

"It's hard to tell, but why not believe she can?" The nurse smiled and stepped to the end of the hospital bed. She lifted the bed linens from Belinda's feet and lower legs, checking for discoloring and splotching, which gave a clearer picture of what was happening in the process and how fast the end was approaching.

He clutched Belinda's cold, lifeless hand. "Belinda, I'm here. So are your mother and Rachel. You're not alone, we're here with you—" He crumbled.

Rachel stepped to Paul's side, putting her arm around his waist and leaning forward nearer Belinda. "We love you, Belinda. And don't worry; we'll take care of your beautiful babies. You know we will." She reached back to grip the shoulder of Belinda's distraught mother who was slumped over in the chair, sobbing.

A few moments later, a deep, throaty gasp escaped from Belinda's lips . . . and her beautiful young life was over.

Rachel fell back into one of the bedside chairs, her face buried into a towel the nurse had left behind. She wept and mourned her dear friend and all the good times they had together. But now she was gone just like all the others, five soulmates, all dead, all in a heap.

Beatrice moved to the chair beside her, wiping her own tears from her eyes. "Rachel, my dear one, she is at peace. She wanted to go. She said so. The pain was too much for her to bear; it had taken over her body. I find solace in the fact that she no longer has pain. You must do the same. We must think of

Baby Jake and little Paulie now. Our dear, darling boys who have lost their mother—" At that, Beatrice too lost control and wept.

Rachel wrapped her arms around Beatrice, resting her cheek against her head, nestling in her grey, curly hair. *This woman has just lost her only daughter, her only child. How tragic is that?*

Beatrice looked up into Rachel's face. "My dear, I have found that when a loved one dies, there is always another to care for. Always someone who needs us, who loves us. There is always room in our hearts for more. When my folks died, Belinda's father became my life. He filled the void. Then when he died all those years ago, I had Belinda to love. She needed me. I had my sisters. After my sisters passed and close friends died or drifted away, I always had my memories to sustain me. And I cling to those memories to help me get through difficult times. Belinda was a blessing for me while she was here, my dear. And now her children will take up that space. We have her children to love."

Beatrice straightened up and took a deep breath. She wiped her eyes and looked at Paul whose head was still lying on Belinda's chest, his arms still clinging to her. "And we have Paul. He'll need us more than ever."

Chapter 47

The day after a small gathering of friends commemorating Belinda's life, Rachel woke up remembering she hadn't telephoned Maxim as she'd promised Della the week before.

So she made a pot of coffee and took it out to the magnolia tree where she settled into one of the garden chairs. She touched Maxim's photo on the contact screen of her cell phone, and placed the call to his cell phone.

When she heard his voice, she took a deep breath and after a few seconds, she finally spoke.

"Hi, Maxim."

"Rachel, I am so happy you are calling. I've tried to reach you but always your voice mail began. You are not answering your phone these days?'

"No, I haven't been available." She took a deep breath. "Belinda died, Maxim. So it's been rather difficult for me to talk. The memorial was yesterday."

"I am so sorry. I know how much you cared for her. So sorry, my dear. Do give Paul my well-wishes and condolences. is there anything I can do?"

"No, nothing," she whispered, still a bit shaky. A silent gap in conversation loomed for a few moments. "Well, I just wanted to call you and try to explain why I left so abruptly. I promised Della I would."

"Was it because of Belinda's health?"

"Partly, as it turned out. But mostly it was because of us, Maxim."

"Please, Rachel, I want to ask your forgiveness for not telling you that I was married. Della said she told you."

"How about *am* married, not *was*."

He sighed. "My wife passed away in the hospital Monday morning, Rachel."

"Oh no!"

"Yes, a fall turned out to be much more serious than they knew. She'd fallen several times the past two years, so they aren't sure which one caused a blood clot in her brain and inevitably an aneurysm which resulted in slow bleeding. She went into a coma and never recovered."

"I am so sorry. Are you in Moscow or Brussels?" She felt badly for being brusque earlier, regardless of what she thought of his infidelity.

"I'm in Brussels making arrangements. Della and Valentin will arrive this evening. You have not spoken to Della?"

"No, not since I returned. Before Belinda died. So she doesn't know about Belinda yet, and I didn't know about your wife."

"Would you like me to tell her to call you when she gets here?'

"If you would, please." Rachel took a sip of coffee while she racked her brain. She didn't know what else to say.

Maxim's deep voice interrupted the silence. "Will you be returning to visit the diamond mines? To finish your novel? Of course you may stay at the cottage."

Rachel's eyes filled with tears. She couldn't answer.

After a few moments of silence, Maxim said in an emotional whisper, "Tell me why you called, what were you going to say?"

She had to be truthful; it wasn't fair to Maxim or to her. "Well, I'll be honest. I was upset that you lied to me, and I am trying to sort my thoughts . . . and feelings."

"Yes? And?" he questioned softly.

She sighed. "I don't feel I'm ready for another relationship. That's the truth of it. And now I've these new responsibilities with Belinda's children. I've decided to stay and help their grandmother with them. They need me, so does Paul. So I won't be doing any traveling for a while. My time will be consumed by my writing and my new adopted family here in Cornwall."

Maxim was silent.

Rachel thought she heard his breath catch. She debated whether or not she should tell him that she also worried about being around the frightening dangers he faced in his line of work and that she was afraid to be caught up in it.

"I see, and I understand," he said quietly.

A few silent moments passed, and then she blurted out: "Maxim, I fear for you and Valentin. And Della. Every single day and night you are in danger. You never know when and from where the next gun shot will come. I don't know how you can live that way. I couldn't."

"But we are progressing, my dear Rachel, we are progressing. With our new freedoms and opportunities, yes, we've become inundated more than ever with the criminal element, just as your country was at one time with your Mafia, and now the cartels. But we too are striving to lessen the danger. And I must remind you, the time is nearing when the Ballenchine family business will close its doors. I am looking forward to a life of peace and leisure."

Rachel hoped it was true, for Della's sake more than anything else. "I do love your country, Maxim, and I hope to come back one day. I've been drawn to it as much as I have been drawn to England." Her voice wavered as she suppressed her emotions. "We will be in touch, won't we? Della and I will be working together, of course, by phone, email, and fax. And next time I'm in Brussels to visit Mandy and Richard, I'll call you. If you're there, maybe we can have lunch . . . or dinner . . . or just drinks?"

"Yes, that would be kind."

Rachel could tell by the tapering quietness of his voice that he was sad; it broke her heart to break his.

"I am so sorry, Maxim."

He didn't reply

She added, "And when you're in England, do let me know. Promise me you will?"

"I will. I will. Thank you." He cleared his throat.

There was nothing more to say.

"Goodbye," Maxim said quietly.

"Goodbye."

Chapter 48

A month had gone by since Belinda died. So many changes had taken place. Paul was still in a stupor, wasn't worth anything to anybody. He couldn't work, he couldn't eat, he wouldn't talk, and he never left the house.

His mother-in-law Beatrice was taking care of the boys in his 'absence'. They were too young to understand what had happened, why things had suddenly changed, why their daddy was ignoring them, why their mommy was not there.

One morning Baby Jake asked Rachel when his mommy was coming home.

Rachel picked him up and sat him next to her on the sofa. "Sweetheart, your mommy lives up in heaven now, with my mommy, and your grandma's mommy. They're watching us from the clouds, and if when you go to bed at night and visualize your mommy sitting up there on those fluffy white clouds in her beautiful angel dress and wings, you can talk to her. You can tell her anything you want and she'll listen to you. She will always love and protect you.

Jake's eyes widened, "You mean she's up in the sky? How did she get there?"

Rachel took a deep breath as her mind raced to find answers. "Well, I'm not sure. But what I've been told is . . . when we die—"

"Mommy died? My mommy died?" Jake started to cry.

Oh God! What have I done? "Sweetie, listen to me. God wanted your mommy to come live with him now; it was his turn to have her. She had done such a good job with you and your brother and was such a good mommy, loving you and taking care of you. But God needed her to come and take care of all the babies that have gone to heaven. He knew you would be all right, because you have your daddy and grandma and me and Uncle Dudley. Those babies up there have nobody." She wondered at her flimsy explanation, whether it would suffice.

"But who will be my mommy now?" Tears still falling, he buried his head into Rachel's lap. "I want my mommy."

Rachel put her arms around him. "Oh, baby, baby. We'll all be your mommy. You'll have lots of mommies. Even your Uncle Peter and Uncle Tom will help. We all loved your mommy, too, and we're going to miss her as much as you do. But we'll all have to stick together and help each other out, okay?"

He looked up at Rachel and wiped his eyes. Then he reached up and wiped her eyes with his chubby little hands. "Don't cry, Auntie Rachel, we can stick together and help each other out. We can do that." He cheerfully jumped down from the sofa. Tears gone. "I have to go tell Baby Paulie that Mommy's in the clouds and she's got angel wings."

Little five-year old Jake ran off to the nursery to tell his three-year old brother the news.

Beatrice stepped into the living room, having heard the conversation between Rachel and Jake. "That was lovely, Rachel. I couldn't have done it any better." She was carrying a pot of tea on a tray with cups. "Here, I brought you some tea."

"Oh, thank you, Beatrice. I really need that. That little tyke is something else, isn't he?"

"Yes, he is. A handful, actually." Beatrice laughed. "He reminds me of Belinda when she was that age, in so many ways. She was curious and talkative, like he is. Didn't know how to stop talking and keep still."

They both drank their tea in silence for a few moments.

"I've been thinking, Rachel. Maybe I should sell the B&B in London and move down here to take care of the boys."

"Oh that would be perfect! For Paul and the boys."

"Yes, I believe so, too. And I'd like to call on you from time to time to help me out when I need a break. Would you be able to do that? The boys love you so much."

"Absolutely! Of course I'll help. I don't plan to do any traveling till next year anyway. I'm on hiatus. Need to sort out some things of my own, here at home. So, any time you need me, just let me know. Have you told Paul your plans?'

Paul entered the room carrying one of Belinda's sculptures. "No she hasn't, and I don't want you to do that, Beatrice." He touched his mother-in-law's shoulder as he passed behind her before setting the sculpture on the mantle. "This was Belinda's last sculpture."

Rachel darted a glance at Beatrice who was reaching for her handkerchief.

"It's beautiful, Paul. Beautiful!" Beatrice whispered hoarsely.

"Yes, it is. My favorite." He turned and moved to the chair across from the two women on the sofa. "So, is there enough tea for me?"

Both Rachel and Beatrice were not only startled by his sudden appearance but by his return to the living. He had not come around them or conversed with either of them in a month. This was a first.

"Of course, there is. And if there isn't, I'll get more. Here, let me pour," Beatrice said, not able to hide her excitement. She handed her refilled cup to him and went off to the kitchen for more tea and another cup.

"I'm so happy to see you, Paul. And to hear your voice, I've been worried."

Paul took a sip before replying. "Jake just told me your story about his mother, her being in heaven and on a cloud. I guess he bought it." He took another sip.

"Oh, well—"

"No no, I'm not complaining. It was brilliant. I wasn't looking forward to having to tell him. I just want to thank you for doing that. It's a huge load off my mind. Thank you." He looked across at her and managed a faint smile.

As she looked into his swollen, reddened, beautiful blue eyes, Rachel felt such sadness in her heart for him. He had lost weight; she could see that, even though he wore pajamas and a bulky robe. His face was drawn, his neck was thinner, his usual shiny blond pony tail was now oily and scraggly, and he hadn't shaven in weeks.

She took a risk and blurted out, "Paul, go take a shower and get dressed. It's time for you to get out of this house. Let's go to lunch. My treat. I won't take no for an answer, either. I mean it. Go get cleaned up, this is ridiculous!" She stood over him.

He stared at his cup for what seemed like minutes, and then raised his sad eyes and searched Rachel's for what seemed like a few more minutes without speaking.

Rachel was about to repeat herself when Beatrice returned with tea and another cup.

"Okay, here we are. Need warm ups, anybody?"

Rachel slumped back down into the sofa, contemplating her next move.

Paul glanced at her and then looked up at Beatrice standing in front of him, teapot poised. "Just one more, please, then if you don't mind, I'm going to get dressed. Rachel's taking me to lunch," he said.

Rachel jumped to her feet.

Paul continued, "Is that all right with you, Beatrice? Will you be okay with the boys?"

If excitement and surprise were electricity, the room would have lit up with so much wattage it would have been blinding. Rachel was ecstatic, Beatrice was relieved.

Their exchanged glances said it all . . . *Everything is going to be all right!*

Chapter 49

It was the middle of March and life with Paul and the boys had consumed Rachel. She spent nearly every day at their 'castle on the hill' handling the day to day activities and duties around the house. Beatrice had gone back to London to put the B&B up for sale and to attend to business.

In the meantime, Rachel cleaned, she baked, she played games with the boys, she took them on outings, she bathed them, read stories to them, and tucked them in every night. Then she would go home and sleep and return the next morning to start the day all over again.

She was doing everything she could to make their little lives much easier and as normal as it could be without their mother to fawn over them and love them to bits as she always had.

It was hard at times, for Rachel missed Belinda too. There were many moments when she had to step out of their sight and re-experience the gutting emotion of the loss of her best friend. But it would never take long until the memory of what Beatrice had said about replacing the death of a loved one with a live one always brought her back to reality. Such a simple concept Beatrice had shared, and it would usually bring Rachel right back to the moment.

Paul came home from the studio for lunch most days. One day when he entered the house through the patio door, Rachel was crying, standing in front of the plate glass window looking out over the bay towards Saint Michael's Mount, her face covered with her hands. She didn't hear Paul come in.

"Oh Rachel, Rachel, I'm so sorry," he said softly as he rushed to her and held her tightly, her back against his body, his arms across her chest.

Her quiet sobs tapered off.

"I forget how much you loved her too. I've been so selfish."

After a few moments she left his grip and walked to the sofa and sat, pulling the extra pillows onto her lap.

He sat facing her on the overstuffed chair. "Will you forgive me?"

"It's all right. I'm sorry I broke down like that. I'm here to console you and the boys, not to act like this. But sometimes I do think of her and then I'm overwhelmed. It's like, well, it's like she and I were so close. We had so much in common and I really loved her. I remember how it was when you both first came here, her living here first, you coming down on weekends. I went to the studio every morning to have coffee with her." Rachel turned her head and looked out the window again. "I can imagine what you and the kids must feel, being even closer to her." She wiped her nose with a tissue.

"I know. I have quite a few of those moments, too. Usually late at night when I wake up and she's not there beside me. That's when it hits me the most. But like you've told me many times before, the boys come first now. They are my life. And I must think of them." He stood up and held out his hand to her. "So, let's have some lunch, shall we? I'll get the boys."

Rachel wiped her eyes and nose again and went to the kitchen. She'd already prepared the meal, just needed to move it all to the dining table. She'd already set the table, so within a few minutes they were all eating, laughing, and talking.

"Auntie Rachel, are you going to live with us in London too?" Jake said with his mouth full of sandwich.

Rachel darted a glance at Paul. "London? Isn't Beatrice selling and coming here?"

"Well, it's all happened so quickly. I was going to tell you about it tonight over dinner. I planned to take you out, Dudley said he would sit with the boys, do you mind?"

"No, that will be fine." She felt a little hurt, being out of the loop so to speak. It seemed everyone but she knew about the move to London.

"You are coming with us to London to live, aren't you, Auntie Rachel?" Jake was persistent.

"No, baby, I'm staying here in my cottage. You know how I love all my flowers and the ocean, don't you? Now you mustn't talk with your mouth full. Chew it up and swallow it, then you can talk. Okay?"

"Okay," he answered with food falling from his mouth.

Rachel chuckled and looked at Paul who was holding his hand over his mouth, hiding his grin.

He gained his composure and poured more iced tea in Rachel's empty glass. "I have a meeting with the realtor on Friday, to sign the escrow papers. So we'll be moving by the end of the month. I know you'll love the house, Rachel. It's perfect for us. And any time you want to come and stay, there's plenty of room."

"So what's happening with this house?"

"I'll probably sell it. You wouldn't want it, would you?"

Rachel laughed. "What ever would I do with a big house like this?"

"Oh, I just thought that it might be nice to keep it in the family. Belinda loved it." He looked down at his plate, solemnly for a moment, and then quickly looked up at Rachel again. "I'd give you a good deal."

Rachel hesitated before speaking. "Well, I don't know."

He stared at the food on his plate. "There's still time to think about it. I won't be doing any advertising just yet."

When he finally looked at Rachel, she saw tears in his eyes. She quickly injected, "I'll tell you what. I will think about it. I can't promise anything, but I'll think about it."

Paul reached across the table and squeezed her hand. "Thank you."

The rest of the lunch was uneventful except for a few dropped utensils during dessert, first a fork from Paulie's little hand, then a spoon from Jake's.

There was a lot of laughter, a lot of conversation, and a lot of love hovering over the table and its lunchtime diners.

Chapter 50

In April Della came from Moscow to Cornwall for three weeks. She and Rachel spent hours shopping and furnishing the house Rachel had decided to buy from Paul. It was quite a challenge, being as big as it was - three stories. The original plans said it contained 8,000 square feet. At first she thought it was ridiculous that she live in such a spacious home by herself, but the more she looked into it and decided how she would use each room, the more the idea appealed to her. She could have a room for everything - writing, painting, reading, music, guest rooms, sunroom, party room, parlor, library, living room and family room, game room, and so on. And as she and Della filled it up, it was getting smaller and becoming pretty darn cozy. Rachel had a unique talent in turning living spaces into cozy spaces no matter how large or small.

Paul and the children were already situated in London and when Della was to return to Moscow, Rachel was going to take the train as far as London with her and they were going to visit the fellas.

But in the meantime, the two bosom buddies were having a grand old time together. In addition to the shopping and decorating during the day, they worked on ideas for writing projects at night and talked about Della's wedding coming up in June.

"Let's go to the Ship Inn for lunch, Della," Rachel said as she came through the double doors leading to the patio from the kitchen. "I fancy some fish and chips, and they have the best."

"No argument there. Let's go." Della closed her laptop and followed Rachel back into the house.

It took them less than ten minutes to get to Mousehole and another five to walk into the village. Parking in the car park on a Saturday was impossible, so they chose to park near a hotel on the outskirts along the beach road.

"Hi, Gina!" Della called out to the bartender as they entered the full bar. It was always crowded on Saturdays, between the tourists and the locals, they would be lucky to find a seat at the bar, much less at a table.

"There they are. How are ya? Champagne, ladies?"

Rachel nodded. "Yep, that'll work. And a couple fish and chips, please." Rachel immediately spied tourists leaving a table. "We'll sit over here by the window today."

"I'll be right with you," Gina said.

"I can't believe we got a table," Rachel said to Della.

"Yea, how about that. Meant to be." Della laughed.

They turned their chairs with their backs to the window to be able to see the patrons, both being avid people-watchers.

"Here you go," Gina said as she arrived with a bottle of champagne in a plastic bucket and two glasses. "I hope you don't mind us being out of champagne glasses. Broke the only four left last night. A gang of people were in here partying and got a bit out of hand." She set the two wine glasses on the table and poured the drinks. "So how's it going with the articles, Della? Are you doing one of Mousehole like you said?"

"Yes, I am. Was working on it this morning."

"Am I gonna be in it?" Gina's wide grin revealed a space where a tooth had once been, but was now gone missing. "You wanna know anything more about me, just ask." She stood waiting for a moment when another customer called her from the bar. "Bloody hell, they can't let me have a moment's peace. Got to get back to work, ladies. Your fish and chips will be right up."

As they watched Gina push her way through the standing crowd at the end of the bar, Della was still chuckling. "She is priceless, isn't she? Tattoos and piercings."

"I know. I love coming in here with all these personalities. Enough to fill quite a few novels. And articles. See that guy over there." She was looking at a tall, stick thin, fisherman. "You wouldn't believe he is a PhD, would you?"

"You're kidding me."

"He is. He's a scientist, decided to become a fisherman instead, and that's what he does. He loves it. Works on a fishing boat out of Newlyn, doesn't even own it. He says he would rather work for someone else, let them pay all the bills. I used to go down to the harbor and watch him when they would unload the fish on the docks. He would go to the Swordfish Pub that's right there by the docks. That was when Pete was running it. That's how I met Jojo, that's what they call him."

"Amazing."

"Yep, that's why I love going to these places and sitting for hours. You meet all sorts and hear all sorts. Perfect for a writer." Rachel took a sip of bubbly. "And you know what; no man in this world would ever want to sit with his woman in a pub while she watches and talks to people for hours. And he definitely wouldn't want her to go there by herself. That's another reason I need to stay single. With Pete it worked, he knew how I was, and he didn't mind me traveling. He was gone most of the time anyway. It would be hard to find another man like that." Rachel sighed heavily.

"But I see you're doing better, accepting the fact that Pete is gone and that you have to move on with your life, right?" Della wasn't sure she should have asked the question, but she did it anyway.

"Oh, you would think the more you go through it, the easier it becomes. And in some things that's probably true, but losing someone you love doesn't qualify. I do feel as if I'm making progress, though. I accept the fact that Pete is gone and there are other people in my life to love. Like Baby Jake and little Paulie. And my own son, Derek . . . even though he has a wife and a life of his own in the States. But thank God, I still have my memories of Pete."

"And what memories those are, huh?" Della smiled and placed her hand on Rachel's.

"Yep, great ones. He was one of a kind."

"Maxim is one of a kind," Della slipped in the comment as she watched Gina come toward them with their plates. She didn't look at Rachel to see how she was responding. Instead she straightened up in her chair, preparing for her food. "We're all one of a kind, aren't we? So when did you say you're going to Brussels to see Mandy and Richard?"

"Next month, for the grand opening of her second shop."

"That's what I thought," Della lifted her hands as Gina set her plate in front of her.

"There you are," Gina said. "Don't touch the plate, it's hot."

"Thanks, it looks good. When next month, Rachel?"

"The first two weeks."

"Oh, good. Maxim will be there too." Della still hadn't looked at Rachel, she was ogling her food.

But Rachel was staring at her friend across the table while nonchalantly sipping her drink. She wondered if Maxim knew she was going to be in Brussels the first two weeks of

Rebecca Buckley

May. She wondered if Della was now assuming the role of cupid in their relationship.

Della grinned as her glance met Rachel's. "What?"

Chapter 51

The first of May rolled around much quicker than Rachel expected. After Della returned to Moscow, Rachel stayed on in London for a few days visiting Paul and the boys. Then when she returned to Cornwall, she had a little over a week alone in her new hillside home to get ready for her trip to Brussels.

She wanted to surprise Mandy with some pen & ink renderings of early seventeenth century gowns for the new shop in Brussels. She had given Mandy a set of drawings for her first shop and when she saw these in one of her favorite antique stores in Penzance, she bought them for the second shop. They had to be framed and would be ready three days before she was to leave for Brussels.

During the renovation and re-decorating of her own 'castle on the hill', she felt like a new person. She even drove to Bristol to see an antique book case she'd heard about, and a china cabinet. Almost every other day there was something else to go see, to purchase.

The time passed quickly.

Now as she walked through her home the Saturday before her trip, making notes of what she might like to purchase in Belgium to add to her own eclectic mix of décor, she couldn't keep from smiling. It was as if the smile was permanently plastered on her face. In fact her cheeks hurt at the end of each day because of it. This was by far the happiest time of her life. It was puzzling; she didn't know why she felt so good. She just did.

The move had done her good, moving from the cottage that constantly reminded her of Pete, into a completely different setting. And although Belinda and Paul had made their home in the house for those brief years, it wasn't hard for Rachel to settle into it as her own. She'd made enough changes to make it hers, and the memory of Belinda didn't hamper her being there. In fact she loved thinking of Belinda and remembering their conversations and times together. It wasn't the same as remembering Pete in her cottage, although the memories of him were changing too, as were the memories of other loved ones. They weren't provoking sadness and tears anymore.

Being with the boys as often as she could had made her feel as if Belinda was still alive, for they reminded her so much of her. Especially Baby Jake, aside from the orange hair, he was her spitting image. Paulie was a duplicate of Paul, blond hair and blue eyes. So Belinda lived on through them, that's what made the difference. Pete was gone and there was no one who carried on his legacy in Rachel's world, so loving memories would have to suffice.

Rachel reached for the cell phone as it rang, breaking into her thoughts.

"Hello? Hi, Dudley. We have to leave here at eight. Yep. No, Monday, not Sunday. Right. Okay, luv. I'll see you Monday morning then. Bye."

Dudley was driving her to the airport in Newquay to catch the plane to Brussels. Although she would have to make a stop on the Isle of Man, it was a godsend not to have to go through the London train stations and airports.

Monday came before she knew it.

Rachel was up early, sipping coffee as she dressed. Everything was already packed and waiting. She took one last look in the mirror, hesitated, and then fondled the diamond pendant on the chain hanging around her neck. The pendant fell into her cleavage, so sometimes it didn't show, depending on what she was wearing. Today she wore a V-necked black sweater and the brilliance of the five-carat stone was blatantly obvious.

She stared at the necklace for a moment and unclasped the chain. Carrying the diamond set in white gold with matching chain, she went to the jewelry armoire and placed the precious remembrance in a velvet-lined drawer in which lay various other precious gems. She locked the drawer with a key that was tucked into a pouch inside another jewelry case.

She stepped back and sighed deeply, but without tears this time. It was over. There would be no more tears shed for the dead. She thought of her father and the great fun they had after his and her failed marriages. She and her father both lived in West L.A. at the time. She thought of her mother and all the wonderful teachings and Indian folklore she had passed on to Rachel those few years before she died. She thought of Ethan and his bouncy, vibrant self that attracted her in the first place, ending in a friendship instead of a love affair. And she thought of how much she and Pete had loved each other. All good memories. Something she could hold on to.

But they had all passed on to another life. They were gone now. And she knew she would meet them all again, because they were her soulmates, traveling together from lifetime to lifetime. It was how it had always been and always would be. Now Belinda was in that number. This she chose to believe, because it made it easier, knowing she'd be with them all again.

Rachel was standing in the driveway when Dudley pulled up at seven thirty that Monday morning. He put her bags in the car and off they went.

She arrived early afternoon in Brussels to an excited Mandy and Richard Miller shouting and waving beyond the customs section. It was so good to see them; she hadn't realized how much she'd missed their happy faces till she saw them grinning from ear to ear. They exuded happiness, wreaked of it.

"You look terrific, Rachel," Mandy said as she hugged her friend.

"And look at you, you're pregnant? You didn't tell me?"

"We wanted to surprise you," Richard said as he took his turn to hug Rachel. "It's a boy! We're going to have a boy."

"No wonder you're so radiant. I saw the glow from way back there."

Richard took her bags - a satchel and a roller bag. "You travel light."

"Finally learned how to do that." She laughed. "I FedExed a package to you, though. Did you get it yet?"

"Yes, it came this morning," Mandy answered. "It said not to open, so we didn't. What is it?"

"It's a surprise."

"Come this way," Richard said. "Are you hungry? We'll have lunch in town if you'd like?"

"I'd really love to go to our favorite café, you know, The Roy at the Grand Place. I've missed that so much. We went there almost every day when we were getting the shop ready to open. Remember?"

Mandy grabbed Rachel's hand. "Oh boy, do I! How could I ever forget all the stuff we did to get that shop up and running." She laughed.

"So how's it going, the opening of the new one?" Rachel asked.

"Great. We're all set for Saturday. I'm so glad to have you here, Rachel. I can't tell you."

Rachel stopped walking and turned to hug Mandy again. "I wouldn't miss it! And I'm thrilled to be here, honey, I really am. I've so much to tell you."

They began walking again, taking an exit to the parking garage.

"What is this I hear about Maxim being married?" Richard asked.

"Well, he is. He was married all that time he said he was a widower. Can you believe that?"

Mandy added, "But his wife just died, right? So now he is a widower."

"Yep." Rachel said quietly.

"He knows you're here, you're aware of that?" Richard said. "He's been calling."

"I figured he would, Della knows I'm here." She laughed. "I'm sure she told him. She's hoping we'll get together."

"Oh, I'd love to meet that Della, she sounds so much fun. And Anastasia, Maxim's sister, when is she coming? You said you might bring her with you one of these times. I can't wait to see some of her designs. You tell her she can put them in my stores if she wants."

Rachel loved Mandy's exuberance; she was one of the most energetic and ambitious young people she knew. The girl was unstoppable. Here she was pregnant and even before she had opened her second shop; she was planning for a third one in Bruges.

"Well, I don't know when she can make it. We'll see. So when is the baby due?" Rachel wasn't ready to get into all the nitty gritty of the Russian faction, she would do that later. Right now she just wanted to absorb and get caught up with the Miller family.

"Baby's due in August," Mandy replied.

"Here we are. Go ahead and get into the car, I'll take care of the bags."

"Rachel, you sit in the front seat, I'll take the back," Mandy was already opening the back door and stepping in.

"You don't have to do that, Mandy. I can sit in the back."

"No, you're our guest."

Rachel had to marvel at how the two were so compatible; it hadn't changed a bit, if anything their love was deeper. And now they were having a baby.

Mandy was a late bloomer, in her twenties, tall and lanky, long straight blond hair. She had the look of Gweneth Paltrow. Richard was in his forties, also tall and slim, but muscular, graying blond hair, blue eyes. He adored Mandy, had pursued her for months before she gave in to his insistence that she marry him. His daughter from a previous relationship married his foreman and the two of them were running his cattle ranches in California. In all he owned twenty-two ranches throughout the country. This would be his first son.

Mandy's ex-husband had disappeared on a Christmas Day in the seventh year of their marriage, leaving her penniless, without any means of support and without a vehicle. It had been a desperate time for her, to say the least, but she recovered within a year and never looked back. She pursued a dream and a vision and here she was in Brussels, Belgium, a lacemaker, clothing designer, shop owner. It was incredible, a poor little girl from the Ozarks in Arkansas ending up where she was now.

Mandy had saved her money, waitressing, and had come to Belgium for a holiday, with the intention of finding work, and possibly staying. One thing led to another, she went to the lacemaking school at the Kancentrum in Bruges, began selling lace aprons, and that was the beginning of a new life for her.

Richard had met Mandy in the restaurant where she was a waitress in California and after she left he couldn't bear living without her. So a few months later he appeared on her doorstep in Belgium, prepared to do anything to convince her to marry him.

Now they were married and lived outside of Brussels in what they called their camellia castle. And it actually had been a castle at one time, beautiful camellia gardens still. All of Mandy's dreams had come true. And now she was going to have a baby.

Mandy and Rachel had first met in Bruges, an hour west of Brussels, at the historic Craenenburg in the *Grote Markt*.

But today they entered the *Grand Place* in Brussels and were glad the Le Roi d'Espagne, The Roy, as they called it, wasn't as busy as usual.

The same waiter that had been their daily waitperson during the weeks Rachel was there before was on duty, his eyes brightened when he saw them enter.

Later in the afternoon at the Miller manor, or rather, Miller's Camellia Gardens Estate, 'la-di-dah' as Mandy would say, Richard poured a glass of champagne for Rachel, then got a beer for himself. Mandy was drinking tomato juice.

"He should be arriving any minute now, Rachel," Richard said as he walked to one of the giant diamond-paned windows that looked out towards the long drive from the main road. "In fact here he comes."

Rachel was nervous. She hadn't seen Maxim since before she left Moscow on New Year's Day - over five months ago. She still wasn't sure how she felt about him, it was all very confusing. But she did know she had to be calm for everybody else's sakes and just pretend all was well and that they were still friends, no matter what. One thing she had to do, she had to be in control of her emotions. She could do it. She was getting better at it lately.

263

The butler ushered Maxim into the parlor where they were waiting.

Richard broke the silence by greeting Maxim and putting his arm around his shoulders, leading him to Rachel.

When Maxim saw Rachel he extended his arms and she went to him. "Ah, my dear Rachel, I am in heaven now that I see you." He held her in an embrace for a few moments and then kissed her lightly on the lips.

She felt a thrill surge through her body, and pulled back to look into his handsome face that was in the process of melting her heart. "You are such a charmer." She leaned forward and returned the kiss. "I'm glad to see you too." *Something about this man . . .*

They wined and dined at the estate until late in the evening. Maxim and Richard talked about business for over an hour in the study at one point, while Rachel and Mandy went onto the veranda to relax and enjoy the soothing music of Diana Krall and Michael Buble wafting through the French doors.

"So what do you think of Maxim selling his home in Brussels?" Mandy asked.

"It really doesn't matter to me what he does." Rachel took a sip of her drink. "I don't mean that harshly, I just mean it's up to him, not really my concern."

Mandy sat thoughtfully for a moment then asked, "Do you love him, Rachel?"

Rachel sighed. "I don't know, Mandy. I honestly don't know. Something is holding me back."

"Could be you're still hurt that he didn't tell you the truth. You loved him before you found out, right?"

"I thought I did. But now I'm not so sure. Life has changed since then."

"Well, what is it you want, Rachel?" Mandy asked.

"I want— "

Richard and Maxim stepped into the cool night air, carrying their drinks.

"Here they are. Out here, gossiping," Richard said before he bent down and kissed Mandy's forehead.

Maxim sat in a chair next to Rachel. "Are you warm enough, shall I get you a wrap?"

"I'm fine, thank you. Have you two solved all the problems of the world?" Rachel asked with a grin.

Richard sat next to Mandy. "Oh yes, we did that most assuredly."

They all laughed and smiled, but were feeling an awkward moment.

"Maxim was just telling me if he retires completely and sells the Brussels house he may buy in Paris." Richard looked at Rachel.

"Really? I have a place in Paris, Maxim, as you know. In Montmartre. Will we be neighbors?' she asked cautiously, not sure if that appealed to her or not.

"I would want to be in the country. City life is too much for me on a daily basis. Too crowded. I must have space around me with gardens and trees. So Montmartre would be out of the question, I'm afraid."

Mandy was the only one who saw Rachel breathe a sigh of relief.

As the evening passed and conversation and laughter wore them down, it came time to call it a night.

Richard invited Maxim to stay and join them for brunch around noon, and Maxim accepted.

Mandy stood up and hugged Maxim. "Your room is ready; it's the first door on the left on the second floor. The Purple Iris room, name's on the door. I hope you rest well."

Rachel was impressed at Mandy's new manners and use of the English language. When they'd first met she still was that endearing shy girl from the Ozarks using *ain't* and *y'all* in every sentence. One thing about Mandy, when she put her mind to something, she accomplished it in a blink of an eye. She wanted to improve her speech and she did just that.

"Good night, Rachel," Mandy said as she hugged her friend.

"Good night, honey. See you in the morning, or rather later this morning."

They laughed.

"Good night to you both," Richard said and he and his wife turned and left the veranda arm in arm.

"Let's go inside, shall we?" Maxim took Rachel's glass and his own and led the way. "It's getting a bit chilly out here. Do you mind if we talk some more?"

"Sure. I'm quite awake, not tired at all." She moved to a settee near the piano.

He filled their glasses and joined her. "Tell me about your new novel."

"Well, it's about a young woman in Montana who leaves the family ranch after her mother is murdered to start a career in Hollywood. Not as a starlet, but as a screenwriter."

"Are all your heroines writers?"

"I guess they are, in some sense of the word, sometimes they're journalists, or novelists, or as in my new novel, a screenwriter. Writing what you know is the key to creating believable fiction." Rachel took a sip while staring at the man before her. Not many men would even show an interest in her writing, much less know about the heroines. "Have you read any of my novels?"

"Yes, all three of them." He lifted her hand and kissed it. "I kiss the hand of a very talented woman."

Rachel caved. Why couldn't she love this man? What would be wrong with it?

"My love, I wish to explain something to you. Would you please allow me?"

"What is it?"

"About my wife."

"There isn't any need to explain. I know the story. Della told me." She pulled her hand from his grasp and placed one of the small sofa pillows on her lap, a sure-fire defense tactic. "What else is there to say?"

"I want to tell you how I felt about her. I did love her when we married many years ago. She was beautiful and a bright spot in my life. We did everything together. She helped me in the business; it was her father's you know, before he died. She supported me when I needed her. She was right beside me when money was scarce. But when she could not have children, she withdrew from me. Slowly over the years she became a recluse and an alcoholic, let herself go, weighed over 200 pounds and could barely walk. I couldn't get through to her. Nothing I would say or do could bring her out of the hole she had dug for herself. She became mean and violent towards me. I began to stay away; I lived in Moscow while she lived in Brussels. I felt helpless, felt guilty that I couldn't help her. And now—" He turned away and cleared his throat.

Rachel reached for his hand. "Maxim, please stop. Don't talk about it. It's too painful for you still, I can see that. You needn't tell me."

"But I want you to understand that I was afraid, I was afraid you would walk away if you knew the truth."

"You were right. That's exactly what I did. I made a vow to myself never to be involved with a married man." Her eyes filled with tears when she glimpsed a tear on his cheek. Seeing someone else cry did it to her every time. If they cried, she cried. Didn't matter what the reason. She reached up and blotted his tears with her finger tips, as Baby Jake had blotted hers. "Don't cry, Maxim. Please don't."

Her gentleness got to him, that's all it took. His chin quivered with suppressed emotion as he spoke, "I love you,

Rachel. I do not want to be without you." He grabbed her and held her so tight she couldn't breathe.

Finally, he released his hold on her. "I'm sorry." He kissed her on the forehead and stood up. "I am so sorry this has happened. You must think very little of me for sniveling like a child and being such a brute. Please forgive me." He took a handkerchief from his pocket and wiped his eyes and face as he left the room before Rachel could say anything.

She was stunned. She stood and poured another glass of champagne, wondering why she wasn't feeling the effects of all she'd drank that night. She felt stone cold sober.

When the house awoke later in the morning, Maxim was gone. He had slipped a note for Rachel under her door.

It read:

My dearest Rachel,

I understand your rejection of me. I am not worthy of your love, I understand that now. Please let us remain friends. I will not impose myself upon you in the future. By the time you read this, I will have left for Moscow. I beg that this does not interfere with your plans to come to the wedding next month. Della and Valentin are looking forward to you being the maid of honor.

As Always, Maxim Ballenchine

Rachel wept.

Chapter 52

May and June in Cornwall could be hot as hell, if one believes in that kind of hell - fiery hell way down somewhere. And this June was no exception.

Rachel was wearing a halter top and a pair of shorts, barefoot, and lounging on one of her new lawn chairs on the main deck of the Newland house (which is what she called it, in honor of Paul and Belinda Newland). She was reading a magazine. A tall glass of homemade pink lemonade was sitting on the glass table beside her. Maraschino cherries gave it the pink color and the extra-tasty sweetness.

She rested the magazine face down on her lap and closed her eyes behind oversize prescription sunglasses, thinking about what she'd just read. It was an article by her dear friend Della Doheny. Her first published article about the diamond trade in Russia. It was absolutely fascinating and Della had captured the true story without posing a threat to the Ballenchine Brothers.

Rachel reached for her cell phone and called Della in Moscow.

"Della, I just read it. It's terrific. You got it right," she said as soon as Della said hello. "I mean, it is fabulous!"

"Oh, thank you. I'm so glad you like it. Thank you so much. I did what you suggested, wrote it in first person as an observer. So what do think about how I portrayed the Popov brothers? I'm sure those who are really close to them will get it, will know they're Valentin and Maxim, but for the most part, no one will know."

"You were very clever in telling their story without giving them away. Very clever! I love it. What's next?"

"I'm working on a piece for a travel magazine, would you take a look at it if I email it to you? It's the one about Cornwall."

"I'd love to read it."

"Great, I'll send it as soon as I finish."

"So how're the wedding plans coming along, are you ready?" Rachel reached for the lemonade and sipped.

"I'm really nervous, Rachel. I wish you were here right now; I could use the moral support. Anytime you want to come, your rooms are ready, you know that."

"And how is Maxim?" She hadn't told Della about what had happened in Brussels, or about the note.

"He talks about you all the time, asks if I've heard from you every time I see him. Retirement seems to suit him; you know he's retired, right?"

"He said he was thinking about it."

"Well, he doesn't waste time. He made the decision one day and retired the next. He's sculpting again, beautiful stuff. But he's in Brussels right now. I think he's made up his mind to sell the house there, at least that's what he told Valentino he was going to do. And he's thinking of buying a place in London instead of Paris. I wonder why he's going to London. Any ideas about that?"

Rachel could hear the teasing tone in Della's voice. She laughed.

"I wouldn't know, Della. I haven't talked to him since Brussels. He didn't mention it then, he was still thinking about Paris." She set the glass on the table and rose from the chair to walk to the edge of the stone terrace.

"Well, I think he's trying to get closer to you, that's what I think."

Rachel thought for a moment before answering. "I don't think so."

"Why not? Didn't you get along with him in Brussels?'

"Yep, but—" She turned and walked towards the open patio doors leading into the expansive kitchen.

"He's quite a catch, you know."

Rachel laughed. "I know he is, and that alone is enough for most women. But I'm not most women, Della. Money has never turned my head, has never made a difference. You know that. I know it's nice to have everything one could ever want, money coming out the ying yang, but you know what? That isn't what does it for me. Besides I'm comfortable with what I have, what I can get for myself with no strings attached. And I'm really loving this house now. You should see it, I've added more stuff since you were here. And sure, he's as handsome as they come. But that isn't the most important thing in a relationship, either. It's got to come from the heart and soul. Like it did with Pete. I loved that man. He didn't have money, and he wasn't pretty, either. We had fun together. We were like teenagers. I want that back. I want to have silly fun as well as all the rest. It took me a while to find out how much I loved Pete, and I realized it almost too late. He made me feel like I was the only woman in his world, and that is what's most important, Della. Like Valentin makes you feel."

"I believe Maxim truly loves you, Rachel. Please don't wait till it's almost too late with him too. Don't mark him off, yet. Will you promise me that?"

271

"Well, there certainly aren't any other men pounding down my door. And I'm not out there looking, so— anyway, send me the article and I'll get back to you later. Okay, luv?"

"All right, and we'll see you in a couple. How's your book coming along?"

"It's formulating. I think I'll go to California this fall. You know my son lives in Brentwood now and we're partners in a construction business, it might be a good time to go there for a couple months and check on business while I soak up inspiration for my next novel. I might put my heroine in Malibu. That would be a terrific setting, don't you think? Lots of rich people there, lots of sexy, sordid stories. I'm sure I can conjure up a murder or two." She laughed as she ran a brush through her hair. "I've got to go, Della. I'm meeting Paul and Dudley for lunch. Paul's here for the weekend finalizing the paperwork on this house."

"You going to the Ship Inn in Mousehole for lunch?"

"Absolutely."

"Say hi to Gina for me, will you? She was hilarious."

"I will."

"Okay, luv. Talk to you later. Love you. Bye."

"Love you, too. And give a hug to Valentin for me. Bye."

Rachel stood thoughtfully for a moment, smiling. She missed Della. She really did.

Quickly she changed into a pair of jeans and her standard black T-shirt, slipped into sandals, grabbed her purse and was out the door in a flash.

Chapter 53

Her heart always skipped a beat when Paul came into view. From the first moment when she and Ethan had stood waiting for a taxi outside the Ritz in London the eve of the Millennium, when Paul had bolted through the hotel's doors and their eyes met and held for what seemed like forever, he had that effect on her. It seemed that everywhere she and Ethan were that weekend in London, there was Paul.

And then when she ran into him and Belinda two months later in Cornwall on the walk between Newlyn and Penzance, that's when their special friendship began. It was meant to be. That's the way it happens with soulmates.

They'd talked about the coincidences or more accurately, fate, surrounding their lives in Cornwall. Paul too felt they were part of a group traveling together from lifetime to lifetime as soulmates. Whether they were first layer or third layer soulmates was yet to be determined.

According to the theory, as Rachel's mother had explained to her, being the spiritual teacher that she was, soulmates are friends and lovers with whom you've shared previous lives. There are companion soulmates and twin

273

soulmates. Companion soulmates are those who you feel good about, who help you in reaching a goal or accomplishing a specific purpose. Twin soulmates are those you've shared a special bond in many lifetimes and you feel completely natural and open with them. You immediately feel comfortable with them and you pick up where you left off in a previous past life. And it isn't uncommon for a companion soulmate to become a twin soulmate at one point.

Sometimes Rachel felt Paul might be her ultimate soulmate - her twin flame soulmate, her one and only.

'There is only one who is your perfect counterpart,' her mother had told her.

But then Rachel thought her twin flame could also be Pete, not to mention Ethan, but especially Pete. Both had been a huge part of her life, and she had felt good with each of them. She wished she had the vision to see it as it was before, to see which one was that one person for whom she was created and with whom she would eventually feel complete and fulfilled in the final lifetime together. Her thoughts shifted to Maxim. She wondered how he fit in the equation.

But all thoughts of Maxim, Pete, and Ethan immediately dropped from her mind as she opened the door of the Ship Inn and saw Paul sitting with Dudley at the bar.

The sunlight beamed on Paul, making it appear as if he were in a spotlight. He looked ethereal, spiritual, as if he should be wearing robes of an angel. His shoulder length blond hair and startling blue eyes seemed brighter than ever. *He* seemed brighter than ever. Rachel was hypnotized on the spot. It had been several weeks since she'd seen him.

"Rachel, come here," Paul stood and held out his arms towards her. "Are you all right?"

She quickly gathered her wits and moved forward. "Oh my goodness you look good! How are you, Paul?" She hugged him heartily and moved to Dudley to give him a lesser version of a hug. "Dudley, you clean up pretty good too, my man."

"For you, I do," Dudley said as he reddened and chuckled.

Paul directed her to a stool between them. "Let's have a drink before we move to a table for lunch. Is that okay with you?"

"Of course," she replied.

"So, you're writing another novel, I hear," Dudley said.

"Yep, set in the States this time. I'm going to California for a few months this fall to do research."

"Did you finish the one about Moscow? About the diamond mines?" Paul asked.

"Actually, no. I've set it aside until I can go back. I usually have two or three projects going at the same time anyway, so I'm just going to work on one of the others for now." She poked Paul on the arm. "And you are painting up a storm again, I hear."

They both glanced at Dudley, their purveyor of news and updates between them.

"I just happened to have finished what might be my best yet, I'm told." Paul signaled the bartender for the bottle of champagne he'd pre-ordered. "I have a meeting with the art distributor on Tuesday, we'll see how it goes. Living in London makes it much easier for me, I must say. Did you sell the cottage?"

"No, I decided to keep it. Am renting it out to a nice little old lady who's on a pension. Perfect for her. And she loves my garden." She took a sip of her drink. "So are you really happy in London, Paul?"

"Yes, for the most part. The boys are glad to be there with their granny. And like I said, it makes it easier for me to go about my business, having her right there to help. And now she doesn't have to neglect her hotel, either. The boys will be in school soon and that will free up her time considerably. And mine too. Speaking of the boys they send their love and said they miss you terribly."

"I miss them, too. Tell them that. And I'll come spend a week with them before I go to the states."

"They'll love that. So will I."

Rachel averted her glance to the glass of champagne that was being poured for her.

Paul spoke up, "So let's make a toast to us. C'mon Dudley, you can have one glass, can't you? If I can, you can, being the hopeless reformed alcoholics that we are." Paul held his glass in the air.

"I shouldn't, but I will take a sip. Nothing more, mind you. Can't start up the whole business again, you know. Took me too long to get off the bloody works as it was."

"Hey, I've been drinking lemonade and herbal teas more and more lately, I was drinking too much champagne there for a while. Drinking it like water. So I've cut back on it. Now I have it for special occasions only," Rachel added. "So, we'll all watch each other today, and slap hands if we overdo, or immediately go to an AA meeting."

They laughed together for the first time in months. It had been eons since they'd been their old selves. Since before Belinda's illness.

"So, Dudley. Are you taking that holiday you were talking about last time I saw you?" Rachel slapped his knee.

"I bloody well am. Leaving on Monday, going to Spain for some rock hunting in the mountain streams, and will be in Pamplona for the running of the bulls."

"You aren't going to run with them, please tell me you're not." Rachel clenched his shoulder.

"That would surely be the end of it, I can bloody well guarantee you of that," Paul said with a chuckle.

"No, I'm not going to Spain to kill myself, or to become a bloody drunk again. I've a few more years left in me. Have to be here to take care of my godchildren now, don't I? Which reminds me, I'll be taking them to Pamplona one day, Paul, when they're old enough. Just want you to get used to the idea ahead of time."

"You will not, I won't let you," Rachel said. "Over my godmother dead body, that's for sure."

"Then you'll have to go with us, won't she, Paul?"

"Good idea! We'll all go together, that's a date. Alright with you, Rachel? When they're old enough?"

Rachel shook her head, looking back and forth from Paul to Dudley, her eyes sparkling, feeling her happiest sitting at the bar in the Ship Inn with the two of them. They provoked feelings no one else could. Feelings of comfort, contentment, safety, friendship, love . . . yes, love. She felt it emanating from them, and she willingly gave it in return.

She set her glass on the bar and stretched one arm around Paul's neck, the other around Dudley's and almost pulled them off their bar stools.

"I love you guys," she said as she squeezed them close together in the crooks of her arms. "I love ya."

Paul slipped his arm around her waist and whispered in her ear.

She wasn't sure, because the noise level was so high in the pub, but she thought he said, "I love you, too." He couldn't have meant it the way it sounded. And it was surely in the same spirit she said it, not as she thought it sounded. Surely not.

Chapter 54

It was June in Moscow. The weather was sweltering, reaching nearly a hundred degrees. Because of the high humidity, it seemed to be hotter than it actually was. Being landlocked always made Moscow summers uncomfortable in the city for the over ten million inhabitants, smog was prevalent, so most people would head out to the countryside to be near bodies of water as often as they could.

But the trees were green and the summer gardens were in full bloom, including the Alexander Gardens along the Kremlin walls, Bitsevski Park with its hundreds of species of trees and plants, the Moscow Botanical Garden and its 20,000 different species of plants, a wonder to behold . . . and other gardens throughout the city.

But out in the countryside away from it all, Maxim Ballenchine's gardens were spectacular. He practically dwelled in his gardens where blossoms appeared year 'round. Now more than ever, being retired from Ballenchine Brothers Inc., he would work with the gardeners, tending the roses especially, a carry-over from his dear, departed mother. She loved gardening and cooking - paving the way for Maxim and his love of gardens and Valentin's love of food.

For the wedding Maxim had made special plantings of chamomile, azaleas, orchids, roses, lilies, gerbera daisies, chrysanthemums, and carnations in gigantic containers leading up the drive to the portico and spaced all around the perimeter of the mansion. The flower-filled verandas at the back of the mansion were set up with round tables, umbrellas and chairs, seating ten at each table, and would be used for dining after the wedding. Containers of flowers were also placed along the driveway to the cottage where Valentin and Della lived.

The plan was to have the bride delivered by horse and carriage from the cottage to the main house where Valentin would be waiting at the door. The ceremony would take place in the grand ballroom that had been converted to accommodate two hundred seated guests. After the wedding the chairs would be removed from the ballroom and there would be dancing with a live band. Dinner would be served on the verandas at dusk.

Rachel had arrived early that morning and was with Della at the cottage. Valentin was already with Maxim at his house on the huge country estate.

The wedding was scheduled to begin in two hours, at three in the afternoon.

"Do you have the ring, Maxim?"

Both brothers were wearing full-dress gray tuxedos, tails, cummerbunds, pleated silk shirts and wide bow ties. They looked as if they had stepped right off the pages of a high-end fashion magazine.

Maxim said to his nervous brother, "How many times are you going to ask me if I have the ring?" he laughed. "Yes, yes, yes. I have the ring. Look." He reached into his waist pocket and pulled out the ring. "Here it is. It is right here in my pocket."

"I am so afraid something will go wrong. I want this to be perfect for Della." He hugged Maxim. "I love you, my brother. I love you." He couldn't hold back the tears; he reached for a handkerchief in his pocket. "I am so emotional today. I think of our mama and papa, how happy they would be that I am to be married."

"I have a surprise for you." Maxim reached into his jacket inside pocket and pulled out an envelope. "My wedding gift to you, my brother."

Valentin opened the envelope to a travel itinerary with hotel reservations and airline tickets to Paris, Rome, London, Dublin, and New York City for the month of July. A check for a generous amount of money was also included.

"For your honeymoon. I was happy you hadn't made any plans yet. I am right, am I?" For a moment he thought maybe Valentin had already made plans.

Finally, Valentin answered, "Yes. I mean, no, no. We have not. We could not decide where to go." He grabbed his brother and hugged him harder than before. "You are dear to me. I can never repay you for the life you have provided for me and the rest of our family. If it weren't for you, I don't know—" His voice broke off and he turned his head, obviously shaken.

"Here, here . . ." Maxim patted Valentin on the back and guided him towards one of the portable bars that had been set up in the shade of the portico for the event. "Let us have a drink to calm us. It is your wedding day, not a time for tears."

After gaining his composure and downing vodka, Valentin excused himself. "I must check on the food, Maxim."

Valentin was using the occasion to advertise his Moscow restaurant that would be opening in December. At Della's insistence, it would be called *Valentino's* - Italian, French, and Russia cuisines would be the specialties. He had already hired the chefs and wait staff for his restaurant and they were on duty today at the wedding. It was a test for them as well as a test for the public's response to the food they prepared and served for dinner.

Guests were already arriving for the wedding and were milling around the entrance and finding seats in the ballroom.

Libation in honor of the bride and groom and hors d' oeuvres were being served by waiters carrying silver trays.

Security was flawless. No one would be able to reach the house carrying a weapon of any kind. When they pulled up to the gate, a valet would take their car from them. Their vehicles were not allowed inside the gates. Parking had been provided across the road in an empty field that had been mowed and graded to accommodate the autos.

Then they had to produce the engraved invitation along with ID at the first checkpoint before entering the gate. They were screened and had to match the photos that were on file with their names. The second checkpoint just inside the gate was a body and weapons scanner, similar to airport screening devices. Then further up the driveway, horse and buggies were waiting to transport the guests to the manor. So they only had to walk a short distance. It was a beautiful touch . . . the horses and carriages . . . period top hats and tuxedos . . . gowns and flowery hats.

One hour before the wedding Anastasia Ballenchine arrived with both her sister Irina from Paris and their brother Leonid who traveled from Switzerland to be there for their older brother's wedding. They had been staying in Moscow rather than at Maxim's house to keep out of the way. They knew it would be a madhouse during wedding preparations, and they were right.

Valentin rejoined Maxim just as their siblings pulled up in the carriage together.

"Ah! Here they are, Valentin! Our family! Our beautiful family!" Maxim rushed to the carriage to greet them, Valentin was right behind him.

Hugs and kisses, tears and laughter were flowing. It was a reunion of the Ballenchine family, and it had been years since they were all together. There was Irina Ballenchine, who Maxim had sent to business school in Paris after a failed marriage to a crook; Leonid, the youngest brother, who was a college professor in Switzerland - Maxim had paid for Leonid's schooling. And, of course, Anastasia, who Maxim had encouraged and helped in her design business that was now going strong. All five of the Ballenchine family members, successful, and together again.

And now they would greet a new member into the fold - Valentin's American bride Della. It was a wonderful occasion. New beginnings all around.

Chapter 55

Rachel was in awe of Della. She was mesmerized with how she looked in her wedding gown, how her brilliant Irish red curls framed her freckled face, some of her thick tresses had been lifted to fall down her back with the billowy tulle veil fastened to a tiara on top of her head.

"You look like a princess!" Rachel said to Della who was looking into a full-length mirror in her bedroom. "A real princess."

Della's gown had been designed by Anastasia, created to give the illusion of Della being engulfed in a cloud. The full fluffy tulle skirt rose to the ankles in front revealing pearl satin shoes trimmed in lace, then the skirt extended into a five-foot train in back. The upper part of her arms were covered with puffy see-through sleeves with fitted lace from the elbow to points on the back of her hands. Her bodice was studded with a V panel of lace and pearls. A fabulous Anastasia creation. Della fell in love with the design the first time Anastasia showed her the sketch.

"Yea, right, a forty-year old princess. Do you think it's a bit tight around the middle?" Della said as she smoothed her hands at the waist on the fitted crème-colored silk cummerbund.

"No, it shows off your new tiny waistline. I can't believe you lost that much weight in that short of time. Wow! I need to go on that diet."

"Well, the Spanx helps a lot. It does wonders in smoothing out the rolls." Della laughed and turned to face Rachel. She took Rachel's hands and looked into her face. "Do you think I'm doing the right thing?"

"Della! Come on, I would hope you know whether or not you are doing the right thing by now. You do, don't you?"

Della turned and walked to the window, lifting her billowing skirt as she moved. "I feel I am, but then there's this little niggling thought that it just might not work."

Rachel bent down and straightened the train to trail behind her.

The princess bride stared across the lawn to the north gate. "I've never been married, so I don't know what it's like. It's sort of scary, you know? I think about my parents and how they were so happy then, out of the blue, one day they weren't." She turned around and looked at Rachel. "I love Valentin, I really do. He is the love of my life. But what if he doesn't feel as strong about it as I do? They say that one always loves more than the other. And I don't see how he could love me more than I love him. So that means he loves me less, doesn't it?"

"Della, that's enough. You're driving yourself silly with thoughts like that." She reached for the glasses of champagne that had just been poured by the maid. "Here, let's make a toast to the wedding of a lifetime! To the gorgeous bride and groom and to the happy married life that you've always wanted. It's here, honey, it has arrived. This is what you've wanted, you're already living it. This is what you left New York for, a life in

Russia that you love, with a man that you love, your dream come true."

Della took the glass with tears in her eyes. "You are so right, Rachel O'Neill. What's the matter with me?"

"Buyer's remorse. So drink up!"

Chapter 56

It was time for the wedding.

After helping Della into the carriage seat, Rachel positioned herself in the seat opposite.

Rachel couldn't believe she let herself be talked into wearing a pale blue chiffon gown. Although it did make her feel feminine and young. It had a beaded V panel on the ruched bust, a straight strapless neckline, empire waist, with a flowy, floor-sweeping skirt and fluted hemline. The silk fell in soft fullness, not as full as the bridal gown, not even a tenth as full, just a slight fullness that caused it to flow with movement without touching the body. It was another Anastasia creation.

She wore full-length matching gloves and her broad-brimmed hat was of open-weave straw with flowers and matching pale blue chiffon covering it. Although she didn't ordinarily wear hats, she joined the crowd this time. It was the least she could do for her dear friend, Della, on her very special wedding day.

For a moment Rachel felt like a princess herself. She remembered when she was a girl, growing up in the San Joaquin Valley of California, when she dreamed of being a princess and finding her Prince Charming. At times she had felt like a

Cinderella - motherless, living with a father who didn't care. His third wife turned out to be a wicked stepmother, so she had felt unwanted and unloved even more. She had spent many hours living in her own head, creating a vision of the life she wanted, always believing she would one day meet her Prince and would live happily ever after. She had surrounded herself with volumes of fairytale books and lots of paper doll books. She would use the cutouts as characters in her stories she would tell herself. She'd enact the stories on rolls of plain white shelf paper where she drew castles and villages that filled her imaginary world.

Even today as she sat across from Della riding in the carriage to Maxim's house, there was a moment she imagined she was on her way to marry her own prince charming. But only a moment, because she knew it was idiotic to hang on to adolescent dreams.

She snapped back to reality and immediately began wishing she had worn her comfortable black. Black on black. She always felt conspicuous in colors, bright or pastels.

And my god, a hat! What was I thinking?

"I'm nervous, Rachel." Della put her hands up to her cheeks.

"No, no, no. Don't be. Why would you be nervous?"

"Well, for one thing, I'm the star of the show. I don't particularly like that. Not at all. I'd rather sneak in through the back door and be married behind a screen."

Rachel laughed. "I can't believe you're that nervous."

"Yea, I am. I've always been that way. Never could get up on a stage or be the center of attention. Even running my own company was a challenge, especially at executive meetings or presentations. Just don't like it."

"Well, there won't be any more of those meetings now that you're a full-fledged free-lancer, it's nothing but fun and freedom from here on out. So all you have to do is get through today and then you're home free. Me too. I'm feeling like I want

287

to disappear. I'm so uncomfortable in this color. I need my black."

Della laughed and leaned forward, squeezing Rachel's knee. "You're beautiful in baby blue. You really are. With that body you should wear pastels all the time, show it off."

"Yikes! That's just what I don't want to do."

Maxim and Valentin wearing their top hats, canes hanging from their wrists, were waiting at the entrance when the bride's carriage arrived. Footmen helped the ladies from the buggy and Valentin, beaming, handed Della a lovely bouquet of lilies and orchids encircled with lace and then offered his arm to his lovely bride . . . Maxim, beaming as well, handed Rachel a bouquet of pink and yellow baby rose buds with streaming ribbons and offered his arm to her.

All four entered the manor to music chosen especially for the walk up the newly created aisle in the ballroom. Two hundred people, friends and associates of the Ballenchines, were standing in rows of chairs, turning towards the bride and groom, watching with wide grins, some with teary eyes.

Although it wasn't a traditional Russian Orthodox wedding, and the ceremony wasn't taking place in a church, the bride and groom held to the Russian tradition of standing just inside the entrance while a Russian priest blessed them. Then he handed them lighted candles to carry up the aisle and hold throughout the ceremony.

The four of them, lead by the priest, made their way to the platform in front of the room - the bride and groom carrying candles, the best man and the maid of honor who were the caretakers of the rings.

The Ballenchine siblings, Anastasia, Leonid, and Irina were on the first row, full of emotion, soaking up all the happiness and love that permeated the atmosphere in that moment. They were a close knit family, headed up by Maxim, strong and wise, the protector; second in the sibling line was

Valentin, full of admiration of his older brother but possessing a quiet strength and ambition as well; Irina was the third in the pecking order, also tough and ambitious, knew what she wanted and went for it in Paris; Leonid their youngest brother, loving his professorship in Zurich; and Anastasia, the baby, having at last found love and carving out a successful niche in the fashion industry. A proud family was the Ballenchines, and they were most proud of their Valentin on this his wedding day.

The traditional Russian wedding normally included the betrothal ring ceremony, the rings being put on the right hands of the bride and groom, followed by the crowning ceremony - each having a crown placed upon the head and entering into a procession with the priest. But they had decided to forego all that and opted to mix it up a bit, using a few American and Russian traditions, but not all of both.

An Irish Catholic priest joined the Russian Orthodox priest standing on the riser before the bride and groom. They took turns reading scriptures in their native tongues, and then Della and Valentin were asked to profess that they were marrying of their own free will and that they had not promised themselves to another.

After that, the priests took the candles and placed them in ornate candelabras standing behind them on each side of the stage.

Then the ring ceremony took place. The Russian priest directed Valentin to put the ring on Della, and the Irish priest directed Della to put the ring on Valentin's finger. The bands were identical, ornately etched platinum.

Two prayers followed, one by each priest, and then the sharing of a "common cup" of wine by the bride and groom.

The Russian priest blessed them once more and then motioned to them to kiss.

It was a soft, loving, passionate kiss and embrace. The guests oohed and ahhed for a good reason, for the bride and groom were obviously in love and they were obviously meant for each other. They emanated their passion and affection for one another without even trying. It was truly real.

The Irish priest stepped down from the platform off to the side and gestured with both hands towards the bride and groom while saying to the guests, "Ladies and gentlemen, I give you, a match made in heaven, Mr. and Mrs. Valentin Ballenchine!"

Music and applause filled the room.

Later, after the breaking of the glasses ritual, cutting and serving of the cake, the first dance as man and wife, and the rest of the reception, Rachel removed her hat and made her way to a shaded table in a corner of the veranda, outside the library doors. She needed to get away from the noise and she found a spot where she felt peaceful, sipping champagne and watching other guests stroll the grounds, laughing and talking. It had been the first chance to get away from the crowd and be quiet in her own thoughts.

How she admired Maxim, regardless of the lie he had told her. Something within her always cringed and fought against anyone who lied to her, and she had come to the conclusion only recently that it probably had stemmed from the lie her father told her all those years ago about her mother's death, and the lies of her two husbands. But she realized she couldn't forever mistrust because of it.

And in spite of it all, and in spite of Maxim's lie about being a widower, she knew he was a good human being. He was loving and kind to his family and friends. Even while his wife was alive, he did all he could to make her life livable and to save her, Rachel knew that. She could even understand and couldn't blame him for finding solace elsewhere. There wasn't anything Rachel could see that was negative about him now. Nothing.

And now that he was retired, he was away from the dangerous, life-threatening business dealings that had been thrust upon him. She believed he even had had his own brand of exemplary ethics; he would never intentionally harm anyone, even in his dealings with the Russian Mafioso. On the contrary, he was his own man. Did it his own way. And she admired him for that. She did. Both he and Valentin were amazing men. Della was lucky to marry into that family. And they were lucky to get her.

She was feeling a little depressed when a server came through the open doors from the library carrying a tray of filled champagne glasses. Rachel handed him her empty, he gave her a full one. As he turned to go back into the library, Maxim walked through the doorway.

"Ah, there you are, Rachel. Mind if I join you?" he asked.

"Please do," she said. They hadn't spoken at any great length at all. It had been all about the wedding and Maxim had been the perfect host, tending to the guests. They hadn't spoken before the wedding, either.

Rachel arrived that morning at the north gate where Della had met her to let her in, and then they went directly to the cottage to dress for the wedding. She hadn't seen Maxim until he took her arm before the nuptials and they followed Della and Valentin into the ballroom.

"You are lovelier than ever," he said as he lifted her hand and kissed it. "Blue is your color."

"My goodness, that just tops off my day," she said with a smile. "I've never seen such a wedding, Maxim . . . so much charm and elegance. A fairy-tale wedding. I love the elegant, old-world feel you created, having everybody dress the part. It was perfect. I was just sitting here thinking about it all. It was beautiful."

"I am happy you approve," he said as he leaned back in his chair and looked over his drink at her while sipping, seeming to stare straight through her eyes into her soul. He felt as if he was walking on eggshells. "Della tells me you have moved from your lovely cottage to a larger home in Newlyn."

"Yep. Actually you know the house, it belonged to Paul and Belinda. He and the boys are living in London now. I bought the house and rented mine out."

"I can imagine how cozy you have made it, if it's anything like your cottage."

Rachel hesitated, and then said, "You'll have to come see for yourself."

"Is that an invitation?"

"It is. So I understand you are sculpting now that you've retired."

"Yes, I have decided to do it again. I don't know how far I will go with it, but for now it is working for me. However, I had forgotten how difficult it is, so I do not know if I want to work that hard." He grinned at Rachel; his eyes glancing discreetly over her body from head to toe. "And how is your new novel coming along?"

"Oh, the writing is flowing. I'll be going to California this fall to do some research for it."

He shifted his gaze out across the gardens and took another sip of vodka. "But will you be coming to Russia to finish your novel about diamond mining before you go?" he asked, waiting for an answer, not wanting her to know that he was disappointed by what she had just said.

Rachel heard the shift in his voice; it was almost as if he had suddenly become sad. Up to that point he had been bright and happy. "I don't know," she said.

Maxim stood and reached for her hand. "Come with me, please. I want to show you something." He led her into the library and up a hidden stairway behind one of the bookcases to another floor. They entered what had to be a bedroom that was a self-contained apartment unto itself. There was a seating area, an entertainment center in an alcove, a giant bed with swaged draperies surrounding it, an ornate bar area, the room was actually a rotunda. It jutted out from the rest of the rooms on that floor, had a roof of its own. They walked out onto the balcony that overlooked the veranda below where they had been sitting.

"Wow! This is something else."

"It is my special bedroom. This is where I spend most of my time when I am at home alone. My desk is in the alcove, my computer. Everything is here that I need. No one can bother me here. There is only one doorway and it locks itself." He looked at her for a moment without speaking and then lowered his eyes and turned away, appearing to watch the guests on the veranda below.

She had read his eyes, knowing he wanted to say something but was having trouble saying it. She touched his arm, "Maxim—"

He turned and looked at her, tears glistening on his cheeks, his chin quivering.

It took Rachel completely by surprise. She reached up and held his chin with her hand. "Maxim, what is it? Why are you crying?"

He set his glass on the balustrade and took her glass and placed it next to his. Then he put his arms around her waist and looked into her eyes. "I am sad because you are going away. You are going back to England, to America, to everywhere else, but not to me. I can't help myself, Rachel, I love you. I wanted you to see my room so you can visualize me here, heartbroken without you."

Rachel rose to her toes tilting her face to his. "Kiss me, Maxim. Please kiss me."

He wrapped his arms tightly around her, lifted her, and with a guttural moan he kissed her lips, her chin and her neck, all in one passionate swoop.

He loosened his grip till her feet touched the floor and their lips found each other again, this time in excessive fervor, and Rachel knew, right then and there, at that exact moment, she was in love with Maxim. Nothing else mattered in all the world. She loved him. That's all there was to it. Her heart felt as if it would burst.

"Rachel, my darling Rachel . . . I don't know what I will do without you." He picked her up in his arms and carried her to his bed. "Do not be afraid, I will not make love to you. Let us please just lay next to each other for a few minutes, my darling. I need to feel close to you. I will not impose myself." He removed his coat and tie, unbuttoned his collar.

Rachel kicked off her shoes and didn't resist, they lay in an embrace, exchanging kisses and caresses that reached momentum almost to the point of no return.

Maxim finally pulled himself away and sat up on the edge of the bed. He took deep breaths as he ran his hands through his hair then smoothed his clothing. "We need to get back to our guests." Then he turned and offered his hand to her.

She didn't move or take his hand. "So what if . . . ," she said, still lying on the bed. "What if I do fall in love with you, what then?"

His heart skipped a beat. It skipped ten beats. He immediately stretched across the bed and took her face in his hands. "Is it true? Do you love me?" His voice cracked and his eyes told on him, not only was he afraid to ask the question, he was afraid to hear the answer.

"So what if I do?" she smiled and planted a light kiss on his nose.

"Rachel, you must tell me. Please, no more teasing." A reluctant grin was beginning to spread across his face. "Do you love me?"

"Yes. I do. You win. You got me. Now what?"

He actually rolled over, stood up on the bed and jumped up and down on it; as if it were a trampoline and he was a child.

She would not have ever imagined a grown man, the size and age of Maxim, especially Maxim, jumping on the bed like a wild little kid.

She laughed so hard she cried.

He finally stopped and pulled her up into his arms and they both stood in the middle of the bed, laughing and gazing into each other's eyes.

Maxim was out of breath. "Now I am happy," he said. "We will work it out, you will see. No need to worry."

Rachel couldn't stop giggling, she wanted to find Della and tell her what had just happened. She felt like the little kid Maxim had mimicked jumping up and down on the bed. She nuzzled under his chin, and planted kisses on his sexy, hairy chest where he had unbuttoned his shirt.

He held her tightly as he rested his chin on top of her soft curls and closed his eyes, absorbing the thrill of her kisses. "Will you marry me, my darling?" he whispered.

Rachel thought of her mother Lily, about the advice Lily had given her, about Rachel first loving herself and living happily and healthy, about how, then, and only then, true love would find her. Her true soulmate would find her. And then she thought about how Maxim kept coming back into her life, and how they had met by chance that New Year's Eve in Brussels, but seemed to know each other so well, what were the chances of that ever happening? And how he appeared at a time when she needed him desperately, and he needed her.

Rachel leaned back and looked up at Maxim's worried expression. Obviously she was taking too long to answer his question.

"Will you marry me?" he asked again, frowning.

She hesitated before saying: "Uh, when?"

"You are driving me mad." He laughed as he helped her off the bed and they stood and swayed in each other's arms. "So is that a 'yes'?"

"Yes."

"Yes? *Yes?*"

"Yes."

He feigned a faint and fell on the floor, spread eagle.

Rachel swooned on top of him and they rolled in laughter back and forth across the Persian carpet.

"I love you more than I have loved anyone else," he said to her as they stopped rolling, exhausted and breathing hard, but still wrapped around each other.

"And I love you like I have never loved anyone else," she said, and she meant it with all her heart.

Maxim and Rachel entered the ballroom downstairs, arm in arm. They were acting like a couple of young lovers.

Della watched as her dear friend and brother-in-law went up on the stage and stood by while the singer finished her song.

Valentin moved to Della. "What do you think they are doing?" he said to her.

When the music stopped, Maxim reached for the microphone.

Anastasia joined the newlyweds watching what was to unfold. Leonid and Irina had been talking to friends across the room, but they became silent when the music stopped and joined the crowd who were quizzically staring at Maxim and Rachel on the platform. All the celebratory toasts had been made a couple hours before, what could be coming next?

Maxim looked out over the crowd and motioned to Della and Valentin. "First I want to say that dinner will be served on the verandas in thirty minutes. Our restaurateur Valentin Ballenchine of the soon to be *Valentino's* in Moscow is providing the cuisine. *Prijatnovo appetita!*"

The crowd applauded.

Maxim waited for the applause to die down and then took a deep breath before continuing. "Secondly, I do not wish to steal the attention from our beloved bride and groom, but I have something I must tell you that is most important." He put his arm around Rachel and pulled her closer, his breath catching as he looked down at her glow, and said: "Today I have asked this lovely lady, Rachel O'Neill, to be my wife. And she has accepted!" he shouted.

The crowd cheered. Della and Anastasia rushed to the front of the stage screaming and clapping their hands. Valentin joined his younger brother Leonid and sister Irina and together the three of them hurried to the stage too. Everybody was applauding.

Maxim continued. "We do not know when or where this special event will happen, but I am saying to you and to my love, today, my wish is that it will be a Christmas wedding." He replaced the microphone and turned to his bride to be.

He motioned for his valet who hurried onstage and handed him a small dark blue velvet box.

"What is this?" Rachel asked with widened eyes.

"I had this made for you weeks ago." He opened the box and took out a brilliant ten-carat diamond ring set in gold, the center stone surrounded by emeralds. He reached for Rachel's hand and slipped it on her finger.

"Oh, Maxim. It is so beautiful!" Rachel looked up at him with tears in her eyes and said in a soft voice, "I've always wanted a Christmas wedding."

"I know," he whispered. "I know." His eyes were filled with love.

And then they kissed in front of everybody to the resounding *hip-hip-hoorays!* and the *Vashe zdorovies!* that echoed through the grand halls of Ballenchine Manor.

COMINGSOON
Fifth novel in the Series
Midnight in Malibu
Rebecca Buckley

Excerpt:

Allegra scrambled underneath the giant medieval bench and began praying that the perpetrator would not find her as she peered around the folded edge of a seventeenth century Aubusson rug that was draped over it.

Just a few moments before, when she heard glass smashing downstairs, she had bolted out of her Edwardian antique four-poster into the adjoining parlor. Her double wide bedroom doors opened onto the landing above the foyer below, so her automatic reaction was to go into her parlor and then sneak through those doors to the end of the balustrade without being seen, just in case someone was downstairs in the entryway, looking up.

She had slowly opened one door from the parlor onto the carpeted hallway beyond the landing and then had crawled to the far end of the balustrade and its ornate balusters. She saw what appeared to be flashlight rays on the ground floor bouncing off the walls in the library to the left of the dark entryway. The massive, carved wooden doors leading from the front portico and colonnade were ajar, for she could see a sliver of reflection from the outside lights onto the glossy marble floor in the foyer.

She had quickly turned and crawled farther down the corridor before she stood up and ran to the last bedroom on the second floor. Why she had chosen to hide in that particular guest room, she didn't know. It was just a reaction. Maybe it was

1

because it was as far away from the noise as she could get in the part of the house where she was trapped.

She could still hear the rummaging noise that seemed to be going on forever, thuds and things falling, being flung to the floor most likely. She scrunched up even smaller trying to disappear into the darkness beneath her shelter of the bench. The mustiness of the centuries old rug gave her a strange feeling of safety, and her thoughts drifted to the novel she'd been reading about pre-Arthurian times, *The Singing Sword* by Jack Whyte.

Suddenly the noise stopped.

She didn't move.

She could hear footsteps on the marble staircase.

A light came on in the hallway beyond the guestroom door that was slightly open—it hadn't closed securely, and it was too late to close it now.

Please, please, God, don't let them come in here, please!

Allegra was afraid to move, afraid she'd make a noise and was wishing she could stop breathing just in case the intruder could hear her. She could always find her cats in hiding by listening for their purring. Her heart was pounding in her ears so loudly she was sure he or they would be able to hear it if they came into the room.

Now someone was in the room next door.

All she could think of was how her mother must have felt when the same thing had happened to her. She wondered if this was to be a repeat event.

She wished she would have thought to switch off the television in her bedroom and had grabbed her coffee cup and brought it with her. She always drank coffee as she read in bed, and the cup still sat on the bedside table. The home invaders would surely feel the warmth of it and know that someone had just been there. She could bet they had discovered the coffee by now. She couldn't hear what was happening. There wasn't any movement going on.

How she wished that the outside staircase leading from her bedroom veranda to the patio below was usable. The age-old wooden stairway had rotted and fallen away a few months before, and was being rebuilt. She'd hired a contractor to design an elaborate winding staircase with stone steps, but he was slow in getting it done. So, there was no way she could have escaped from the second floor of the house even if she wanted to, while someone was on the first floor. There was only one curved stairway, indoors, leading down from the catwalk around the second floor perimeter above the foyer. Other corridors branched off from it to all the second floor rooms. The stairs leading up to the third floor weren't safe either, they needed to be rebuilt, so hiding up there was out of the question too.

Downstairs, to the left of the entry were the library, an office, and a ballroom and spacious sitting room to the right. A formal dining room was straight across the foyer (under Allegra's bedroom), leading into a family room and a kitchen towards the sunroom and indoor pool. Beyond that were the beach and the Pacific Ocean.

She didn't know how many burglars there were, or whether or not they were male or female. *Burglars are usually male,* she thought to herself as her breath quickened. The thought of a home invasion had always terrified her. ADT was scheduled to install a more effective and elaborate alarm system on Friday, but that was two days away. The burglars must've been able to disarm the existing one, it was so outdated. Her mind was racing. She knew she had locked the doors and windows; she always checked them before she went to bed. Yes, they must've disarmed the security system.

Problem was she'd left her cell phone recharging downstairs on the kitchen counter, a big mistake. She didn't have time to try the house phone in her bedroom, there wasn't one in the guest room, but it didn't matter, she figured they

3

would have cut the lines before entering. Professional burglars would have done that.

Now she could hear movement again, doors opening and closing.

Oh how she wished she'd listened to her big brother Arlie! He had been nagging her over the phone just that week to buy a gun to keep in the house, but she couldn't bring herself to do it. She was thinking that she should have listened to him. If whoever found her under the bench, she'd sure as hell feel much safer if she was lying there pointing a gun up at the bastard prick. If she survived, the first thing she would do tomorrow was to buy a gun. Three houses had been broken into on Hollingsworth Drive during the past month in the upscale gated community of Malibu, which was why her brother had begged her to buy a gun. Burglars were drawn to the area for the valuable pickings. Supposedly security was patrolling more than usual, but obviously not, for they hadn't prevented this break-in.

Someone opened the guestroom door slowly and switched on the light.

Oh God, please don't let this happen to me, too! Mama!

Tears filled her eyes as she blinked hard to clear her vision and thoughts of her mother.

Now she could see a man's shoes through a space between the folds of the rug. They didn't look like the shoes of a low-life crook. They were shiny dress blacks, patent leather, like those worn with a tuxedo. In fact, it looked like a satin stripe on the side of his pants, same as on a tuxedo pair of pants. *He's wearing a tuxedo?* She pressed her body against the wall, making sure there was plenty of space between her and the front of the bench. She was silently thanking her mother for passing on her small genes to her. Her mother had been 4'11", weighed 98 pounds – same as Allegra.

God, why didn't I listen to Arlie and buy a gun? The McAdams had always been a gun family, so it wasn't like

4

Allegra didn't know how to use one. She'd handled guns since she was a pre-teen when she was living at home on the ranch in Montana. She and her brothers had been taught by their father how to shoot when they could hardly hold a gun up to aim. Allegra was a crack shot and usually won first, if not second, in shooting competitions with her brothers and friends in those days. But ever since her mother had been brutally beaten and shot to death two years ago with her own gun, Allegra hadn't owned a gun and didn't want one near her. She felt if the gun hadn't been in the house, her mother might still be alive. Allegra had lived in fear ever since, thinking it could happen to her, too. Now she was having second thoughts, having a gun for protection wasn't such a bad idea.

"Allegra, are you in here? Allegra?"

Allegra's heart stopped. "Connie, is that you?" she squeaked, but didn't move, her body was still stiff with fright.

Connie moved towards the small voice and bent down to lift the edge of the Persian Carpet. "Yes, it's me, darling. Here, let me help you out of there." He shoved the rug off of the heavy ornate bench, and lifted the bench as if it was made of balsa wood. "I was leaving the Hildreth's anniversary party, saw your light upstairs, and then noticed that your front door was standing wide open." He set the bench down and helped Allegra to her feet. "Are you all right?"

Allegra wiped the tears from her eyes with her fingers as she stared up at the tall, handsome man. She collapsed into his arms and sobbed, "I was so afraid, Connie. I didn't know who was in the house. Someone was downstairs, did you see them? I was afraid they were going to come up here and find me. It was awful! All I could think of was my mother. I was afraid they were going to kill me, too."

Her mother's murder had never been solved. It hadn't been a burglary; nothing taken from the ranch house. Allegra's father had died three years before that, so her mother had been running the ranch with the help of Arlie and the ranch hands.

Her youngest brother had been living in New York City since before her father died, so he hadn't been there when his mother was killed. Allan and his father didn't get along once Allan's effeminate ways and his homosexual tendencies became more obvious. So he took off to New York to find himself. Arlie had been pleading with Allegra not to send Allan any more money for he'd already gone through his trust fund. Allan had been more of a mama's boy, not a daddy's boy like Arlie, and had always felt like a misplaced member of the McAdams family. He had artistic abilities, but hadn't quite found his niche in New York City, so he partied instead, ran with the jet-setters and lost his money in one quick scheme after another.

Allegra McAdams had moved to Brentwood when she turned 22, after she graduated from USC Film School. That was seven years ago. Her first two screenplays became successful films and she bought an estate that had once belonged to the silent film star - Marla Scott. Marla wasn't as famous as Greta Garbo and Gloria Swanson, but she had married a prominent film producer and they had lived in one of the most luxurious mansions on Hollingworth Drive in the '30s, although it was smaller than most. Allegra was lucky, bought it at auction for a little over four million.

Living in California's La-La-Land was a far cry from growing up on a cattle spread in Montana, but it suited her. She missed the ranch, missed the simpleness and realness of it. And she was always happy to take a few weeks off and go home in between manuscripts. In fact, she was wishing she was in Montana at that very moment.

"Someone was downstairs before I came in, darling. They must have heard me come up the walk because the French doors in the office were standing wide open, they must have gone out that way. Saw no sign of anyone in the house, but could hear someone running down the driveway. I called the police on my cell as soon as I saw the damage downstairs."

Allegra was listening, but couldn't speak. Her face was nestled in the ruffles of Connie's shirt.

With his arm still holding her close, Connie pulled his cell phone from his inside jacket pocket and punched a number with the thumb of the same hand. "Gladys, yes. I'm at Allegra's. Will you please send Trudy and Carl over to spend the night with her? Someone's broken into her house. Yes, tell Carl to arm himself. The police are on the way, yes. Thanks. Are Eric's rooms ready? Good. I'll be home soon."

"I don't need any babysitters. I'll be alright."

"But it'll make me feel better. I need to make another call, do you mind?"

"No, go ahead." Allegra reluctantly pulled away from his embrace. She went to the stairway landing and flipped the switch for the four chandeliers hanging over the foyer. She could see that a rare Ming dynasty vase, usually sitting atop a pedestal, was now smattered to smithereens on the marble tiles.

That was the crashing sound I heard.

She could see strewn papers and books on the carpet inside the office. She sighed heavily and looked back into the room where Connie was still talking on the phone.

Allegra had had a crush on Connie ever since she'd moved into the neighborhood and had met him at her first home owners' association meeting. He had greeted her at the HOA meeting that welcomed new residents to the community, and she had melted at the sight of him and even more so when he had taken her hand and held it for what seemed like forever. She'd wished it had been forever. But he was at least 25 years older than her and she knew she wasn't his type; she didn't feel sophisticated or fashionable enough for him. She was an inexperienced girl from a ranch in Montana, had never had a serious relationship, while he had his choice of all the beautiful women in the world according to the tabloids. But she fantasized about him anyway. She even wrote a character based on him in one of her film scripts. He either didn't see the movie or didn't connect the dots; she never mentioned it, and neither did he.

Usually she'd go to the parties thrown by the neighbors on Hollingsworth Drive, hoping he'd be there, and he usually was if he was in town. Hollingsworth was a community made up of quite an assortment of residents. There was a top model, two movie starlets who bought a house together - lesbians, a famous comedian turned dramatic actor, several film and television producers, two other writers other than herself, an academy award actor, a jewelry store family, a clothing designer, and Connie Brown, the local philanthropist.

"Okay, luv," Connie said as he put his cell phone away, "Let's go downstairs and wait for the police, I'll pour us both a glass of Scotch, if you don't mind."

"Sounds good to me, I'm still a bit shaky."

He took her hand and put his other arm around her as they went down the stairs into the library that housed an elaborate bar.

"How did you know I was in that guest room?"

"I didn't. But the only doors that were open were the doors from the room off your bedroom and that guest room. I thought that if you'd fled your room, possibly you were where the other door was ajar. Just a lucky guess," he reached for a bottle of Scotch. "But I checked all the rooms, anyway. As I recall this is your favorite single malt?"

She was surprised he knew. "Yes, it is. How did you know that?"

"I've been to enough parties with you present to see what you drink. Last one was at our girls' engagement party." He grinned and winked at her. "Nice party. I've never seen so many women; the men were outnumbered ten to one."

Allegra laughed. "Well, that's what happens when two women become engaged. They invite all their female friends. Were you uncomfortable?"

"Not in the least. I adore Millie and Julie. Did it bother you?"

"No, of course not. My youngest brother is gay. Doesn't bother me at all."

"Here you go, darling." He handed her a half-filled crystal old-fashioned glass of golden liquid.

"Thank you, I really do need this."

"I thought you might." He lifted his glass to hers and said, "To finding the bloody culprits and locking them up forever."

"Hear, hear!" she responded and took a big gulp of the drink. "Okay, I think I'll sit down now. My legs are feeling a bit wobbly."

"What am I thinking? Of course you're wobbly … here," he said as he set his glass on a cocktail table in front of the leather sofa and then guided her carefully to the seat. "There you go. Oh, damn, the siren, they're here. You stay; I'll meet them at the door. Just relax, take a deep breath and collect your thoughts. They'll want to question you." He left the room before she could say anything else.

As he stood waiting outside the open front door, he could still feel Allegra's tiny, curvy body pressed against his. He'd had to train his thoughts on something else so that she wouldn't know how she'd aroused him. He'd wanted to hold her close ever since he had first met her. And more still, he had wanted to kiss her. She was an innocent little dream angel to him, someone unaffected by the crassness and brashness of the Hollywood scene. How she'd managed to stay apart from it all, he didn't know. Even at the gatherings and parties on Hollingsworth—and he went to as many as he could in hopes of finding her there— she maintained and never clung to or climbed all over the studio executives, producers, and directors like the other female film types. She never pitched her scripts at parties like other writers; she never asked for favors, she was cordial and behaved like a well-put-together young lady. If only she weren't so young and innocent. He knew she would never be interested in anyone his age, and surely not him. She didn't even need his money. How he wished it were different. She was about the same age as his son, he figured.

His thoughts switched to his son Eric. He was arriving tomorrow afternoon from England where he'd lived for the past eight years with his grandmother, Connie's mother. Eric had telephoned the week before, first time in four years his dad had heard from him, although his grandmother gave Connie monthly reports.

Connie took a deep breath of the cool night air and faced the policemen coming up the walk, "Right this way, gentlemen. She's in the library."

"Good morning, Miss Allegra," Trudy said as she opened the draperies to let in the bright sunlight. "How are you feeling?"

"I'm a bit weary, but other than that, I'm feeling good. And you? Are you and Carl comfy in your rooms?"

"Oh yes. Thank you." Trudy grinned widely, secretly knowing that they'd shared the same room, hadn't used both of them. "You have a beautiful home, Miss Allegra," she replied as she continued opening the draperies on all the windows.

Allegra threw back the covers and stood on the fluffy Flokati rug next to her bed and stretched. "What I need now is a good cup of coffee. Would you like one, Trudy?"

"Oh, Carl and me have had ours already, Miss, and we made a fresh pot for you as well as your breakfast. I hope you like biscuits. Are you ready for it now, you want me to bring it up here, or wait till you're dressed and come downstairs?"

"You didn't have to do that, hon. I'm not used to being waited on. I do it all myself, you know. I only have a housekeeper who comes in twice a week and that's all."

"You livin' in this big ol' house by yourself, and no one to help you? Well, then, I'm glad we did it for you, Miss Allegra. Why don't you have servants, miss? In this mansion, I would think you would need them. My sister Callie is available, I know you'd love her. She's no bigger than a minute, like you. She just moved here from New Orleans. All my family is here in California. We all lost our homes during Katrina. Where do you keep your linens, Miss? I'll change your bed and do your laundry while I'm at it."

"Oh no, you don't have to do that. The housekeeper does it when she comes. Really, now. And please, tell me more about your sister Callie, I just may take you up on that offer. But first, let me get dressed, I'll meet you down in the kitchen. You can tell me down there. Okay?"

"Alright, Miss. But is there anything else I can do for you before I go back downstairs?"

Allegra was overcome with the politeness and sweetness of the young black girl standing before her. She felt like Scarlet O'Hara in *Gone with the Wind*, felt the charm of the old south through Trudy's genuine helpfulness. "That'll be all, Trudy. Thank you."

Trudy actually curtsied and backed through the doorway. It was all Allegra could take. She felt transported to a different time and era. She giggled in spite of what all had transpired the night before and the memories that had been conjured in her usual nightmares.

Her cell phone rang.

"Hello?"

"Hello, Allegra."

"Connie. How are you this bright sunshiny Monday morning? Did you get any sleep at all?"

"Not much, but I don't need much sleep. How about you?"

"I did sleep some. Yes. And I must say, you have quite a jewel in Trudy. She is something else."

"I thought you'd like her. Keep her for a few days, I've a house full of servants at the moment, since my son is arriving today."

"Oh no, I wouldn't dream of it. She told me about her sister Callie, I may hire her, she needs work."

"Oh yes, you'll love Callie. She's worked a few of my parties. Yes, she's a good choice. And I'm sure if you need more staff, Trudy can supply them. Her whole family is in L.A. now."

"Yes, she told me. Katrina."

"Unfortunately, yes. So, have the police come back this morning? They said they would."

"I don't know. I just got up and am going downstairs now."

"Well, let me know if you need me. Even though my son will be arriving, I'm sure he'll be off on his own. Pretty independent, you know. By the way, I'm having a little get-together for him, welcoming him back sort of, you know, inviting a few of his old friends and some of the neighbors. Another excuse for a party. Will you come Friday night at eight?"

"I'd love to. You can count on me. Will it be formal or casual?"

"Casual."

"I'll be there."

"Great! I'll see you then, unless you want me to come over before then, you're certainly welcome. You have my cell number."

"Alright. I'll call you if the police need you for something."

"Okay, bye."

"Bye." She closed her eyes and held the phone to her ear for a few moments even after he hung up. His voice sounded sexy over the phone.

After breakfast with Trudy and Carl, for Allegra insisted they sit down and eat with her, Allegra took her laptop to the patio by the pool and began writing her new screenplay. Just the day before she'd decided to take some time off before starting the next one, she had been thinking of going to Montana for a month, a vacation. But all that had changed. She wasn't going anywhere now.

She leaned back in the cushioned wicker chair and took a deep breath, smelling the mixed aromas of the climbing Wisteria and lilac shrubbery and the roses near her. Carl had cut fresh roses and put them in a glass vase on the table beside her while she was writing. She hadn't seen him on the patio at all; he just suddenly appeared with the bouquet of roses and set them on the table. Trudy followed with a fresh pot of coffee. They were spoiling her in the short time they'd been there.

Her mind was forming a plot, this time a departure from the previous detective stories. She wanted to write a love story - a simple love story with two main characters. Maybe a period piece. She loved British history. Maybe something to do with early British history, and then again, maybe not. Her thoughts shifted to Connie Brown. He was British. Although it was difficult to hear the accent, he'd cultivated more of a worldly accent. He sounded more American than British.

"Miss Allegra," Trudy interrupted. "The PO-leese are here to talk to you. You want them to come out here?"

"I'll come in." She set the computer on the table and followed Trudy into the house.

Detective Worthy greeted Allegra with a hand shake and a bright grin. He introduced himself and his partner Detective

Johnson. Both were young, in their 30s most likely, as far as Allegra could tell. *Probably early 30s,* she thought to herself as she showed them the major damage in the library.

"Is there anything missing? Or is it hard to tell in this mess?" Detective Worthy shook his head as he took in the room of chaos.

"Well, my neighbor and I both agreed that they were definitely looking for something. I don't think they were vandals, but as far as I can see, nothing of any value is missing. They didn't find the safe. Maybe that's what they were looking for. They certainly cleared the bookshelves, though, didn't they? The antique vase in the foyer was broken to bits, but that's about all the major damage. Can we start putting the books back on the shelves now?"

Detective Worthy reached down and picked up a leather-bound, gold inscribed book. "You've quite a collection here."

"Yes, most of them belonged to the previous owners. I bought the house with the library intact. Strange, but then I guess the heirs to the decedents didn't want to bother with the books. Some of them must be valuable; there are some signed copies and first editions in the lot. Do you think the burglars might have been after one of the books since they didn't go into any other part of the house?"

"Could be. But I'm more inclined to think they were looking for a safe. That's how it's been happening in the other homes that have been burglarized in this area. They're after money or jewelry. They don't even bother with electronics."

"I'm glad I had the safe moved then. They would have never found it. But I wonder what made them think it was in the library."

"The best part is that you were smart enough to get out of harm's way."

"True, and I'm going to buy a gun now. I think I need one to protect myself, just in case. I've been foolish in not doing it already. My mother was murdered with her own gun a few years ago and ever since then I've been afraid to have one around. But it's time."

"I don't know that that would be the best thing to do, Miss. Do you know how to handle one?"

"Hell, yes! I'm a crack shot and I've won shooting contests up in Montana and all over the northwest. I'm a ranch girl; I was raised holding a gun, owned my first one when I was nine. In fact I used to do trick shooting. Would stand on a galloping horse and shoot at moving targets. So you don't have to worry about me. I can hold my own with the best of them."

Both detectives raised their eyebrows and glanced at each other as she was talking.

"In fact, my dad's collection of guns fills a room the size of this library. I should have some of them shipped down here. I just might do that. My brother Arlie doesn't need them. He has his own collection. Yes, that's what I'll do." She smiled mischievously and added, "I could display them in my bedroom and the parlor next to it."

"Well, that ought to hold the burglars at bay, not to mention the suitors," Detective Johnson said through a wide grin.

They all laughed.

Allegra couldn't decide on what to wear to Connie's party. She'd been trying on outfits for an hour and still hadn't found the right one.

"How about this one, Miss Allegra?" Trudy was holding up a short rust-colored silk dress that was almost the same color as Allegra's long wavy hair. "This is your color, you know. And I saw some shoes in there that match the dress."

It was Trudy's last day at Allegra's. Her sister Callie was arriving in the morning as well as her cousin Ben. Both were going to live with Allegra and 'take care of her', as Trudy had put it. She told Allegra that Ben was a big man, 45 years old, and he could help with the remodel of the house and do some odd jobs that Allegra wanted done. So with Callie and Ben and the Swedish housekeeper Esther and the two gardeners – Carlos Ramirez and his brother Juan, it was becoming quite the little ethnic community.

"Yes, I like that dress. I keep forgetting about it. It's casual enough, a shirtdress. Okay. Perfect. Thanks, Trudy."

"Don't mention it. You gonna wear your hair down or up in a ponytail like usual?"

"Down, I think. Makes me look more mature, don't you think?"

"Ha! That's funny. Most women want to look younger. Why is it you wantin' to look older? Why is that, Miss Allegra?" She cocked her head and grinned at her mistress. She had seen the way Allegra had been looking at Connie Brown. When he came over and helped put the books on the shelves in the library on Tuesday, she saw a bit of chemistry popping between them. But her boss made a quick exit after the job was done, maybe too quickly, even though Allegra had invited him to stay for dinner. His excuse was that he needed to get home and discuss something with his son. Poor excuse in Trudy's estimation. She felt his son wasn't worth the trouble. Eric was disrespectful of his father and didn't show any appreciation to anyone. She'd be glad when he went back to England.

"So what do you think of Eric, Trudy? Is he like his father?" Allegra pulled the dress over her head and fastened the belt.

"No m'am! He ain't like his daddy at all."

"How old is he?"

"About your age, I guess. You better watch out for him, Miss Allegra. There's something wrong about him that gives me

16

the willies. You know? Something's just not right with him. My Carl says the same thing. "

"What do you mean, exactly?" She sat at the dressing table and brushed her hair.

"Well, I can't put my finger on it, but he's got an odd look in his eyes. His daddy bends over backwards for him, gives him everything he wants, but Eric doesn't appreciate it. He just keeps taking advantage of Mister Connie. It just ain't right. And he lives over there in England with his grandma, doin' nothin'. Hasn't worked a day in his life. Sends invoices to his daddy for his living expenses. Can you imagine that? And his grandma ain't much better, she gives him all the money he wants, too. They've spoiled that brat, yes they have."

Allegra chuckled at Trudy's seriousness. "Well, you know how it is with the wealthy, they just hand everything to their kids not realizing how important it is for them to learn how to make their own living. My father stressed that importance to all three of us. Of course my brother Arlie has always been pegged to run the ranch, it's always been his. But my other brother, Allen, poor Allan, he couldn't find his way. He ran through his trust fund in no time flat and I don't know what he's doing now. He's in New York. The last time I sent him money, Arlie jumped all over me. But I couldn't let him just die on the vine, you know? Maybe that's how Connie and his mother feel about Eric. Maybe Eric just doesn't know how to take care of himself. It's a hard call sometimes."

"I suppose. But I just don't understand people like that. We all work for a living. We always have. I think if we had lots of money we'd still work," Trudy said as she brought the matching patent leather shoes to Allegra. "Here you go."

"I'm going to miss you, Trudy."

"You'll like Callie, you will. She's just like me, only a younger version, and half my size. She wears her hair in braids all over with beads. And I know you'll like Ben. He is our favorite cousin. Maybe a little simple-minded, but he's fearless and good with his hands and is loyal. You'll be happy with them both, Miss.

I'm sure I will be."

"And you know, I was thinkin', if you might one day want to get a different housekeeper, you know, one that lives in, my auntie Talutha is the crème of the crop. She cleaned houses for some of the richest people in New Orleans and she's here now, looking for work. She lived at a famous doctor's house for seven years before Katrina came. She could come at a moment's notice; I'd make sure of that."

"You mean she'd live in?"

"Yes, ma'am. She'd need to live in. She'd work for her board and keep. She doesn't ask for much."

"Well, I'd give her a wage, too. I wouldn't ask anyone to work for nothing. I'll think about it, Trudy. It would be nice to have someone here all the time. Does she cook?"

"Oh my goodness, does she ever cook! She is the best cook in our family. She even learned how to do the gourmet stuff when she was at the doctor's. They paid for her classes."

"That settles it then. Tell her she can start in two weeks. I'll have to give Esther two weeks' notice. Okay? Actually she isn't all that much of a good housekeeper, so this will work out great. And Callie can help her."

"Oh, Miss Allegra, that makes me so happy. You don't have any idea how happy. Between you and Mister Connie, I'm gettin' all my family placed. He's been helping me get them here from Louisiana and has been paying for them all a place to stay until I can find 'em all live-in jobs. Some of his friends have hired some, too. I'm so happy I could cry." She wiped her eyes with the hem of her apron.

"Oh, no, don't cry, Trudy. You'll make me do it and then I'll have to redo my makeup."

They both laughed through their tears.

What Allegra thought was going to be a small gathering of Eric's friends turned out to be a gala. There had to be at least 300 guests in Connie's ballroom that night, and Allegra discovered that the Brown mansion was more than a mansion. It was a palatial estate that stretched unending it seemed. She couldn't believe the size of it. She'd seen the columned entry and the front of the house set back from the gate on Hollingworth Drive every time she drove by, but she had no idea that the structure was U-shaped, extending farther back on the property, four stories on all three sides, surrounding gardens fit to be included among the grandest in the world. It certainly had to be the grandest in Southern California. Allegra had seen nothing like it in the U.S., and she'd seen most of the major ones, she loved gardens. Got that from the genteel side of the family, her mother's.

As soon as she arrived, Connie gave her a tour. After an hour of him telling her its history, she was overwhelmed and suggested he get back to his guests, said she didn't want to monopolize his time, said she'd roam on her own and would meet him back in the ballroom. She was actually tired of hearing about it, too much information all at once.

So he excused himself and she continued on the journey through the Brown Palace, as she dubbed it.

I have never seen anything like this in my life! She looked up at the massive portraits of what had to be Connie's British ancestors lining the staircase. *So many of them.* The frames alone had to be worth a fortune.

"So, what do you think of our little family?"

Allegra turned to the voice and was almost nose to nose with Eric who was standing very close, two steps below her. She was surprised at how handsome he was; Trudy had neglected to tell her that. He was a younger version of his father, except his hair was blond, not black like Connie's, and his eyes were grey blue, not cobalt like Connie's.

"Oh, you startled me!"

"Sorry, didn't mean to do that. That one is my great grandmother, Lady Arlington. She was a grand old dame."

"So you knew her?"

"Yes, for a short time. She died when I was seven. But I remember her. And I've heard Dad and Gram tell the tales." His broad grin revealed perfect white teeth and dimples in each cheek. His father didn't have dimples in his cheeks, but had one in the middle of his chin, a Cary Grant cleft.

"I think it is wonderful to have such a display of ancestors. It pays homage to them, actually. It's respectful. Not many people in America do that, you know. We have photos of our grandparents in frames in Montana, but not paintings, and maybe some of our great grandparents, but not as far back as these go. It's fabulous!"

"Well, I find it boring. So, I understand you live on Hollingsworth Drive too?" He joined her on the step where she was standing and leaned against the wall.

Stepping back to the railing she answered, "Yes, just up the street. But not in a palace like this. Mine is much smaller."

"I'd love to see it, if I may."

"Sure. I mean— well, maybe you and your dad would like to come to lunch tomorrow or one day next week. I'll ask him."

"You'll ask me what, my dear?" Connie reached for Allegra's hand and led her to the bottom of the staircase.

"Eric asked to see my house. Would you like to come to lunch tomorrow or Sunday?"

Eric frowned. "Actually, that won't be good for me; I'm meeting up with some friends for the weekend. Maybe next week. We'll be in touch." He turned and walked towards the bar.

20

Allegra was puzzled at his sudden departure. "Did I say something—"

"No. That's just Eric. He wanted you all to himself, I'm sure. Sorry I interrupted."

"I'm not sorry you interrupted."

Their eyes met and held for a brief moment and then they moved, arm in arm, toward the ballroom.

Allegra was dead on her feet. When her head hit the pillow she was nearly asleep already. But as she lay there she thought back over the events of the evening. She thought of Connie and his charming behavior, she thought of his son Eric whose aggressive manner and actions were a bit strange and scary. He had come on to her very strongly as the party had begun to wind down and the guests were leaving. Eric had insisted on walking her home, was being very pushy, but Connie stepped in and took her arm and as they headed down the driveway, Eric stood on the portico glaring after them.

She was grateful Eric had said he'd be busy over the weekend and couldn't come to lunch, for she didn't think she could bear to be around him any more than she had to be. She felt sorry for Connie. His only son was ungrateful and downright rude to him. It was just as Trudy had said. He was a spoiled brat.

After she turned over on her side and pulled the comforter up to her chin, she remembered she'd left her cell phone downstairs again. "Dammit!" She threw the covers back and snapped on the bedside lamp. "I'd forget my head if it weren't attached."

Now she was wide awake and feeling hungry. As she headed down the stairs to the kitchen she thought she might have a turkey sandwich and some carrot juice. And some potato chips. Yes, that sounded yummy to her. Trudy and Carl had the weekend off, and Trudy had left her a note about the turkey and trimmings she'd cooked and left in the refrigerator for Allegra to munch on that weekend.

"Wha—?" Her heart nearly stopped as she came face to face with Eric. The adrenaline rushed as she stepped back through the kitchen doorway. The door leading out to the patio was standing wide open. "What are you doing in my house?"

"I thought I'd come give you a proper good night kiss since you rushed away with my father before I had a chance to," Eric replied in a raspy, breathy voice. He reached for her and grabbed her shoulders before she could do or say anything.

"Stop it, Eric!"

"Just be still, I won't hurt you. You know you're attracted to me. C'mon, just a goodnight kiss. What's it going to hurt?" He pulled her tightly to his body, pinning her arms to her sides.

She struggled to break his grip to no avail and she dodged his face as he tried to kiss her. "Stop it, Eric! I mean it! Let me go!"

But that was not Eric's intention, not at all. In the struggle his body was pressing and rubbing against hers and he was aroused. No way was he going to let her go now. She felt good to him in her skimpy little night gown. The moment he saw her standing in the kitchen doorway, he knew he was going to have her. He could see her naked body right through the thin fabric. Yes, he had to have her, he'd convince her to want him.

"Eric! Don't!"

He was holding both her arms behind her with one of his hands and began to fondle her breasts with his other hand while he watched her eyes.

She glared in contempt at him and spit in his face. "Your father will kill you for this."

"My father will never know, Allegra. You're not going to tell him. If you do, I'll have you shot and killed just like your mother was and no one will ever think that I'm responsible.

They'll think it was another burglary, or even your mother's killers finishing you off, too. I have contacts, Allegra. Don't think I don't. I have assassins at my beck and call and I'm not afraid to use them." He turned her while holding her arms behind her and shoved her towards the stairs.

"How do you know about my mother?"

"I do my homework. Keep going."

She tripped on one of the stairs and almost took them both down, but he caught himself and grabbed her as she was scrambling to get out of his reach. She fought him all the way up the stairs, cursing and yelling, but there was no way anyone but the two of them could hear her.

Once in the bedroom, Eric rummaged in a dresser drawer for something to tie her hands behind her back. He found a pair of pantyhose and wound them around her wrists and secured them with a double knot.

"Now the fun begins," he said through a wild and slobbery grin.

"You're crazy." Allegra growled at him. "Why would you want to do this? Huh? What's the matter with you?"

Without saying another word he pushed her, face down, onto the bed and held her down with one hand as he unzipped his pants.

"Please, Eric. Please don't!" She kicked and screamed, was humiliated and terrified as he roughly spread her legs with his. "Oh, God! Stop it, Eric!"

He repeatedly forced entry into her in spite of her body's resistance.

"You're hurting me, Eric!" She cried in pain. "Dear God, make him stop!"

Loud, piercing cries and screams continued to resound through the high-ceilinged rooms of the 1930s mansion, but nobody heard.

The rape went on for over an hour. Eric used her to exhaustion—his and hers.

She had nothing left in her, no more resistance, no more sounds, no more tears. She lay motionless on a blood soaked bed.

He untied her and left.